To my family
who allowed me to become who I am,

to all my friends
for loving me in spite of me,

and to my readers.
You made all of this possible.

Special thanks to UFOP: Starbase 118 for teaching me how to write,

and to Shane Michael Murray,
my tireless proofreader, motivator and partner in crime.

Lacuna

空
白

The Spectre of Oblivion

What the caterpillar calls the end of the world the master calls a butterfly.

- Richard Bach

The Milky Way
A two-dimensional representation

Prologue

"The Prodigal Son Returns"
*****

Forge world of Belthas IV
Deep within Toralii space

November 2037 AD

Ben planned his arrival to be as the coming of a God.

The Toralii Alliance forge world of Belthas IV, a world of sand and oceans. A planet nestled snugly at the centre of the Alliance's web of worlds, the manufacturing heart of the vast, star-spanning empire. It was here that all manner of construction work took place: steel for ships, hydrogen for fusion reactors, silicon for computers.

Computers such as Ben.

His vessel, the *Giralan*, appeared in the upper reaches of the planet's atmosphere, its 200,000 tonne bulk displacing an equal volume of thin atmosphere at nearly the speed of light. The incredible force of matter moving at such a speed flung the hydrogen and oxygen in the air's moisture apart, the intense heat immediately igniting newly created fuel and accelerant in a colossal ball of fire. The effect was a white flash in the sky, so bright it illuminated the land and turned night into day before slowly fading to a red, ominous glow.

Wreathed in flame, the colossal Toralii ship plummeted from the conflagration towards the surface like a burning comet, a little streak of light slicing through the tranquil twilight. Ben, the ship's sole sentient occupant, watched impassively through a myriad of sensors as the planet's dusty surface raced towards him, the lights of a small cluster of buildings twinkling directly below. Ben's records showed that the small town was home to 8,211 Toralii and was a residential settlement.

With a thought Ben activated the *Giralan*'s worldshatter device, a Toralii weapon specifically designed for orbital bombardment. A white lance of light leapt from the tip of his ship's bow, bathing the town below in the cleansing fire, vaporising the entire settlement and leaving only ruin and debris, a red glowing crater in the surface of this world. Dark red clouds of immolated matter mushroomed up from the impact site, glowing a fierce crimson at its heart, the dust of those who lived below, their lives instantly snuffed out.

The worldshatter device's heat was comparable to ripping out the heart of a star and transplanting it onto the surface of the planet. The likelihood of survivors was statistically improbable aside from those who happened to be in hardened bunkers, but the Toralii who lived on this world had known peace for far too long. There would be no survivors. Their destruction would be swift and without error.

The sand rushed up to meet him, but the *Giralan* jumped away before it smashed into the surface, reappearing high in the atmosphere again, almost six thousand kilometres away. Another colossal ball of flame amongst the stars, another suicidal dive down to the surface, another wave of light, another white-hot crater aimed at a slumbering town.

16,930 souls blasted to ashes, and the planet's primary barracks turned to glass and molten iron.

Belthas IV's automated defences had, finally, began to track him. He could see their fingers reaching for him through his ship's infrared sensors as easily as though he were looking through his own eyes, infrared beams like great searchlights sweeping the atmosphere for his vessel.

But searchlights worked both ways.

He waited for the targeting sensors to reveal the position of the Toralii weapons system, his colossal vessel winking away again before their energy weapons could fire. His ship reappeared with a white flash further back into space, only a dozen kilometres from the orbital station that coordinated those defences. The worldshatter device spoke again, silencing the Toralii guns forever.

Given the amount of planning Ben had put into this operation, his stunning success cheapened the victory somewhat. The worldshatter device's energy was spent now, but his message had been transmitted loudly and clearly, far neater and more articulate than mere language could convey.

You are beaten.

If Ben were addressing synthetic life words would now be superfluous, but the tiny minds of his creators, the biological creatures who scurried around like tiny insects on the planet's surface, would not grasp even such a simple message so quickly. In their ineptitude they would stumble, confused and disorientated from their rest, and they would spend minutes—whole minutes!—attempting to discern what had happened. They would meander through the grossly dumbed down reports from whatever remained of their systems, reading with flawed optics the inescapable fact that their entire world had, in mere moments, been brought low, humbled before Ben's unstoppable power.

The planet's population was on its knees and didn't even know it.

Ben had planned out exactly what he would say. He had, for some time, intended to make a grand statement, to lay his intentions out in full so the denizens of this world would know, fully and completely, how total was their defeat. But, having considered, he felt that perhaps keeping things simple would be preferable.

His synthetic brain reached into his ship's systems much as a Human might move their lips. He engaged the long-range communication device and tuned it to a frequency he knew the Telvan faction of the Toralii who lived on the planet would be listening to.

["I am Ben. Your world, Belthas IV, is now mine. Any vessel leaving the surface of this planet will be destroyed. Any attempt to reach the jump points near this planet will result in failure. Any attempt to harm my vessel, or impede my will, will fail. You are to offer your unconditional surrender immediately or face oblivion."]

Just as he had predicted, the responses came in. They doubted. They threatened. They pleaded. They blustered and fumbled and attempted to negotiate, but Ben's demands were simple and direct. The squawking of the biologicals, their pointless prattle, didn't interest him. They spoke loudly but said nothing, so whenever the surface dwellers transmitted anything that was not their total, unconditional surrender, Ben merely jumped his vessel to a randomly selected settlement, blasted it to a molten crater, then repeated his demands.

Sixteen minutes later, the forge world of Belthas IV, the place where his processor's silicon was shaped from the endless sands and his body forged from its iron, capitulated to his demands. With supreme magnanimity, Ben lowered the *Giralan* through the atmosphere, the planet's landing lights bathing his colossal ship in illumination.

The *Giralan*, once a mighty and proud Toralii warship, was now pitted and scarred with rust, burned from its appearance through the atmosphere and degraded from a half-century resting under the sands of the barren desert world of Karathi. Visible gaps in the surface of the ship's hull, spots where the rust had eaten through to reveal the bones of the ship, belied its true nature; it was not pressurised and could support no life, its systems in disrepair, the entire vessel rotting like a dead thing. It was a destroyed, zombie vessel lurching through the stars, a mere hunk of corroded metal and composite materials.

Yet it was not all dead. Fresh, clean metal had been recently grafted to its surface in scores of places, a patchwork of old and new. The square boxes of weapon turrets, seemingly attached at random, dotted the less corroded sections of the ship's hull, shining, clean, chrome spires forcefully welded onto the ruined exterior of the ancient warship.

The vessel, in many ways, began to resemble its owner. Pieced together from whatever technology it could find, the new grafted onto the old, taking what was optimal and discarding form for function.

With a pained groan, the gargantuan vessel landed on the surface of Belthas IV. There it sat, silent, the bloated victor resting on its rusted landing struts, a faint cloud of steam rising from its still-hot surface. The Toralii who rushed to see the spectacle watched fearfully, the ship creaking and groaning as it cooled and its metal skin contracted.

Hissing, the escape of pressure, heralded the descent of a ramp, slowly lowering to touch the synthetic stone that covered the landing site. In silhouette Ben's form appeared, backlit by the ship's internal lighting, an eight legged creature the size of a horse, striding down the ramp, metal legs hitting metal deck with a faint *tink-tink*. His body was flattened like a cockroach, with a raised head that had two luminescent blue eyes. Twin energy cannons of recent manufacture articulated themselves independently, sizing up the gathered crowd of Toralii.

One stepped forward, his dark red fur streaked with grey. His figure cut a clear shadow in the bright luminescence of the landing lights.

["Who are you?"] he asked, his posture cowed and fearful.

Ben inclined his head, cobalt eyes flashing as he spoke. ["I am Ben, Worldleader Jul'aran."]

The Toralii stared at him. ["How... how could you know my name?"]

Gesturing out with mechanical arms, Ben's limbs clicked as he took a step forward. His tone was tinged with sarcasm. ["Do you not know of me? I was forged here, as were millions like me. Landmaiden Mevara tested me herself not far from this very site, in fact."]

["I... you are no model we have ever built here."]

The construct's mouth, an articulate and expressive mechanical opening, widened. ["This body, no. It is my own creation, my evolution of your designs. My datacore, however, was born from the furnaces of this world. I am as much a child of Belthas IV as any biological creature. And now the prodigal son has returned."]

Jul'aran regarded the construct warily. ["What do you want with us?"]

Ben's mechanical smile, an action that he had learnt from the humans, only widened.

It was important to smile.

Act I

Chapter I

"Reckoning"
*****

Military Court Building J
Gunzhou, China

Meanwhile

"This court-martial has now come to order."

Naval Commander Melissa Liao was the last to sit, her hand on her swollen abdomen. Most women found they were fairly mobile right up until delivery, but possibly owing to her age, at six months pregnant, she felt as though iron chains had been laid across her back. Her body strained with the effort of moving, a toll made worse by the knowledge that she had three months of the process left and things were only going to get worse from here on in.

The honourable judge Dewei Qu, a portly and serious man with grey hair and an efficient expression, gently rapped his gavel.

"Commander Melissa Liao is charged with dereliction of duty with regard to turning over command of her vessel to a construct, with conduct unbecoming an officer for engaging in and perpetuating a relationship with another commanding officer, and reckless endangerment of fleet assets. The court will now hear an opening statement from the prosecution."

The advocate for the prosecution, a well-dressed man whom her court documents identified as Deshi Fang, stood and opened his briefcase. He removed a small, paper-clipped and dog-eared stack of paper and began to read.

"Ladies and gentlemen of the court, June 18th, 2029, is one date among many that will forever live in infamy. Despite a worldwide economic collapse, the People's Republic had launched the robotic probes that began the automated construction of our lunar colony; this was the first time our species had established a permanent presence on the moon. Independently but concurrently, the People's Republic of China, the Islamic Republic of Iran, and the Commonwealth of Australia researched a wondrous new technology called the spatial coordinate re-mapper, or jump drive, was set to change the future of our species forever. Plans for interstellar vessels were drawn up. The stock market was strengthening. Women and men were starting to come back to work, and galvanised by industry, we began the long road to recovery."

Fang lowered the piece of paper as though he no longer needed the notes to give his address. "Everyone in this room knows what happened that idle Monday. The Toralii arrived, detecting the jump drive technology through a process that still eludes us. They destroyed the cities of Beijing, Tehran and Sydney... then vanished."

Liao had been in Sydney during the attacks with Summer and James and was almost killed when the building she had been visiting collapsed. She still had a wicked scar on her hip where a steel beam had sliced her open.

"Eight years later and our lunar colony, along with the three vessels constructed there, was complete. Commander Liao was given command of one of the ships built on the lunar colony, the TFR *Beijing*. She obeyed her orders unquestioningly and her devotion to her duty was impeccable; Liao was, for a period of almost a year, a shining symbol of hope and triumph against the Toralii. Under her skilled leadership, our ships took to the heavens and scored numerous victories. Although her ship was, on two occasions, significantly damaged, Liao emerged victorious each and every time—a radiant testament to the power of the Human spirit, of our indomitable courage, an exemplary woman for us all to emulate and admire."

Fang laid the stack of papers on the desk. Liao could see now that it wasn't notes for his opening address; it was a partial transcript, written in Chinese, of a report Liao herself had authored.

"Or so the official record would have you believe."

A subtle murmur, shuffling like waves on a pond, rippled through the court. Fang waited until it passed, then continued.

"The reality of war is never perfect. There are no clean battles, no struggles of pure good and evil, and the cackling, moustache-twirling villains are never reliably, righteously and soundly defeated by plucky heroes. War is a dark, bloody place where the young go to die at the behest of old men, where every single day our soldiers, sailors and airmen commit acts that, in the civilian world, would not just be criminal but shocking, twisted and insane. Military commanders are human. No Human is perfect, so the People's Republic Army Navy, and mankind as a whole, was not expecting Captain Liao's command to be perfect."

The lawyer turned to Liao, their eyes locking, and she held his gaze. "But we were not expecting her to shoot dead her own XO on the bridge of her lover's ship. We were not expecting the *Beijing* to be willingly compromised by an alien artificial intelligence, leading to the deaths of fifty thousand Toralii of the Telvan faction—a number that represented the only allies that our species had in the entire galaxy. We were not expecting Liao to leap into bed with the commanding officer of the *Tehran*, then fail to protect herself against the potential consequences. You can follow the footsteps of Liao's command by following the trail of mistakes she has made, and if you get lost and wander off the scent, just breath in and follow the stink of our dead."

Liao felt her fists tighten at her sides, but she kept her gaze even and unyielding. She stared at Fang and he at her, the two engaging in a silent, noncommunicative standoff. Almost everything the man said could be tolerated, but pointing out her sexual relationship with James, and subsequent pregnancy, in front of the court invoked a primal protectiveness that was difficult to keep restrained. It was true that the child was James's, Captain James Grégoire, the CO of the Tehran who spent two months in a Toralii prison. The child was not planned, but it was a welcome addition to her life, even if it would ultimately cost Liao her command.

Fang returned his attention back to the judge, his finger lying over Liao's report. "The Pillars of the Earth have been a rousing success, the *Beijing* the foremost among them, but successes have also come from the *Sydney* and the *Tehran*. The *Tehran's* weapons accounted for double the amount of Toralii tonnage versus the *Beijing* during the attack on the Kor'Vakkar shipyard, while the *Sydney's* crew has been working towards forging an alliance with the Kel-Voran Imperium, much to our benefit. We now have allies again, and allies have value... unlike a ship constantly in a shipyard, and a captain who can no longer lead.

"The prosecution intends to demonstrate that these outcomes, and others, were the result of Captain Liao's negligence with the aim of having her removed from command." Fang inclined his head respectfully towards the judge. "Thank you, Your Honour."

He sat. Liao digested his speech. While eloquent and articulate, there was nothing in there she had not expected. She anticipated, in fact, a much more malicious and scathing opening; she expected the prosecution to crucify her for her lack of command experience and for being a woman, but neither point had been raised... yet. For this, she was grateful in a strange kind of way.

Her lawyer, Craig Martin, stood to give his own opening presentation. She had declined a lawyer from the People's Republic, instead seeking one from their allies instead. She felt that it was necessary for her to do so. A former Queen's Council, Martin would be able to defend her in a much more impartial manner than one of her countrymen; he would be able to point out where she had genuinely erred and would be more open and more honest with her in regard to her failings. Martin had a reputation for being as cold and blunt as stone to both his clients and to the court itself, and this was exactly the kind of man she needed defending her.

"Your Honour, first let me thank you for allowing me to represent Captain Liao in this court. It is a privilege to be here."

The judge nodded slightly and Martin continued. "My esteemed colleague, Mister Fang, in many ways articulated my case better than I could, so for that I am grateful. However, he is incorrect on one substantial part: that Commander Liao's actions, while in some cases rash and impulsive, were made with the best of intentions and with limited information. In plain terms, she did the best she could with the limited means at her disposal. Accordingly, her actions should be seen not with the benefit of hindsight, as we relax in this air conditioned court room so far removed from danger, but seen through the lens of the situation at the time."

Martin paused to let his words sink in, then continued. "I am not one for large speeches, Your Honour, so if it pleases the court, I would like to call my first witness."

*****

"Please state your full name for the court records."

["I am Airmaiden Saara of the Telvan. I have no other names."]

Saara, the six foot eight Toralii female, glanced to her translator as she spoke. The Toralii were physically incapable of speaking English, and the guttural, rumbling language they had was unpronounceable to humans, but both species could hear and understand the other just fine.

Over the year Liao had been in space, the Telvan dialect had been well documented and studied. However, the dialect had not been made available to civilians, so Lieutenant Yu from the *Beijing* was assigned to translate. Apart from Liao, he was their best Toralii speaker.

Yu repeated her words.

Fang nodded in understanding. "You are, or were, a member of the Telvan military, correct?"

["That is correct, Lawyer-man. My current status is best described as 'Away Without Leave'."]

"I see. And Airmaiden was your rank, yes? Somewhat similar to our Lieutenant?"

["The ranks are vaguely similar, yes, regarding the tasks I was assigned and the responsibilities I had."]

"That's quite a remarkable shift, to abandon your own people in favour of aliens who tried to kill you... who successfully killed every single other Toralii on your ship, isn't it?"

Saara's golden eyes narrowed at the question, her thick paws resting comfortably on her thighs. ["This is the truth."]

"Can you explain to me why you took this rather dramatic step?"

Saara seemed nervous and out of place for more reasons than her species. The whole procedure would be entirely foreign and uncomfortable to her, but Liao respected that she was willing to do it for her sake.

["Toralii believe that to save a life is to earn a life's gratitude. I owe Melissa Liao a great deal, and that debt can only be repaid with my service to her species. I give what I can to her cause."]

"I see. Please describe for me the circumstances under which Commander Liao earned this debt."

["The Human called Gaulung Sheng, the one appointed as Commander Liao's Executive Officer, he disobeyed her orders, betrayed his oaths, and took command of the ship named the *Tehran*. His men believed I had intelligence which could help your people. They proceeded to apply what you euphemistically call 'enhanced interrogation'. I barely survived, and only because of Liao's timely intervention. My jaw was shattered, my organs bruised... Liao and Captain Grégoire rescued me, and Doctor Saeed repaired my injuries. In return, I willingly shared what I knew."]

"And Liao trusted you?"

The Toralii's eyes flicked to her, then back to the prosecutor. Liao's heart went out to Saara. She had promised the alien that she would see Earth's many wonders, but her first few hours on their home planet were in a sterile court room.

["We... developed a bond during my time as her prisoner, a friendship."]

"Granted, but what evidence did Liao have that you were not simply lying?"

Liao saw the fur on Saara's neck rise but the Toralii was obviously making an effort to control herself. The question, Liao knew, would be insulting: to suggest duplicity was, for Toralii, a very aggressive act.

["I gave her my *word*. What I told her was true."]

"I understand that, and yes, the assault on the Hades system—the place you call Kor'Vakkar, the Gateway of Eternal Ash—was successful. You clearly *were* speaking the truth, but we know that with the benefit of hindsight. I'm asking you what evidence, at the time, did Liao have that you were not leading the crews of the *Tehran* and the *Beijing* into a trap?"

The tips of Saara's claws, ever so slowly, became visible at the ends of her paws.

Keep it together, Liao silently pleaded.

["She had no evidence."]

"So she trusted you meant what you said?"

["Yes."]

"She trusted you with her ship, her life, the lives of her crew, *and* those of the crew of the Tehran, including her lover? She risked all this on your word?"

["... Yes."]

"Did you think this was reckless?"

Saara's hesitation answered the question better than her words could. ["I... believe Liao took a calculated risk that resulted in a very favourable outcome."]

Fang nodded, inclining his head. "Thank you, Airmaiden Saara. No further questions." The man sat and nodded to Martin, who stood and approached the seemingly exasperated, stressed Toralii.

"Airmaiden, thank you for your time. Can you please describe your relationship with Commander Liao?"

Saara looked to Liao, and Liao held her gaze, smiling slightly. ["My parents died when I was young, but do not misunderstand; I was at no disadvantage. The Toralii raise their children differently than Humans do; children are the responsibility of the community, a great treasure, the continuation of the species. Such a delicate, important task cannot be left in the hands of a single pair of individuals, so for me to have no living biological parents is not as significant an emotional trauma as it might be for one of your species. Still, I miss them often, even in my adult years.

["However, with Captain Liao, I felt as though, in some way, she and I have a mother-daughter relationship. She allows me to assist her crew aboard the *Beijing* and, in return, she... protects me, keeps my well-being in my heart as I work to repay my debt."]

"And once your debt is repaid, you'll return to your people?"

Saara gave Liao a long, unreadable look which created an uncomfortable silence in the court room. Liao did not know how she would answer. ["I am uncertain at this time, but currently, I do not believe I shall."]

"Would you consider enlisting in the People's Republican Army Navy?"

["Liao's grace in battle and her ability to make accurate, timely decisions with limited and imperfect information is one of the cornerstones of her success. If I was inclined to serve in the military once again, I would consider a posting under Liao's command... Although, I am uncertain of the formal requirements for enlistment."]

"So you believe Liao to be a competent commander, one who treats her crew well and not only achieves the objectives set out for her by her superiors, but who enjoys great success against targets of opportunity when they appear?"

["That would be an accurate assessment of her skills, yes."]

Martin's voice softened slightly. "And you still feel this way after the destruction of the Velsharn research colony, after Liao allowed the construct known as Ben to interface with her ship's systems? Were they not Telvan, like you?"

Saara's features clouded. ["The Toralii are hardened against suffering, Lawyer-man. I weep for the loss of my fellows, but I harbour no resentment towards her for the tragedy, because the events that transpired were not her fault. Liao trusted the construct you know as Ben, and it betrayed that trust. Any commanding officer would have done the same, if they had the courage."]

"Can you elaborate on that?"

["Your species lives in dark times, Lawyer-man. The iron fist of the Toralii Alliance fleet hovers over your species, waiting for an opportunity to crush you all. Our most rigid, inflexible law is that no other species can possess the voidwarp technology—the technological marvel you call a jump drive. The destruction of your cities pales in comparison to what the Toralii Alliance has done in the past, and will do again if you continue to defy them. Every single woman and man who dons a uniform to fight the Alliance risks death every single day, but truth be told, the battlefield stretches beyond those brave souls. Your entire *species* is the price you will forfeit if you fail, if the Toralii Alliance gains the opportunity strike at Earth. There are no civilians, no noncombatants, no parties who will be spared the wrath of the Alliance if and when they come for you. The construct warned you of this, and yet Liao remains ready to stand against the Toralii. Despite her mistakes, despite her pregnancy, despite her losses... she remains ready to fight."]

"I see."

Saara kept her eyes focused on Martin. ["This, in my mind, shows her courage. Courage will be in short supply for your species in those dark times, so I suggest you take whatever you can get."]

Martin inclined his head. "No further questions, and you are excused. Thank you for your time."

*****

Liao had begged Summer Rowe, her eccentric genius engineer, to wear suitable clothes to court. Smart and business-like, she had said, like you were going to a job interview.

Apparently, in Australia, businesswomen wore jeans and a baggy, over-sized black shirt that read I EAT EVERYTHING I FUCK in white lettering to court. Liao was amazed the fiery redhead was not held in contempt.

"Please state your name for the court records."

"Summer Katelyn Rowe, Your Grace."

The judge frowned slightly. "Thank you, but I'm not a king just yet. 'Your Honour' will suffice for now, Miss Rowe."

"Right-o then, Your Honour."

Did she think the court proceedings were a joke? Liao stared daggers across the court room, willing Summer to treat the court seriously.

Fang stood to address her. "Miss Rowe, you are currently the chief of engineering aboard the *Beijing*, are you not?"

"Yep."

"Yet you are not a member of the People's Republican Army Navy, are you?"

"Nup."

"Nor a citizen of the People's Republic?"

"Nope."

"So, can you explain to me how you came to earn this prestigious position aboard the crew of the *Beijing*?"

Rowe stretched her arms upward, her back cracking as she did so. "Sure. Basically, you know the jump drive? I invented a fair chunk of it. Not all of it, but some of it. Nobody knew it better than I did, though, and I wanted to make sure my little baby was taken care of. Liao has her crotch-fruit; I have my devices. We're pretty much the same like that."

Breathe, Liao urged herself, forcing herself to remember that Summer was just being Summer. This was how she was. She was on her side.

Fang nodded. "And you were offered this post by Liao?"

Rowe shook her head. "Nah, actually Sheng handpicked me, technically. Liao found out about it when she was on a rocket to the moon. We met just before the attacks, and boy, was Liao surprised to see me... when she wasn't too busy puking her fucking guts out."

Liao felt herself flush at the memory. Despite commanding a spaceship, she became queasy when in zero gravity, such as when the ship had to use its jump drive or in more conventional means of space travel.

"I see. But Liao had the right to remove you and she did not. Is that correct?"

"Yep and yep."

Liao studied judge Qu. Although the man was clearly very patient with the task set before him, Rowe's terse answers and flippant attitude were clearly testing his patience.

Fang, seemingly pleased, continued. "Can you explain to the court why this would be so?"

"Liao wants her ship to fly straight. I don't walk around with a stick up my arse. And yeah, I got a bit of an unconventional approach to technology and, well, everything. That's true." She paused, glanced at Liao, then back to Fang. "But Melissa could see I knew my stuff. This is highly experimental tech with all kinds of crazy fucking side effects and weird behaviours. It sometimes goes spastic for no reason, or doesn't work, or needs software patches on the fly. Same goes for the whole fucking ship, actually. It's a damn miracle that piece of shit could ever even get into space, let alone take on the Toralii. Without me, it'd be a giant piece of flying scrap within two weeks."

"So Commander Liao did not care that you were not a member of the military and were not subject to the same oaths and training that the rest of the crew were bound to, and believed your expertise to be invaluable?"

"Yep."

"Would you say that you were irreplaceable?"

"Sure."

"And were there any apprenticeships put into place during your whole year aboard the *Beijing*? Were any provisions made if you were to be killed?"

Rowe snorted. "I'm immortal. I'm a vampire and I sparkle in the sun. Besides, I'm either in Engineering or in Operations, both of which are the most protected parts of the ship. The chances of me getting killed are about fucking zero, they'd have to blow up almost all the ship to get to me anyway."

"But you are not *always* in Engineering or Operations, are you? Liao's report specifically states that you were actually performing an extravehicular activity in the midst of a pitched battle no less than three months ago. You were also part of the team that visited Velsharn, exposing you to risk there, and this excludes other risks such as illness, disease, or misadventure. Despite your insistence, none of us are immortal. If something did happen to you without a suitable replacement on hand, your absence could very well have significantly affected the combat readiness of the *Beijing*."

Rowe shrugged and didn't seem to have an answer.

"Would you say it's irresponsible of Captain Liao to place the working operation of her ship in the hands of one individual, without whom as you so accurately put it, the entire ship would be flying scrap within two weeks?"

Rowe's cockiness evaporated and she threw up her hands. "Look, I didn't *literally* mean the ship would fall to pieces!"

"Well then what did you mean?"

"I just meant that... ugh. The engineers are smart, a'right? And other people can do the job I do—the *Sydney* and the *Tehran* are doing just fine after all—but the point is that I do it best!"

"I'm not contesting that; I'm simply asking you if Liao recognised your value to the fleet and sought to protect that value by passing along your skills to others."

Rowe apparently gave up, folding her arms and looking away. "Whatever."

Fang turned to the judge. "I'll take that as a 'no'. No further questions for this witness, Your Honour."

Martin pushed back his chair and approached the witness stand. He didn't ask anything right away, giving Rowe a chance to compose herself.

"Miss Rowe, my esteemed colleague Mister Fang drew specific mention to an 'extravehicular activity' you performed during a combat involving the *Beijing*. Can you elaborate further on the circumstances behind this?"

Rowe, seeming to recover quickly, gave an eager nod. "Oh, sure. Basically, we blew the shit out of this prison station called Cenar, right? But on the way back, Ben, the psychotic robot, ripped out our jump drive and activated it, teleporting him away, which left us without one. Fortunately, the Kel-Voran we'd allied ourselves with—insane bastards that they are—had a spare jump drive. You see, the jump drive can only carry 200,000 tonnes no matter what. It's because gravity messes with the drive. So normally, they can only work in Lagrange points, which are naturally occurring points of extreme microgravity found near celestial bodies. Once you hit 200,000 tonnes, your own mass is generating enough of a gravity field to throw it off. Anyway, the Kel-Voran ships break in half, so they're really two parts which jump separately, a really cool—"

"Thank you," said Martin, "for this enlightening segue, but please, the battle."

"Uh, right. Yeah. Anyway, so Ben took the *Beijing*'s jump drive. Fortunately the Kel-Voran had a spare. They gave one half's jump drive to us while the other half bought us some time. We didn't have time to carry the jump drive inside, so we just attached it to the hull and jumped away. And by *we*, I mean *I*."

Martin nodded understandingly. "And nobody else on board had the potential skills to complete this operation, right?"

Rowe gave a nasally, heaving laugh. "Nup."

"Do you think anyone does?"

"Nah. Maybe the combined teams of the *Sydney* and the *Tehran*, but probably not as fast as I could."

"So you would say Liao's decision to keep you on board, to add you to her crew despite your lack of military rank and service, was a wise one? That despite the risk of the loss of your knowledge, your presence provided a unique boon to the crew that could not be replicated through any other means?"

"Damn straight."

"And without you, the *Beijing* would not have returned from the assault on Cenar?"

Rowe leaned back in her chair, grinning widely. "Sounds about right."

Martin pursed his lips thoughtfully. "Can you describe for me a standard work day?"

"Well, I tend to not sleep much, so I usually crawl out of bed at 0700-ish to fix whatever broke while I was asleep. I usually check on the reactors first, unless something's on fire or the problem's with the jump drive. See, when we have active missiles in the launch tubes, sometimes that causes fluctuations in the jump drive's power levels. I think it's because they had *idiots* doing the wiring. I have no idea. Anyway, it requires manual balancing or the ship can't jump." Rowe took a deep breath, then began counting issues on her fingers. "Then there are problems with water supply and air filtration units, CO_2 scrubbers going down all the time, the reactionless generators we use as artificial gravity shorting out, even squeaking deck plates. I somehow get everything done and crash into bed by about midnight, or 0100 hours if I'm feeling like I like pain."

"And so there's no real recreation time in your work day, then?"

Rowe shrugged. "Not really. Even when I'm off the job, I'm on the job. It's not your usual forty hour work week; it's pretty full on."

Martin nodded in agreement. "So there's really no time for training anyone else, since you're so busy with your actual work."

Rowe gave a loud, long, pronounced laugh. "There's literally no way I could train some minion up at the same time as I kept that ship sailing."

"So Liao's decision to keep you working, although risky, was the best choice for the ship and its crew?"

"Pretty much, yeah."

Martin turned to Qu. "Very well, no further questions."

*****

"Please state your full name for the court records."

"Commander Kamal Bashiri Iraj, Your Honour, representing the Islamic Republic of Iran Navy."

Kamal Iraj was Liao's XO, her second in command, and someone she had relied on considerably during her time in command. He was taller than Liao, with Persian features and a completely shaved head. His most distinctive feature was a thick, jagged scar running from between his eyes down the left-hand side of his face. He'd earned that scar fighting off a second wave of Toralii boarders who had attacked the ship during their encounter with the *Seth'arak*. Liao had been unconscious.

She gave him a reassuring nod and the questions from Fang began.

"How did Liao handle having an Arab as her first officer? Was there conflict between the two of you?"

Kamal narrowed his eyes slightly. "I wouldn't know, as I am *Persian*, much like most Iranians. I can say that my ethnicity had no bearing on Commander Liao's conduct. I suspect, based on both her words and her actions, that she valued my input. I believe she considers me a confidant and good friend."

"A confidant? But she did not reveal her pregnancy to you until after she had told the Toralii on Velsharn, after she had told Saara, and Doctor Saeed."

Kamal looked at her, but Liao met his gaze and did not look away.

"That is correct, Mister Fang. I was... offended, I admit, but I understand her reasons for doing this. I do not hold it against her."

Fang paused, flipping over a page of his notes, skipping a section. "Very well. Is it true you were made aware of Commander Liao's relationship with Captain James Grégoire?"

"I was."

"And is it true that you did not act on this knowledge because Commander Liao reciprocally concealed your relationship with Lieutenant Bai Peng?"

Kamal affixed an icy stare at the lawyer. "You know a great deal about a ship you've never stepped foot upon, Mister Fang."

"Please answer the question, Commander Iraj," said Qu. "Did you not act upon this information because you knew of Commander Liao's relationship with Captain Grégoire?"

"As you wish, Your Honour: No. There was no reciprocity and we did not 'collude' to disguise the truth. It is true, though, that we as commanding officers exercised discretion where it was appropriate in an unusual situation to preserve the ship's day-to-day operations."

Fang shuffled his papers, laying one on top. "So you were engaged in a same-sex relationship with Lieutenant Peng?"

Kamal leaned forward slightly. "Did he tell you that?"

"That's irrelevant, Commander. Answer the question."

Liao watched as Kamal stared down the lawyer.

"Yes," he finally answered, "but it was brief. It ended when Peng was transferred away from the vessel after Lieutenant Jiang regained consciousness and resumed her post as chief tactical officer. To the best of my knowledge, Peng is now serving a post aboard the Cerberus Mars Lagrange Point blockade."

"So he is not aboard the *Beijing* any longer?"

"I already said that he is not, no."

"Was he transferred away because of your relationship?"

Kamal shook his head emphatically. "No. That decision was made because Lieutenant Jiang has much experience with the *Beijing*'s weapons systems, including actual combat experience. Peng, while eager to learn, did not adapt as well as Jiang, and his expertise was better suited to a less demanding position." He turned to Qu. "In short, Your Honour, Jiang was better and the *Beijing* needs the best."

Liao had taken no pleasure in that transfer, but she was glad that Jiang had recovered.

"Very well," said Fang. "No further questions."

Liao looked to Martin expectantly, but he just stood and addressed Qu without looking at her. "No questions for this witness, Your Honour."

She stared at him as he took his seat. No questions? She wanted to ask him why, but instead, bit her tongue. It would be her turn next.

*****

And then it was her turn. Liao eased herself into the chair provided, exhaling as she made herself comfortable. The view from this side of the stand was remarkably different than from the defendant's box; she had imagined it to be empowering, staring down the entire court, but instead, she found it to be intimidating.

Perhaps this was by design.

"State your name for the court records."

"Commander Melissa Liao, People's Republic of China Army Navy."

Fang faced her directly for the first time. As he stared at her, seemingly examining her and judging her all at once, Liao slowly gained a new respect for just how skilled the lawyer was. She felt as though Fang's gaze were made of iron, piercing her mental defences and laying her secrets bare.

"Thank you. Can you please, Commander Liao, in your own words, describe your last year of service."

"I was offered command of the TFR *Beijing* in July, 2036, a year before her scheduled completion. At the time, I had been serving as the Executive Officer for the Han class Type 091 submarine 404, then later the 410. Admiral Tiong, my CO in that post, was originally to command the *Beijing*, but a minor heart issue disqualified him from service in space. Similarly, Admiral Ng, Captain Chou, Captain Lo, Commander Liáng and Commander Xiè were deemed unsuitable for reasons of ill health or other commitments, so the duty fell to me."

Fang consulted his notes. "That seems like a remarkably short list for such a desirable post."

"It was," Liao said, "primarily because of the loss of nearly thirty-seven officers of rank commander or above during the attack on Beijing city. Since then, the People's Army Navy has focused on decentralised training exercises."

"Do you find it odd that the PRC appointed a woman to be the commanding officer of the vessel that would carry the name of their capital city?"

Liao found it surprisingly easy to keep her posture even. She knew he was baiting her, trying to shake her nerve.

"I do find it odd, yes. Most high ranking naval officers are male. That doesn't mean I couldn't do the job they asked of me or that I would be a suboptimal choice. The role of Commanding Officer is genderless."

"An interesting statement, Commander, given your current condition."

"The People's Republic Army Navy allows officers of both genders parental leave. I fail to see how my pregnancy is a significant issue."

Fang lowered his notes. "The issue is, Commander, that the *Beijing* is no standard deployment, nor is the Task Force Resolution a standard military operation. The Toralii are out there, Commander, and your unwise and ill-timed pregnancy has endangered us all. If you were commanding a seagoing vessel or a naval base or any other operation, this would be a non-issue."

Liao straightened her back at considerable difficulty. "And, pray tell, how is it different?"

Fang twisted his head, looking around the court room with incredulity. "The Toralii are the greatest threat our species has ever faced, Commander. You of all people should know that. Your trivialisation of this issue is bad comedy."

Liao shook her head emphatically. "No, I'm not trivialising anything. I meant what I said, Fang. The *Beijing* technically operates under Chinese law and under the authority of the People's Republic of China Army Navy. Task Force provisions aside, it is absolutely no different than a seagoing vessel."

"Surely you can admit that's being facetious, Commander. The Pillars of the Earth are, by far, the most important endeavour humanity has ever embarked upon. Our very survival rests in the hands of the commanding officers. They have to be treated differently. We have to make sacrifices to ensure their work is done."

Liao stared at Fang unblinkingly. "If you think that all we have to do is give up everything you hold up as a value, and this will be enough to defeat the Toralii, then I'm afraid you do not know them very well at all." She pointed to Saara without looking at her. "Maybe, when she was sitting where I'm sitting, you should have been more direct with your questions. Saara, is it true what Ben said right before he destroyed Velsharn? Does humanity have a chance against the Toralii?"

"It is not Saara's turn to speak," said Qu, "and I ask you to refrain from further outbursts of that nature, Commander Liao."

Liao's finger trembled, pointing directly at the Toralii she considered her closest friend. "Saara? Saara, I want you to answer my question!"

"Commander Liao, you are out of order."

Liao rose from her seat, both hands squeezing the hard wooden railing of the defendant's box. "SAARA!" Her voice rose to a roar. "ANSWER MY QUESTION!"

The judge banged his gavel, and a grinning Fang gestured helplessly to the packed courtroom, shrugging as though Liao were a lost case. Reporters scribbled in their notebooks, whispers and mutterings drowning out Saara's muttered response.

["No."]

*****

When order was restored, Judge Qu called for a brief recess. Liao took the opportunity to get some fresh air, slipping out the fire exit at the rear of the court building after a quick check to see that it was not alarmed. The front would be swarming with reporters crowding under the overhang to avoid a particularly strong seasonal storm, and she did not feel she could handle facing the horde again.

But her cunning earned her only a moment's peace. The door swung open and Martin stepped into the puddle of water, the whizz-click of an extending umbrella immediately following.

"I told you to keep your calm."

Blunt as she had expected. "You did," Liao said, "but it had to be said."

"Really? You had to tell the court that our species is basically done for?"

Liao looked away down the side of the large brick building. "It was necessary for Qu to know the stakes, to know my mind, to understand what occupies my thoughts every day when we're out there."

Martin rested his back up against the stone wall, rain pattering against his umbrella. He held it over Liao's head. "You picked a poor way to do it. What you did made you look unstable. We don't want unstable."

Liao fixed her gaze upon him. "Right. So why no questions for Kamal?"

He looked at her for some time, the rain pattering down on the umbrella he held over her head. "The practice of law is not as fluid as people think. The justice system, flawed though it is, is not a wild courtroom drama, not normally. It's intended to be the solemn, sober collection of facts with an aim at the approximation of the truth of a matter. However, that said, each side in a legal dispute is expected to put forward their case in the best possible light. Mister Fang has nothing personal against you; he's merely doing his job."

"I know."

"Good. Some clients take these things very personally, which I can understand." Martin shuffled, his expensive shoes sloshing in the water. "With this in mind," he said, "sometimes the best move you can play is to do nothing."

Liao reached up and pinched the bridge of her nose. "I thought you said we didn't want to look unstable. Fang made it seem like my ship was a gay bathhouse and everyone was shagging the whole time we were up there."

"Well, maybe," Martin admitted, "but I believe Fang erred in this case. Kamal's relationship was inappropriate, yes, but it was understandable. Kamal has an excellent service record, and the court took his answers favourably, I think. Sometimes, the best thing you can say is nothing at all, especially when you're ahead."

She looked at him, trying to gauge his honesty. "You think we're ahead?"

Martin pursed his lips a moment. "Fifty fifty," he said. "It could go either way. Your little outburst didn't help."

"Sorry. I was going for the 'strong and determined' look."

"There are better ways to make that work. Your redheaded friend's little show-and-tell didn't help either. I thought you said you told her—"

"I definitely told her."

He laughed, a low, happy laugh that Liao felt was strangely out of place in the dank, smelly alley, rain pattering down all around them. "No worries, mate. What's done is done. For what it's worth, if we were home, it'd be less of an issue. There's a saying in Australia... The only person who wears a suit is the defendant. I doubt Qu will see it that way though."

Liao absently rubbed her abdomen. "The shirt was funny though."

"I would have chosen 'Fuck The Police' myself."

She gave a snorting laugh, then eased herself away from the wall. "Okay, well, whatever. Time to face the music again, right?"

"Yes, but this time, it's my turn to play," promised Martin, snapping his umbrella closed as Liao stepped back through the open door and into the court building.

*****

"I apologise for my disturbance."

It was difficult to say. Liao was of the firm belief that being pregnant didn't make a woman helpless, so taking advantage of the leniency many would give someone in her position rubbed her the wrong way, but she knew it had to be done. Martin had counselled her in the strongest possible terms to set her pride aside and seek every advantage she could. As she finished speaking, she saw him gave her an approving nod out of the corner of her eye.

"I want to be clear," Qu said, "That the court understands how stressful this whole thing has been on you and recognises the difficulty of your pregnancy." His voice became pointed. "Although there'll be no further outbursts, will there?"

Liao looked to Fang. "No." Then back towards Qu. "And no, Your Honour."

Qu seemed satisfied, so Liao turned her attention to Martin. "You can ask your questions."

"Very well. For the benefit of the court, can you please detail how you report to your superiors when the *Beijing* is out in space?"

"Simply put, it's not possible. The nature of our FTL technology is limited. The jump drive allows our vessels to travel anywhere without gravimetric interference, but the number of ships we have that are jump capable is limited. We can't afford a Broadsword messenger unless the situation is truly dire, so by and large, unless we're travelling back and forth ourselves, it's just us out there."

Martin turned a page on his notes. "And while covered in your training, this is unusual for a modern military, yes? To be out of communications with their command structure?"

"Very."

"This must make command decisions difficult."

"To a significant extent, yes, since the command staff are acting with imperfect and outdated information. There are times, such as the assault on Kor'Vakkar, where contacting Fleet Command wasn't possible. Then we were on our own."

"That couldn't have been easy on you."

"It wasn't. Sometimes we had support though. The destruction of the prison station of Cenar was one such operation."

"So, just to be clear, after you'd launched that operation, once the ship had jumped away, was there any way to stop the operation if you were ordered to?"

She shook her head. "No. Once a ship is out of radio range, there's no way to receive support from Earth. No way to get in contact with your superiors."

"And yet both of those operations were successful, despite significant damage to the Pillars, correct?"

"I'd say they were a success, yes. The primary mission objectives were accomplished, along with significant success with secondary targets and targets of opportunity. All the ships made it back, more or less. Against the Toralii Alliance, I'd be reluctant to classify that as anything other than complete and total victory."

Martin, leaning forward slightly, seemed to get to his point. "So even though mistakes were made and the decisions you made were never perfect, you still did the absolute best you could do—and you succeeded despite long odds against a foe you, conventionally, had little chance against."

"I'd say that's an accurate assessment of the *Beijing*'s mission history so far."

Martin moved to the next section of his notes. "Aside from the Toralii, you encountered another species, yes?"

"Correct. The Kel-Voran, a warrior culture who frequently skirmish with the Toralii. Their representative was Garn, who held the rank of Starslayer."

"And what did Garn say the Kel-Voran call you?"

"The Butcher of Kor'Vakkar, The Bringer of Terror, Slayer of Varsian the Immortal." Her lip curled up slightly. "I told him Miss Rowe was the one who actually killed Varsian, and I wasn't sure about the rest of it."

Martin inclined his head slightly, gesturing to the courtroom. "It sounds like they respect you, maybe even fear you."

"Something like that, yes. Very few have stood against the Toralii and lived to tell about it. Fewer still, more than once. Garn seemed to know who I was, despite none of our ships having any contact with their species. The Toralii are talking about us."

"About us as a species, or about you, specifically?"

Liao smiled slightly. "About me by name."

"And what happened to Garn?"

Her face fell and she let it happen. "The construct known as Ben ripped the jump drive from our ship, disappearing with it and leaving us stranded. The Kel-Voran gave us one of theirs while the other half of their ship held off the attackers. He died defending us."

"It's interesting that an alien who you'd just met would give his life for you, isn't it?"

"That's their way, but I admit that it is extremely odd. My reputation must have spread far."

Martin nodded. "I think we can all agree that it has been well earned." Then to Qu. "No further questions, Your Honour."

*****

Time passed. The arguments were made, back and forth, and the judge was left in deliberation. Finally, when he returned, Liao steadied herself for his judgement.

"All rise for the verdict."

She did, and Judge Qu took a moment to collect his thoughts before speaking again.

"Humanity and all its nations exist in an unprecedented time, a time where the ordinary, the routine, the expected, must be treated with a critical, lenient eye. Our first contact with alien species has not been peaceful and we know now that if the species of man is to exist in this vast universe teeming with life, we are going to have to fight for that right. The actions of Commander Melissa Liao while under the command of the TFR *Beijing* have not been perfect, but they have been shown to be effective. She has, for the large part, acted within the framework of the behaviour we all expected her to, and she has accomplished incredible things. For this, she should be commended."

His features hardened somewhat.

"But there is a certain element of recklessness in her command style, and I sense that Commander Liao feels that she has something to prove; perhaps being a woman in charge of the most prestigious posting in the People's Army Navy was not something even *she* felt capable enough to do. Her lingering doubts caused her to overcompensate and to take risks to prove herself, risks that have sometimes paid off and sometimes lead to catastrophic failures. When we are playing with the fate of the entire species, we cannot have catastrophic failures. We cannot allow ourselves to fail, because the stakes are too high. We cannot risk the extinction of our species."

Qu reached for his notes. To Liao, the gesture seemed to be in slow motion, the wait almost impossible to bear.

"On the charge of dereliction of duty for turning her ship over to the construct known as Ben, I find the defendant guilty. I fine her 750 yuan and place a note in her record."

A slap on the wrist. The fine would come out of her wages. Not a concern at all.

"On the charge of conduct unbecoming an officer, I find the defendant not guilty."

She closed her eyes a moment. That was the most sticky of all the charges and, being honest with herself, the charge that she felt least able to avoid.

"And on the charge of reckless endangerment of fleet assets, I find the defendant guilty. I sentence her to be reassigned to a terrestrial post for twelve months so her command potential can be re-examined, pending the completion of her maternity leave. I proclaim this court to be closed."

Qu tapped the gavel against the block and Liao saw her future, in a moment, slip away.

Chapter II

"Their Lives, As They Are"
*****

New York
United States

Six Months Later

The baby monitor in the centre of her bedside table crackled and, just as she feared, the sound of wailing, compressed through the narrow bandwidth of the radio, filled their bedroom. It was night out. "It's your turn," Liao murmured, nudging James with her elbow.

"Mrrmgnrg, wha-? It is? I thought it was yours."

They'd slept more than intended, more than they had thought possible given they were caring for an infant who seemed to enjoy crying as much as she enjoyed spilling the bottles of milk all over her face, chest, the table and the floor. Liao felt James kiss her cheek from behind, his arms around her body like a second blanket, his dark skinned hands holding her close. Safe. Secure.

"Mmm, you don't get it. When you're here on leave, we don't do *turns*. You do it all and I sleep, because it's the only chance. This is my..." she yawned loudly and smacked her lips. "... *biannual* sleep, so go and don't complain. Bottle's in the fridge, middle shelf, usual place."

James groaned and slipped out of his warm bed to feed their child. Liao watched him leave.

Getting the apartment in New York had been something of a necessity. She had initially remained in China, staying with her parents, but Liao had been hounded by the press incessantly. To spare her family the grief and to give herself some peace and quiet, Liao had insisted on going elsewhere. She and James were not to be tabloid fodder, more famous for their illicit affair than the numerous battles they had fought side by side. Although sleep was at a premium for the two of them, even being alone in the room felt intolerable; Liao felt like following him out, to talk while he fed their as-yet-unnamed infant.

That desire died the moment she closed her eyes again and instantly fell asleep.

Hours passed as James tended the child. When she finally reopened her eyes, light filtered in through the cracks in the curtains, and she could see that it was morning. Her nose twinged; the savoury scent of cooking reached it, warm and moist, tinged with garlic, butter and spices. Fish, she was certain.

Climbing out of bed and into the cool, dry air, she made her way across the chilly tiles of their rented apartment following the sound of hissing and frying. James, his ebony skinned body as naked as she, stood by the stove, a large cast-iron frying pan hissing as two slices of fish cooked over the electric pan.

From her vantage point behind the man, Liao could see the grid of scars along his back. She remembered how James had told her he'd gotten them during his stay with the Toralii Alliance. They had a large, square, metal mesh that would be heated to red hot temperatures and applied directly to the skin. Torture was not a particularly effective method of interrogation as the prisoner would often say anything, true or not, to stop the pain, but apparently the Alliance engaged in the practice anyway. It was, as Saara had once explained to her, part interrogation, part the business of extracting information, part pleasure on behalf of the jailers.

"How did she go down?" Liao murmured, sleepily draping her arms around his shoulders, giving him a gentle squeeze and letting her hands stroke over his pectoral muscles. The warmth of the cooking stove and James's body warmed her.

"Pretty well, once she'd been fed. Right back to sleep."

"That's my girl. Is that fish?"

"Yup. You would not believe how much it costs in this country," James said, deftly flipping each of the thick strips so the other side was exposed to the heat. "I knew the American economy was still bad, but jeez. How do people afford to eat in this place?"

"They often don't," Liao answered, squeezing him again, resting her cheek against his shoulders. "Things just haven't been the same in this place ever since the great collapse. Things are looking up for the rest of the world, but... they're still pretty dark for the U.S."

The plate sizzled away as the fish roasted, and Liao realised how hungry she was. "You haven't cooked this before. Is it nearly done? I'm starving."

James laughed, turning his head to rub his cheek against hers. "It hasn't yet begun, love. Watch and learn. First, we apply a second helping of the garlic butter..."

Liao moved with James as he stepped to one side and reached for a sifter, pouring in a small pouch of flour and adding a packet of salt. He sifted it into a plastic bowl, added half a cup of milk, then whisked until completely mixed. A tab of butter was tapped into the bowl, then Liao watched him beat the mixture into a thick, creamy batter. A thick helping of maple syrup, poured out of a bottle emblazoned with a large Canadian flag, was the final ingredient.

"This is for the fish?" Liao stared curiously at the mixture. She was not a cook, somewhat by choice. It was expected of her, in the post-One-Child-Policy China, that she would grow to be a housewife... cooking, cleaning, fucking. But this was not a life for her. Somewhat defiantly, she had never learnt to cook, so the entire process was slightly alien to her.

"Are you kidding?" James twisted his head to look at her. "You're kidding, right?"

She rolled her shoulders helplessly, casually pinching his nipple.

"Ow!"

She laughed, nipping his ear. "Don't make fun of my inability to boil water, okay?"

"Right, right. You can blow up a city from orbit but you can't cook pancakes."

Although the comment was made jovially, Liao immediately thought of Velsharn. The Telvan colony on Velsharn had shown her much kindness, particularly Qadan, their leader, who had shown her hospitality and whom she considered a friend. Yet Ben, bent on revenge, took control of the *Beijing* and attacked them. On her monitors, she had watched her ship's missiles plummet through the atmosphere, little falling stars that burst with a radiant light shining over the island, baking the inhabitants to crisps. She remembered walking through the ashes of that place with Kamal, of finding Qadan's scorched body, and the seared bodies of the children...

Suddenly, the smell of sizzling fish lost its appeal.

"How about just pancakes for me, huh?"

James looked hurt, confused. "You don't want my fish? It's my famous garlic butter! This stuff is divine! It is the flesh of the Gods, battered in elemental *sex* and roasted to perfection on this cheap electric stove. You have to try some."

Liao felt nauseous. It felt like morning sickness, but different. This was entirely emotional. "No. I'm sure it's really good, but seriously, just pancakes for me." She forced a smile, giving his bare chest a firm squeeze. "Make it a double helping."

James seemed concerned for her, but he shrugged it off. "A double helping it is. More ultra-fish for me, I suppose."

She reached down, slowly stroking her hands over his taunt abdomen. "You'll get fat," she cautioned. "Then you'll get thrown off your ship, too."

James began pouring out the pancake batter with one hand, flipping the sizzling fish strips with the other. "Well, if I did get the boot, it would mean more sex, though. That'd be nice."

"Wouldn't it just." Liao pursed her lips, resting her chin on his shoulder and rubbing it back and forth. "How... *is* the ship, anyway?"

"The *Tehran* or the *Beijing*?"

"*The* ship. *My* ship."

James lifted the fish and flipped it again. "Commodore Vong is a fine CO," he admitted. Liao tensed slightly but tried to keep herself under control. "But he's no Liao. He's more experienced at the command side of it, yes, and he actually gets his paperwork in on time, but he's not as... *elegant* as you were when it came to command of a spaceship, nor as bold. The crew misses you, Saara in particular. Rowe mouthed off to him over some trivial matter and got herself replaced as the chief of engineering. She's now just an 'adviser' and not very happy about it. Chang tore a muscle during one of the counter-insurgency drills and has been off recovering for the last two months... Alex and Rowe split up again, but then got back together. The Broadsword *Switchblade* was damaged in a training exercise and only just started flying again... so, you know. Same old, same old, really."

"Nothing too serious, then. Glad to hear it. What about the *Tehran*? How's your ship holding up?"

James put a wide frying pan on the second hot plate, letting it warm up. "Well, the alliance with the Kel-Voran has solidified, thanks to the efforts of the *Sydney* crew. We attacked an Alliance supply convoy headed for one of their shipyards, blew up a fairly impressive amount of tonnage, but that's not the best part. Our marines captured a Toralii scout ship after the *Beijing* disabled its engines."

Liao blinked, slowly raising her head. "I would have thought you'd mention that when I asked about the *Beijing*, but... wait. We took a Toralii ship?"

"Same configuration as Saara's old vessel. We've rechristened her the *Rubens*. We're using her and some ships from the *Sydney* to run black ops, wreaking havoc in the Toralii supply chain... Magnet's leading the wing. Doing a pretty fine job, too."

"Magnet?" The name triggered some kind of memory in her, of a pilot from the *Sydney* who was wounded in the assault on the Toralii mining colony. Captain Knight had told her that he was making a fine recovery; it seemed like he'd survived his ejection and subsequent spacewalk just fine.

James reached out for a stick of butter, slowly smearing it over the empty frying pan. "Flight Lieutenant Mike Williams, call sign Magnet. Some hotshot from the *Sydney*. Ugly mother fucker, but he's a great pilot. He was on the crew that negotiated with the Kel-Voran... Now he's moving up in the world. Their ship is due back shortly, actually. With a bit of luck, you might be able to meet him."

Liao gripped his shoulder, closing her eyes a moment. "I don't think so. I'm nobody now, remember? I get the occasional television interview and that's it. Trust me, caring for our girl is a full time job."

There was a quiet pause as the butter began to melt. "I was thinking," began James. "Did you like the name Jasmine?"

Jasmine. It was a nice name, but Liao shook her head. "Not really. It seems... pretentious."

"My cousin's named Jasmine."

Liao yawned lazily, clicking her tongue. "Well, your cousin has a pretentious name then."

"We have to decide sometime. She's three months old... We can't keep calling her 'the baby'. You have to give her a name soon. She'll be talking before you know it."

"James, I told you about this... Names are important to me. I can't make this decision lightly."

"I know. I'm happy to wait, but still... We should decide sooner rather than later."

"Okay, okay, okay. We will."

"Good."

"Oh, someone's writing a book about our sex-ploits, by the way."

James laughed as he gently brushed the surface of the pan with a little extra butter to grease it. "Oh?"

"Mmm, a fictionalised version of us and our sordid, career-ending affair. She's calling it *Playing Amongst the Stars*. It's some kind of steamy erotic romance. We're going to be superstars. The publisher asked for a raunchy photo for the cover, and I even got a call from a men's mag asking for a naked shoot. They were paying pretty damn well, too: fifteen grand each."

James snorted dismissively. He seemed, for a moment, to be offended. Liao reached around and touched his chin, turning his face to her.

"I said no to both of them. You know that, yeah?"

He smiled. "I know." James reached for the batter, pouring out a pancake roughly fifteen centimetres wide. The smell of it cooking merged with the smell of the fish, helping to dampen the scent of roasted flesh, for which Liao was quietly grateful. Her hands idly explored James's chest.

"So tell me more about this *Rubens*, then. I didn't hear about that on the news."

James smirked at her. "Of course you didn't. Technically, that's top secret, highly classified operating information that'd probably get me put up against a wall and shot if I told anyone, especially someone who was currently on leave."

"Tell anyone what?" Liao remarked, smiling and kissing his cheek. "Don't worry, I won't tell a soul. If you get shot, I'll be sad. Kind of. Who would cook for me then?"

He laughed, testing the pancake's edge with the spatula. "Summer?"

"Phht. That lunatic would burn down my kitchen just to see what the flames look like."

"Saara?"

"Eh, she probably would. How's she doing under Commodore Vong?"

James looked surprised. "You didn't know?"

"Know what?"

"Saara transferred to the *Tehran*. She's just finishing up some things in orbit, then she's going to come visit."

Liao's features brightened. "Well, you're full of good news today."

Liao slid her hand to James's, taking the spatula and cutting off a piece off the pancake. She wiggled it under the fork and brought it up to her lips, blowing on it a few times before popping it into her mouth. "Not bad." She swallowed.

"Just not bad? Phht. It's *my* cooking. It's always amazing."

"Right, right."

They ate, for a time, laughing and joking, the hot pancakes burning their mouths. When their meal was consumed, James tugged her towards the shower, but Liao stopped him.

"You got the condoms, right?"

He laughed. "Yeah. Stop asking me that."

Liao pointed to the other bedroom where their infant was sleeping soundly. "Hey, you want another one of those? Do ya?"

He shook his head and, laughing, the two stepped into the bathroom.

*****

Four days later

Liao, cradling her infant, pulled open the door with a wide smile, barely able to keep her excitement in check. These days, it was rare that she received visitors, even rarer that they were her friends making social calls.

"Come in, Saara. Please. Don't mind the mess."

The Toralii woman, flanked by two marines, stepped through the door. Liao moved out of the way for them, smiling incessantly. Her friend's visit was highly anticipated; Liao had been pestering James to give her time off and it had been, finally, granted. Despite warning her of the mess, Liao had done her best to clean the apartment before Saara's arrival and had even spent some money getting fresh flowers for the vase, something that cost her a pretty penny.

["Thank you, Commander."]

Liao waved Saara's guards away. "I'll be okay with her; I promise."

"Very well, Commander," one answered. "We're here for her protection, not yours. Commodore Vong thought having an unescorted Toralii wandering Earth could be detrimental for her safety."

Liao was forced to agree with his assessment. "Well, she's here now. Thank you." She shut the door, then turned to Saara, beaming. "I was wondering when you were going to visit! Have they been keeping you busy, then?"

Saara bobbed her head. ["They have, yes. Captain Grégoire is a fair commander, but he expects much of those under his command."]

"Well that's good. Wouldn't want you getting bored, then."

["Rest assured, Captain, I am not bored."]

There was something in Saara's demeanour that caused Liao a moment's concern, a little voice nagging at the back of her head. She didn't seem as happy as Liao had expected. Saara was usually a lot more excited to see her, a lot more energetic in her behaviour. Now she seemed reserved, more formal than usual, even distracted.

"Everything okay?" Liao asked. Saara gave a slow nod.

["Yes, Captain Liao. I am well."]

She narrowed her eyes slightly. "You seem... really kind of distracted."

["I... I suppose this is true."] Saara looked away a moment. ["To be honest with you, I had considered not coming at all. The deaths of the Telvan on Velsharn weigh heavily on me, I confess, and seeing your face causes those memories to resurface anew. It has made me reluctant to see you again since my appointment in your court."]

Liao reached out and touched Saara's fur-covered forearm. "I know," she said. "It hurts for me, too. I remember going down to the planet, seeing the devastation firsthand. But you know I didn't want that to happen, don't you? That wasn't what I wanted."

Saara hesitated for a moment, then looked back to Liao, her big yellow eyes hiding a profound regret and sorrow. ["I know,"] she said. ["Although, I wish things had not turned out the way they had. So many dead... all innocent civilians who had done nothing wrong. And children."]

"I wish it were different, too," said Liao, giving a slow nod of her head, forcing a sad smile. "But we're here now. I wish I could have brought Qadan here, shown him Earth, but that was not to be. Sometimes fate deals us a harsh hand, and all we can do is try to make the best of what we have."

["I know,"] said Saara, ["but that doesn't quell the ache in my heart."]

Liao adjusted her hold on the small infant, leaning in and wrapping an arm around Saara's chest, giving her a tight hug. She buried her face in the fur of her shoulder, forcing herself to keep her breathing steady.

"I know," Liao said. "Believe me, I know."

The next morning

A faint knocking on the door awoke her from her rest. Light filtered through the cracks in the curtains. She stretched, cracking her joints, before slipping out of bed. James hadn't stirred yet. She gave his bare backside a gentle pat, pulled a towel off the floor, then headed for the door. She stepped through the kitchen, then to the foyer, passing by a snoozing Saara on the couch. Determined to let at least someone in their apartment sleep, Liao pushed back the cover on the peephole to the outside.

A clean cut, youthful looking man in the uniform of the People's Republic of China Army Navy was standing there. A junior officer by his epaulets, a Lieutenant.

"Hello?"

The man straightened his back. "Commander Liao?"

"Yes?"

"I'm Lieutenant Kang Tai, Commander. I've been assigned to your protection."

Frowning, Liao blinked, eyeing the man through the peephole. "Protection? I didn't request anything like that."

"The request came directly from Commodore Vong, ma'am. Can you please open the door?"

Liao would have opened the door, but this event struck her as unusual. "Got some ID?"

"I'll just get it out. Hang on."

Moments later a thin ID card was held up before the peephole. Lieutenant Kang Tai, People's Republic of China Army Navy, Military Police. The hologram looked authentic.

"One moment."

She discarded the towel, picked up a set of jeans and a shirt, then roughly shoved all the other clothes under the couch. She and James had not been expecting visitors, and it had been nice, she admitted, to discard the routine of dressing in the same clothes every day, especially now she was out of maternity wear.

Satisfied she was adequately dressed, she undid the latch on the door and turned the knob, opening it. "Please come in," she offered, "but don't mind the mess. We weren't expecting visitors."

Tai stepped through the threshold, smiling slightly. "It's quite fine, ma'am."

Liao raised an eyebrow sardonically. "Aren't you going to say something in Chinese just so I can rebuke you and ask you to speak in English only?"

Tai laughed at that, rolling his eyes. "They warned me about your preference in languages, and I was specifically picked because of my English fluency. So no."

She folded her arms, frowning. "Really?"

"They told me you wouldn't be happy about me telling you that, either."

"So far 'they' are two for two." Liao shook her head. "I still don't know why you're here."

"There was a threat against you," Tai said. "It came from the Kel-Voran embassy. I suppose there are downsides to being famous, ma'am."

She raised an eyebrow curiously. "The one in Melbourne? I'm not sure I understand; what do the Kel-Voran have against me?"

"Nothing. The message was relayed through the Kel-Voran by the Toralii Alliance. Fleet Command believes the threat is credible, so they've assigned a guard to your person."

Liao tried very hard not to roll her eyes. "This has absolutely nothing to do with the alien crashing on my couch?"

Tai shook his head emphatically. "No. Security's vetted Saara. She's not a threat."

"Well, right. I'm not sure how an armed bodyguard will assist against the Toralii. Their method of assassination seems to be orbital bombardment, and while I'm sure you're good at your job, I don't think you can prevent that kind of thing. Takes a little more than pepper spray."

Tai gave a firm nod. "No, you're right of course..." His features brightened somewhat. "But the powers that be had to be seen to be doing something, which is why they sent me. Of course it's all political, I'm afraid."

Liao nodded. "Well, thanks for your honesty. I appreciate that."

"They said you would."

She tried, and failed, to keep her mouth closed. "I wish 'they' would put as much effort into finding out more about this supposed threat, and avoiding unnecessary politics, as they did in predicting my every move."

Tai smiled an apologetic smile. "You and me both. Alas we are but mortals, Captain."

Liao waved her hand at that. "To be a captain you have to have a ship. It's just Commander now, but you know what? These days I'd prefer simply Melissa."

"That's a little informal, isn't it?"

She gestured down to her jeans. "My official post in the People's Army is Person of Interest to the Parade and Propaganda Unit. Literally, my job for the last six months has been to simply *exist*. I think I can throw away silly things like ranks and titles at this point." Her voice softened slightly. "I'm not a captain anymore. I'm basically a civilian. Might as well act like it."

"Very well, as you wish." Tai stepped into the room, casually putting his hands into his pockets. "I'll note that in my paperwork."

She wrinkled her nose. "Yeah, you make sure you do. As well as the filthy state of my apartment, I suppose?"

Tai smiled. "Nah, that one can remain our secret, assuming you kept some of that scotch you were famous for having."

"I kind of hoped I'd become famous for blowing up not one, but two Toralii outposts, for winning hopeless battles against long odds... and for fucking another space captain." She gave a depreciating smile. "Well, maybe not that last bit."

"Unfortunately, you're well known for all three. It's an unfortunate problem in our media driven society that one's victories are forgotten and our defeats immortalised."

"Yes, well, until we die. Then the process reverses itself; nobody can speak ill of the dead."

"No, I guess not. So, scotch?"

Liao pointed to the kitchen. "Top shelf, third one along. Pour me some while you're at it; the baby will be awake soon."

Tai stepped away to fetch the drinks, and Liao slumped into the seat beside her couch, glancing over at Saara who seemed to be fast asleep. When Tai returned, she had nearly joined her Toralii friend in having a nap, but she accepted the drink without complaint. In seconds it was gone, and Liao savoured the burning feeling as it slipped down her throat.

"So, if you don't mind me asking, what's it like being in space?" asked Tai, sitting on the chair opposite hers, giving Saara a curious glance. Liao had become quite accustomed to the Toralii's presence and sometimes forgot that it would be startling for those who were not used to her.

"Huh?"

"Space. You were there, remember?" Tai leaned forward, cupping his drink with both hands. "What's it like?"

"Hell," Liao answered, resting her empty cup down with a clink of ice on glass. "Back in my day, they used to shoot you up there in a rocket. These days, you get a ride in a Broadsword, but those old rockets didn't have artificial gravity. I don't know about you, but when I'm in zero gravity, my lunch usually makes a cameo appearance. When you get there, you're crammed up with eight thousand crew, most of whom have somewhat lackadaisical attitudes towards bathing, and all of them treat you as some kind of surrogate parent to come crying to with every little detail. They fight, whine, fuck, get blind drunk, break things, get homesick, cry for their mummy, have affairs, their wives or husbands have affairs, get claustrophobic... They have every personal problem under the sun. They devolve into a kind of child-like state. The food is inedible, the paperwork endless, and the job tiresome. You don't get much sleep, and unlike a real ship, you can't just go out and take a walk—it's mighty cold out there. You live in a highly oxygenated environment so your fitness suffers and, due to being surrounded by the void and millions of kilometres away from anywhere, it's dangerous. People call on you at every time of day and night and your life revolves around the Operations room. There's a constant threat of alien attack, aliens who, might I add, significantly out-class you, out-number you, out-gun you. You never see your family. It's intensely lonely, and when you come back from doing the impossible, they throw you in a court martial. And did I mention the pay is terrible?"

He laughed. "Eh, the pay's okay. Beats my old job, working IT for the coal mines." Tai swished his drink. "So why did you do it?"

Liao tilted her head back, staring up at the ceiling, silent for a moment. "Because it was the best job I've ever had."

"You realise how insane that sounds, right?"

She nodded, instinctively reaching for the empty glass, then putting it back down. "Yeah." Liao laughed, shaking away her memories. "Doesn't make it untrue, though. It's... a wonderful opportunity, despite its hardships. I think that year in space was probably the best of my life, and I did a damn good job, too. I think it really was my calling. It was something I could do really well. I was born to be the captain of that ship. It was the best thing I'd ever done, and I was good at it." She cast her eyes to the door that held her sleeping infant. "Better captain than I am a mother, I think."

Tai drank the last of his drink. "I don't know anything about that, really. She's still alive; that would indicate that you've done just fine."

"Maybe."

"You really haven't named your kid?"

"Nope." An edge of annoyance crept into her tone. "I've already had this discussion with James, and it's really something we should sort out ourselves."

Tai held up a hand. "Of course. I'm merely saying, it's very odd. And the press is really curious about why you're doing it. I think they're guessing it's some kind of ploy to throw them off."

"The press can go fuck themselves. I—we—haven't decided on a good name yet, and that's all I have to say. In time, she'll have the most beautiful and perfect name, but right now... we're not ready."

The door to their bedroom swung open with a faint creak. James stepped, naked, into the foyer.

Liao pointed over her shoulder. "James, Mister Tai. Mister Tai, naked James."

"Nice to meet you," James mumbled, yawning as he stretched.

Tai did a double take, but James seemed too tired to care, simply shrugging and walking into the kitchen. "Does he normally do that?"

"We haven't had much time to sleep, what with the baby needing attention every few hours or so," Liao said, "and we don't get many visitors."

Tai grimaced slightly. "Captain Grégoire is supposed to be resting during his shore leave."

"A recognised part of shore leave is to spend time with family," Liao countered. "And besides, it's good for his morale."

Tai laughed, nodding. "Right, right. And I probably shouldn't be telling captains what to do with their time."

Liao waved a hand. "Whatever. I told you; it's fine."

Tai peered at her for a moment as though confused by the surprising informality, then seemed to remember something, snapping his fingers. "Well actually, there was one thing, too. Captain de Lugo was hoping to visit sometime in the next couple of months, as he will be in town inspecting some of the gear scheduled to be put in the TFR *Madrid*."

The name rang a bell. Putting that thought aside for a moment, Liao raised an eyebrow. "They finished that thing?"

"Not quite. It's spaceworthy, but a lot of the systems haven't been installed: flight control, jump navigation, fighter launch subsystems. It has rail guns though, apparently, according to the news."

"No nukes?" she asked. The *Triumph* class ships, such as the *Beijing* and the *Madrid*, carried warheads tipped with nuclear devices. Although the rail guns had substantially more effective range due to their higher speed, and conventional thought had anticipated that the vast distances found in space combat would render more conventional weapons useless, the reality was space warfare took place at extremely close quarters. The same problem was observed when aircraft started to carry long-range missiles in the Vietnam war; although an F4 Phantom could destroy a Soviet MiG from up to twenty miles away, matters of identification and the unreliability of missiles meant that close-range dogfighting was the most common form of engagement. This process of relearning lessons the armed forces of the world had already learnt was painful but progressing rapidly.

"Not yet. Apparently they're being installed fairly soon-ish; there's hope that the *Madrid* can join the *Sydney* on its next operation. There's talk of pairing the two ships on a more permanent basis so they can project more force as a unit."

Although the *Sydney* had suffered the worst of them, all of the first three Pillars of the Earth had suffered various system malfunctions and instabilities during their initial shakedown cruises. She hoped the worst of the issues would be resolved for the new breed of ships. "Good."

["Mister Tai,"] came a voice from the couch. Saara pulled herself up into a sitting position, giving a yawn that displayed a wide array of very sharp teeth. ["Apologies, but I felt I could pretend to be asleep no longer."] She smiled to the guard, a genuine smile, but one Liao thought was somewhat guarded. ["I am Saara."]

"A pleasure," Tai said, nodding politely. "I've read your file. Although I must confess; my Toralii language is not very good. I'm sorry."

Saara shuffled somewhat uncomfortably, looking to Liao. ["I must confess, I served in a humble position when I was with the Telvan. I am unused to celebrity and having my name be known to every stranger. I am not sure I can ever become accustomed to it."]

"You and I both," said Liao. Seeing Tai's confused look, Liao repeated what she had said in English.

James wandered back out, turned down the corridor, then disappeared into the laundry room. Tai discreetly drank until James returned, moments later, now wearing a pair of ill-fitting pants and a shirt.

"So who's this Mister Tai, then?"

Liao grimaced slightly. "My bodyguard, apparently."

"You requested a bodyguard?"

Tai gave an apologetic smile. "No, Captain, it wasn't her. Commodore Vong did."

Liao reached out and patted James on the thigh. "I told him to call me Melissa. You should probably do the same thing or it'll get awkward."

James seemed less enthusiastic about it but reluctantly nodded his head. "Right. Call me Melissa, too."

The four of them all laughed, then Tai nodded. "Right, right. Melissa and Melissa. Got it."

Liao smiled, then the baby started to cry again and she eased herself out of her chair, giving James a reassuring pat as he put his head in his hands.

*****

Tai stood guard the first night he arrived, having spent the remainder of the day sweeping their apartment for bugs, surveying the entrances and exits, and determining vantage points for snipers. Liao thought the process entirely unnecessary, but she understood that he was just doing his job.

It was the evening, after Liao had fed their infant and was preparing to crawl back into bed again, that her phone rang with a blocked number. Curious, for she did not receive many calls, Liao fished it out of her pocket and answered.

"喂?"

There was a faint hiss over the line, indicating it was open, but Liao could hear nothing on the other end. "Hello?" she tried, moving to the window to get better reception.

"My my my," came a low voice, English accented and articulate, "I didn't think Melissa Liao would answer her phone in Chinese."

The voice was instantly known to her. It brought back a surge of memories, too. None too pleasant. That familiar spike of excitement, fear, and anger, she felt, just for a moment, as though she were back in command of her ship, as if she were still the officer and commander she once had been.

The voice of Ben.

"You're alive?"

Ben's hollow laughter filtered down the speaker. "Of course, my dear Melissa. Your jump drive carried me safely away."

"How did you get this number? How the hell are you communicating with me?"

"The advantage of having a jump drive that can take you anywhere, Melissa, is that you can go anywhere. Tautologies like this are typically useless, but they illustrate my point. Your species believes, bumbling and ignorant as they are, that they have this whole system secure... but nowhere is safe from me. I go wherever I wish."

"I'm glad for your new found freedom." She gripped her phone tightly. "What do you want?"

Another faint, hollow laugh. "Just to chat, my dear friend. Don't you have time to talk to me?"

"Not after Velsharn, not after what you've done."

"Oh Melissa, you wound me so. I've been so busy since we last spoke, but it's wonderful to hear your voice again."

Liao fought to keep her tone even. "I have nothing to say to you. Goodbye, Ben. Don't call again."

"I'm sorry you feel that way," Ben said, "because important things are happening. Big things. But... don't worry, Commander. I'll see you soon."

"No you won't."

Liao ended the call then, slowly and deliberately, placed it in her pocket. She stared out the window of her apartment, watching the headlights of cars and the lights of the city, fighting a vague sense of foreboding, and trying to contain her wild imagination.

A faint knock on her door broke her from her musings. ["Is everything okay?"] came Saara's voice. ["I heard your communicator, and you sounded angry..."]

Distracted and half asleep, Liao had forgotten entirely that the Toralii was there. "No, it's fine," she answered, "just a prank caller."

["Very well. Sleep well, Liao."]

Liao smiled at the closed door, then looked back out at the lights of the city. "Thank you, Saara."

Chapter III

Liao slept like the dead.

The eight weeks since Tai's arrival and Ben's mysterious call had gone by faster than she had anticipated. Saara's visit had gone well. Liao had shown the planet Earth to the wide-eyed, excited Toralii. Her poor mood had evaporated once Liao had taken her out of the city. There, she was as bubbly as a child visiting Disneyland, and the smallest thing was something new and fresh for her: grass, cars, highways. It had been good to see Saara, and it was good to keep her promises, but eventually, she and James had returned to duty, leaving Liao alone. Initially, she feared that caring for her infant would overwhelm her, but Tai stepped in to help her better than she possibly could have hoped. He'd done something amazing, something that changed her current situation immeasurably.

He'd arranged for a nanny.

While she'd considered it, usually at the wee hours of the morning while trying to feed her screaming child, Liao opposed the idea with the kind of fiery, defensive, illogical arguments she struggled to justify even to herself. The unnamed baby was *her* responsibility, and if she could manage a 200,000 tonne starship, she could manage a single infant. A child needed her mother for those early years and, despite the considerable effort it took, Liao valued being with her.

But eventually, her resolve wore down and, exhausted and desperate, she gave in.

The nanny Tai hired, Jennifer Pycroft, was a thin, African-American woman in her early twenties and Liao was initially deeply suspicious of her. in Tai's eyes, the tattered American economy meant finding a suitable person for the job was easy; for the simple position of part time nanny he'd received over two hundred applications from people with impressive resumes: scientists whose research grants had dried up, soldiers who could barely live on their benefits payments, teachers whose positions had been made redundant. She knew that, for many young adults, especially those in their teens who had never held a job, it was a struggle to peddle their meagre skills in a brutal job market.

While this meant that he and Liao had their pick of who they wanted for the position, it also planted the seed of doubt back in Liao's mind. She didn't want someone desperate, someone who badly needed money, to have access to her child. What if they were a psychopath? A child abuser? What if they were desperate enough to kidnap her child for ransom?

But Jennifer, in their very first meeting, was shy and polite. Liao could tell that Jennifer very much wanted to make a good impression. She dressed well, smiled a lot, and when Tai finally hired her, Jennifer completely changed everything. Kind and considerate, infinitely patient, warm and loving, Liao saw how Jennifer's eyes had lit up when she saw the baby for the first time, how carefully she cradled the child in her arms, and how she babbled in adorable, loving baby talk. Because of Jennifer, Liao could now sleep through the night without being interrupted by crying. She could go out and do things without being shackled to her apartment. She felt as though her life was her own again.

Her rest, like all things, eventually ended… not with the urgent, despair inducing wail of a hungry child, but with the gentle grace of the sun warming her face. Sliding herself out of bed, Liao brushed the sleep from her eyes and spent a moment doing the unthinkable, fixing her hair.

On board the *Beijing*, Liao had kept it short as a matter of practicality, but her own preference was to wear her hair long. While she did remain on the payroll of the Chinese military, she was effectively out of any actual required work; nobody had come to check that she was maintaining the grooming standard or that her hair was an acceptable length, and Tai wouldn't tell a soul, so she wore it as she pleased.

Satisfied that she was now presentable, Liao pulled open the internal door of her bedroom and stepped into the living area. The apartment was blissfully quiet, and Jennifer's purse was resting on the small table by the door. Pushing open the spare bedroom door, Liao saw Jennifer bottle-feeding the baby as Tai casually looked through the blinds at the outside.

"Hey," Liao said, keeping her voice quiet. "She eating okay?"

"Like a dream, Miss Liao." The baby gave a mindless gurgle. She seemed to respond well to Jennifer's thick, smooth Louisianan accent. Jennifer gave a wide, eager smile and Liao returned it in kind.

"Good." She turned to Tai. "Hey, you up for some pizza from that place across the road?"

"Again? Sure, as long as you're buying."

"Well, you won't be able to be much of a bodyguard if you don't eat something." Liao's gaze fell on Jennifer. "You want anything?"

Jennifer's interest was obvious, but she shook her head, keeping the bottle held snugly so the baby could drink. "No thank you, Miss. I can't afford anything like that. Money's real tight with my Dad and my sisters at the moment. I brought a sandwich; that'll do."

Liao respected her discipline. "My shout," she offered.

The young woman's eyes lit up, but there was a hesitation there, too. An unwillingness to offend her employer even though Liao's offer was made easily and genuinely. This simple job, Liao knew, was important to Jennifer.

But evidently her desire for pizza won out. "Pepperoni?"

Liao gave her a grin. "I'll see what I can do."

Later

Pizza turned out to be just what Liao wanted. There was a street stand just two blocks from their apartment that served the most delicious pizza she had ever tasted, New York style. The man who worked the stand, a heavy set Caucasian man named Anthony who seemed to be perpetually smiling, appeared to have a talent for names. Whenever she and Tai visited, he would greet them by name, asking if they wanted their usual.

Liao wanted to support local businesses as much as she could in these economically dark times. She had a lot of sympathy for Anthony, and it helped that he made an expensive, but tasty, treat.

"The usual, Melissa?" Anthony boomed in his deep, cheerful voice as he saw them approach, beaming to them as though greeting old friends.

"The usual for us both," she answered, finding his smile infectious.

"Fifty bucks a slice, usual price."

The American economy had suffered greatly in the financial collapse nearly a decade ago. The United States had borrowed ever increasing amounts to pay for foreign wars and bailouts of companies too sick to compete in an international market. They had then tried to inflate their way out of the debt. Their creditors had simply indexed the debt in Euros and the US had defaulted. Now the dollar was basically worthless. If it weren't for the construction of the Pillars of the Earth bringing people back to work and creating a market for unskilled labour in the country, things would be much worse off.

"Three hundred, then." Liao flicked through a wad of notes, careful to keep them close to her chest. A number of vagrants sat nearby, watching the proceedings with envious eyes, no doubt eyeing her cash and smelling the pizza. "Here."

Anthony took the money, then looked at someone over Liao's shoulder. "Hey, it's James! Come back for the world's best pizza, 'ey?"

Liao whirled around, her smile intensifying as she saw James. "James! I wasn't expecting you back for—..."

But James's face was a grim mask and he was wearing his uniform. Her smile disappeared just as fast as it had arrived. "What's wrong?" she asked.

He stepped up to her, leaning right up to her ear, whispering so only she could hear.

"Get your stuff. Get the baby. We're leaving for the airport. A Broadsword is coming to take us into orbit later this evening."

"To orbit?" Liao frowned. "What's wrong? What's happened?" she whispered back.

"The Kel-Voranians withdrew their embassy. The bastards just packed up and left without saying a word; a ship picked them up a few hours ago. Intelligence has us at high alert. Something's going down and we don't know what it is. The Pillars are being prepared for combat and the crews are being recalled from leave."

Liao felt the familiar feeling of adrenaline pumping through her body, the rush that came with suddenly being at the very forefront of events taking place around her. No longer was she getting information through the nightly news or the papers; this was *living* in the middle of history being made.

"Why do they need me?"

"They don't, but I put in a special request. I need a consultant I can trust. Given the threat against you, we're taking the kid, too."

She pulled her head back from James, suddenly feeling like her old self again. She'd be going back into space. Not aboard her ship, mind, but *a* ship. It was enough for her. "Let's go," she said. "I can be ready in an hour."

Tai snatched up the pizza slices and the three of them began power walking back towards the apartment building.

"What's happened?" Tai asked, reaching a hand into the paper packet, extracting a slice, and blowing on it urgently.

"I'm being recalled to the *Tehran*." She gave him an apologetic smile. "Sorry."

Tai looked genuinely saddened, but nodded. "Damn. Well, I'll take care of your affairs here. The apartment will be nice and clean when you get back."

Liao grinned at him. "That'll be a nice change." Suddenly she stopped, rolling her eyes. "I forgot Jennifer's, damnit. I promised her."

With Liao leading, the three jogged back to the pizza stand.

"Sorry," she said breathlessly to Anthony, "three more pepperoni."

"It's fine," he said, shaking his head, a broad smile on his face as handed her the extras. "Always happy to sell more pizza."

She hurriedly withdrew her purse and paid for three pepperoni slices, then they started back again to her apartment. Hurrying down the street, Liao pointed down a cramped alley between two apartment blocks.

"Let's cut through here. It's a shortcut."

James seemed sceptical, but she started down the narrow alley and they followed.

"So," James said to Tai, "you feel comfortable staying here while Liao and I go back to space? You should be used to the place by now."

"Hah, you must be kidding, Captain." He chuckled. "Living in this city, surrounded by Americans? I think I'll go crazy by the time—"

A man, unshaven and unkempt, stepped into their path. He was lily-skinned and sickly, gaunt even, as though he had spent his days inside. His hair was a tangled mop, his body cloaked in a worn brown overcoat. Liao glanced at his face. Their eyes met for a moment, and within his hazel gaze she saw... something, something deep and instinctive, primal, a subtle subconscious warning that was too powerful to ignore.

This wasn't just another vagrant. They had passed dozens on the way through the city already, their presence almost invisible by now, but this man was different. This one was looking directly them, not to try to attract pity and sympathy, but with something darker... The desperation was no less or no more with this man than the others, but there was one key difference. He was willing to do them harm.

She stopped walking right as the man reached into a deep pocket, withdrawing a silver revolver and, holding it at his hip, levelled it at Liao.

"Your wallets and phones. *Now*."

There was a tense moment as the three of them stared at the man, surprised and uncertain. His voice was quiet but charged with sincerity. Liao felt her pulse quicken, the same reaction she had when she was in combat. Except this time, she didn't have 200,000 tonnes of warship surrounding her and a battery of missiles and guns.

"*Now!* You first, nigger!"

He looked like a drug addict, Liao mused, although he didn't have the typical bloodshot eyes that addicts usually possessed. A drug addict with eye drops, apparently.

Liao held out her hands, palms upwards. "Look, you're making a terrible mistake. I'm—"

"I don't care who you fucking gooks are." The man levelled his pistol at her and Liao took a step backward.

"It's okay." James threw Liao a side glance, nodding approvingly and slowly reached into his pocket. He withdrew his wallet, passing it over.

The man took it eagerly, shoving it into his back pocket. "Phone?"

"Don't have one."

The man looked like he was going to argue, but instead he pointed his weapon to Tai.

"Fine, whatever. Now you, tough guy. Don't try anything or I'll blow your fucking face off."

Tai nodded acceptingly, his hand already in his pocket. "Fine, here you go. Just don't do anything rash, and let me get my ID chip out. That's of no value to you. How about I just hand you the cash instead?"

The man nodded in nervous agreement, glancing over his shoulder momentarily. For a second, Liao worried Tai was going to do something stupid, but his hand returned with his ID and the wallet was handed over. "I don't have a phone either."

"Fine, whatever. Now you, lady."

"Okay," said Liao. "Let me get my ID out first, too, okay?"

"Fine, fine, just fucking hurry it up."

Fumbling, Liao reached into her pocket, reaching for her small purse. The man extended his empty hand.

"Keep quiet and give it to me real easy, no tricks," he said, the hand holding the firearm trembling slightly. "Hurry up!"

It was gone. Liao tried all her pockets. "Damnit," she said, "I must have left it at Anthony's when I went back to pay for the pizza."

The man's agitation suddenly grew. "You're fucking shitting me. Bullshit. Bullshit!"

Liao held up her hands. "I'm not. I'm not. I just left it—"

"I'll fucking *end* you, you lying bitch!"

Tai stepped forward, moving in front of her. "Everybody just calm down! We already gave you what we have. Now—"

"Who are you, a fucking cop? You're a fucking cop! That's why you didn't want me to see your ID, because you're a cop!"

"What? No! No. Nobody here's a cop, okay? Nobody."

"Look," said Liao, "here. Here's my phone. Take it and go." She reached into her breast pocket, withdrawing the small black brick and holding it out. The strange man, relief crossing his face, snatched the device and jammed it into a pocket.

Then his eyes lit up, wide and panicked, looking at something behind her. On instinct, Liao turned. She could see someone entering the gap between the two buildings. She recognised the rotund form of Anthony, his hand holding her purse.

"Hey, Melissa, ya' forgot yer'—"

Their assailant, now behind her, shouted something incomprehensible and fired, the loud gunshot echoing against the walls of the building. Liao saw Anthony jerk, startled Then he turned and ran. James's strong hands pushed her out of the way, and she saw that Tai's hand now held a small, compact handgun. Tai aimed it quickly, depressing the trigger. Another loud roar and the handgun almost drowned out the cry of their attacker, the round catching the surprised man in his upper arm.

Wounded, he howled, waving his pistol around like a lunatic. Tai fired again, the round knocking a chunk out of the brick wall. The mugger regained some semblance of wit. His pistol barked twice, a loud *crack* like a firework exploding near Liao's head, and she felt James's hands around her shoulders, pulling her down to the ground. Two more shots were fired, Liao recognising the loud retort of the man's revolver as she raised her head in time to see the man, wounded and panicked, as he turned and ran down the alley, stumbling occasionally, his footsteps beating a rapid retreat away from where James and Liao lay sprawled.

"You okay?" asked James.

Liao closed her eyes a moment, hands trembling slightly before she stilled them. "I'm fine," she said, inhaling and opening her eyes, her ears ringing from the loud gunshots. She had fought alien warships. She had repelled Toralii boarders. She was a decorated war hero. But despite the year she'd spent in space staring down death at every turn, a normal man with a gun had managed to rattle her. It was the striking normality of it all, something aside from aliens and space battles, something real and common. "Thanks for that."

James gave a laugh, leaning in and kissing her cheek from behind. "Don't worry; I've got your back. You okay, Tai?"

There was no answer. Liao twisted her body, looking over her shoulder. "Tai?"

Tai lay on his back, his skin ghostly white, his body as limp as a doll. Two blooming red flowers crept over his chest, blood seeping onto the concrete below.

It took her a second to process what had happened, but the moment the reality of the situation hit her, she was moving. She broke away from James's grasp, crawling over to Tai's prone form. She fumbled inside Tai's pocket, pulling out his phone with one hand and tossing it to James. "Call an ambulance!"

Liao lifted Tai's head, cradling it as the Chinese man's blood poured into her lap. She watched as James, ashen faced, flipped open Tai's phone, tapped in 911, then held the device to his ear. Liao looked back down at her bodyguard and friend.

"Kang, Kang, can you hear me?"

He didn't move. She propped up his head, pulling it into her lap, while her other hand searched for his injuries. "Don't worry, okay? James is getting help. We're getting help." She gave a quiet, nervous laugh as she adjusted Tai's head, eliciting a soft groan from the barely conscious man. "What kind of a bodyguard dies from a couple of little boo-boos like that, hey? Suck it up, you'll be fine. You're going to be fine." She brushed a clump of Tai's hair away from his face with a bloodied hand, her gaze turning up to James. "How long...?"

James asked the operator, then nodded to Liao. "Four minutes. They're coming as fast as they can." He spoke into the phone. "Yes, I'll cover the cost."

"Fuck!" Liao pressed her hands to Tai's ghastly wounds, pushing her fingers to his blood-soaked shirt, trying to stem the blood loss. "Kang, you hear that, yeah? Four minutes. You've gotta take care of my apartment when I'm out, you know, so you've got a lot more work to do. And after that... after that, I'm going to get my ship back and I'm going to need... I'm going to need people I can trust. You can work with Cheung. We'll get you a nice cushy position on that boat, okay?"

Tai's blood continued to spill unabated onto the ground. Liao's hands were soaked up to her elbows, but she kept her hands pressed against the entry wounds.

"But you listen to me, Kang," she continued. "If you die, I swear to God I'll have you thrown off my boat. You hear me? If you die, you're getting the boot, and don't you dare think I won't... Don't you *dare* even think that for a second... because I will. I will. I *will*."

She kept her hands there, failing to hold Tai's lifeblood within his body, pressing on his wounds even after the ambulance arrived. She rode with them, keeping the pressure on her friend's injuries all the way through the journey to the Shock Trauma ward, releasing only after the doctors had pronounced Tai's time of death.

6:56pm Thursday, August the 18th, 2039.

*****

New York
8:30pm

James and Liao took a driverless cab back to her apartment, the ride taken mostly in silence aside from asking each other if they were fine over and over like a broken record. She'd had time, at least, to wash her hands before making her statement to the police, two tired looking officers who dutifully took down her details but reminded her that the likelihood of finding the person who had killed Tai, and making a conviction stick, was low. There were so many crimes of this nature every day that the local law enforcement, its funding slashed to almost nothing, had little hope of catching someone who wasn't arrested at the scene.

She felt strangely empty, though, just as she had after Velsharn was destroyed by her ship's missiles. Sadness, self-pity, resentment: none of these things would bring back Kang Tai, his body occupying a tiny block in the district hospital's morgue.

There was anger there, too. Yes, Tai was her bodyguard, but why did he do that? The man who accosted them was only looking for money, and he'd escaped with most of it anyway. Yes, he had fired at Anthony, but perhaps he could have still been reasoned with. Maybe there would have been a way to end this without bloodshed. But he'd chosen to act and now her friend was dead. He was a good man, a useful person. To intervene was a stupid, risky decision, and Tai should have known better.

Or so she told herself, silently, over and over.

The autonomous vehicle pulled up outside Liao's apartment, and a robotic voice read out the cost. James swiped his card over the pay receiver and, with an electronic chime, the doors unlocked.

"Thank you for riding Flexicar New York, your safe, prompt service."

Safe. Liao did not feel particularly safe in this city, and it was with cautious eyes that she scanned the area before stepping out of the vehicle. James held the door open so the car wouldn't leave.

"Don't worry about packing; we don't have time. Just grab the baby and some essentials." He paused a moment. "Are you okay?" James asked, reaching out with his other hand and gently touching her hip. It was almost exactly where her scar was.

Liao nodded, inhaling gently. "I will be. It's okay." She looked up at the towering, concrete pillar. "Jennifer will be freaking out if she's still here."

James shook his head. "She would have gone home by now; it's late."

The idea of her child being alone in the apartment for hours suddenly invigorated her. Without saying anything, she stepped purposefully towards the heavy steel door of the apartment complex, swiping her key and pulling it open. Her immediate destination was the elevator; a swift jab of her finger at the button summoned it to her, the wait intolerable.

After what seemed like the longest ride in the history of the universe, Liao stepped out onto their floor. She broke into a run, swiping her card over the door's sensor and pushing it open. Immediately, the sound of a wailing baby reached her ears and her heart stopped.

"Hello?!"

It was her. Jennifer stepped out from the kitchen, cradling the screaming infant, a distraught look on her face. "Miss Liao! Oh, thank God. What happened? Where did you go?"

Liao leaned her shoulder up against a wall, realising suddenly that she had been holding her breath. "We were mugged," she said simply. "Tai was shot."

The young woman's eyes went wide. "Is he okay?"

Liao reached up and ran her hand through her hair. "Sorry, I would have called earlier, but he took my phone and we left Tai's phone in the ambulance. We didn't have your number."

Jennifer bounced the baby gently, trying to get her to calm down. "Ambulance?"

"He's dead. Sorry. We did everything we could, but..."

Jennifer stopped, freezing completely in place. "I... oh my God!"

"I know. I'm sorry. He just lost too much blood."

"What? What happened?"

"We got to Anthony's place and got the food, but I forgot yours. I went back to get it, and on the way back, this guy just walked out of nowhere and pulled a pistol on us. I guess the guy saw us the first time and had enough time to see we had cash. Anthony chased after us to return my wallet, and it startled the mugger. There was a firefight. The man was wounded, but he got Tai. Then he ran off."

"I... oh God. Sorry, sorry. I tried calling your phone over and over... I guess that's why you didn't pick up." She hesitated. "I... ran out of credit, so I used your landline to call my dad, Miss Liao, just to let him know where I was. He was seriously freaked out. I'm sorry. I'll pay you for the cost, somehow—"

Liao had totally forgotten about the landline. She momentarily cursed herself for her stupidity. "No, it's fine. Don't worry about it. Look Jennifer, something else has happened, too. I'm being recalled."

Jennifer's face fell, her expression one of shock and devastation. "Wh-what?"

"There's something big going down. I needed to be at the airport about fifteen minutes ago." Liao moved as she spoke, stepping into her bedroom, yanking down the biggest suitcase she had, and throwing it open on the bed. Jennifer followed her as Liao started throwing random items of clothing haphazardly into the case.

"Miss Liao, I'm—I'm sorry about Tai."

"It's okay. He was doing his job." Liao felt her voice tighten as she tried to keep herself calm, throwing in her dress uniform's shoes alongside her boots, not caring if the latter got scratched. "And he's gone. We can't do anything to change that. I'm sorry about it, too, especially with all this that's happening."

Jennifer's tone was thick with emotion as though it were she who had pulled the trigger. "I'm sorry, Miss Liao. I'm really, really sorry. I'll pray for him tonight."

"I know. It's okay." Liao took a breath, yanking out and upending her underwear drawer into the case. "He was a good man, and he died doing his duty. His family will be proud." She studied the young woman's dark face, frowning slightly. "Is everything okay?"

"No—well, yes, are..." Jennifer hesitated, her voice cracking. "Are you thinking of replacing him as your bodyguard when you go back into space?"

"James will probably find someone for me on the ship," Liao admitted, "and Commodore Vong will probably insist upon it. The military tends to be somewhat callous when it comes to replacing us. We're interchangeable cogs in a giant machine unfortunately." She met Jennifer's gaze for a moment, then shook her head and looked away. "Bastards will probably dock his Friday pay because he's dead."

"And you're taking the baby with you?"

"Yeah."

Jennifer hesitated and Liao heard her shuffle ever so slightly. "I... see." There was a slight tremor in her voice as she spoke. "And... when will you be back?"

"I don't know," Liao answered, moving into their en suite and gathering anything that looked important. Vitamin pills, deodorant, her favourite comb. "I'm just going to leave most of this stuff here. I don't have time to pack it. The apartment's paid up for the next month. Take whatever you want."

Jennifer followed Liao as she walked, gently bouncing the baby. "And you're leaving right now?"

"Yeah." Liao threw the armful of assorted stuff into the case.

"Can I come with you?"

Liao stopped, blinking in confusion. "Honestly, I could use your help, but there's a lot of protocol to go through before I can just bring a civilian on board a military ship. Trust me; Summer's paperwork was crazy." She laughed. "Besides, believe me; it's not exactly a pleasant life up there."

Jennifer's voice suddenly became pleading. "I don't care if it's not comfortable, Miss Liao. I *really* need this job. Even if it's part time, it's all that's keeping my sister in school. My family needs it. There are five of us and I'm the only one who brings in any income. I know Mister Tai was the one who hired me, and I know I messed up, but I've worked so hard for you—"

"What? No, you've been a gem. You haven't messed up. That's not why this is happening." Liao struggled to comprehend, confused. Her packing was forgotten momentarily. "Why did you say you messed up?"

"It's just... if I hadn't asked for anything while ya'll were out, then you wouldn't have gone back for my slices, and none of this would have happened." Jennifer's voice cracked again, and Liao could see her emotions starting to get the better of her. "I'm *so* sorry. I am. I'm sorry. Just, please..."

She processed Jennifer's words for a moment, then understanding dawned. "It's not your fault. Hey, easy, it's not your fault... I offered to shout you, remember? You're not responsible for what happened."

"But..."

Liao stepped closer, reaching out and touching Jennifer's cheek. "Look, they pay me no matter what I'm doing, so me going away isn't going to change a single thing. And, you know what? I kind of like this place... I want it to be here when I get back." She gave a warm smile. "How about being a full-time house-sitter?"

Jennifer's relief was palpable, written all over the young woman's face. She gave a loud, relieved laugh and took several deep breaths. "Oh thank God. Really? Really?! Really-really-*really*?!"

Liao removed her hand and used it to close the lid of the case, nodding. "Sure." She paused, reaching out for the baby.

Jennifer handed her over without complaint, and Liao could see her hands were trembling with relief. "Thank you, Miss Liao, thank you, thank you."

Liao immediately thought of Velsharn and how, upon seeing its destruction, she blamed herself. It was true that, while she did turn her ship over to Ben's control, and the residual guilt sometimes plagued her, she was not the one who killed all those Toralii. Ben was.

"One thing I've learnt... is that when something bad happens, a million other things could have happened, for better or for worse, but you can't spend your life worrying about what could have been, and what tiny, minute thing you could have done differently. What's done is done. When there are agents of death in the world, the blood they shed is entirely on their hands. Tai's death is no more your fault than mine, or his own, or anyone else's."

Jennifer looked up to her, and Liao could see that she was still struggling to keep herself from crying. "Okay."

"And if Tai hadn't taken the job in the first place, none of this would have happened, either. He knew what he was getting into."

"I know."

Liao nodded, then fished in her pocket for her set of keys, handing them over. "One more thing."

"Yes, Miss Liao?"

She smiled. "Help me carry the suitcase down to the car."

Chapter IV

"Victory?"
*****

Cerberus blockade
Lagrange point between Mars and Phobos

Hours Later

Lieutenant Bai Peng preferred his new post as chief tactical officer aboard the Cerberus blockade to service on the *Beijing* and counted himself lucky that he'd been able to keep the same position on the space station.

The Cerberus blockade was the only open jump point in the entire Sol system. At every other point, gravity generators powered by micro nuclear reactors generated fluctuating pulses of gravity to constantly shift the Lagrange points. With that interference repositioning their location so rapidly and so randomly, no vessel could safely jump into them. In order to permit entry and egress from the system, aside from the far out regions near Pluto, one had to come through Cerberus.

Cerberus was home to nearly thirty heavy gun batteries, one hundred fifty nuke batteries, two wings of fighters and Broadswords, and three gargantuan rail guns on giant pivot turrets in case larger ships jumped in. These gave it equal firepower to two Pillars of the Earth, all focused on one area. Furthermore, a ring of gravity mines meant that if a hostile vessel were to enter, the jump point could be locked out until it was destroyed to prevent reinforcements.

It was safe, secure, but an important position. Perfect for him.

"So Bai," said Yvonne Walker, the strawberry blonde, Australian communications officer who shared his shift, "I heard a rumour that the Kel-Voranians pulled their embassy."

Peng swivelled in his chair. "You serious? The one in Melbourne?"

"Yeah," she answered, "caught it on the fleetwide this morning. That's what Bravo-seven-eight was about."

Bravo-seven-eight was the Task Force Resolution code name for a Kel-Voran ship that had appeared in the jump point nearly eight hours ago, identifying itself as the *B'vall*. It had requested entry to the Sol system under the guise of diplomatic business. Since the Kel-Voran were normally allies of the humans, this request was granted. The jump point between Earth and the Moon was enabled temporarily for the ship to jump. Peng and Walker had tracked the *B'vall* as it landed on Earth, escorted by some of the planet's Broadswords. Hours later, it returned to space, flew to the Earth-Moon Lagrange point, and requested exit from the system. With clearance granted, the gravity generators were briefly turned off and the ship had jumped away.

"Well, that's a bit ominous, don't you think?" Peng said.

Walker shrugged. "Who knows. Maybe they just decided on a change of scenery, or maybe it's a political move."

"Maybe it is; maybe it isn't."

"Well, I'm inclined to think some big shit is about to go down," Walker said, casually tapping a finger on her console. "I heard they recalled the fleet. Everyone who's on leave—boom. Cancelled. The *Tehran* is picking up Captain Liao from Earth, then they're coming here to stand watch with us."

Peng peered skeptically at Walker. For the last ten hours, the *Sydney* had been docked at the blockade station for system checks on the troubled vessel's systems, but it was common knowledge that the airlock was sealed and that nobody had either come aboard or departed. Rumour was that the ship was on high alert and ready to disengage at a moment's notice.

"Really?" said Peng. "They're going to have both the *Sydney* and the *Tehran* guarding the jump point in addition to all this crap?"

"Yep."

He laughed. "You're mental if you think Fleet Command is so fucking shit-scared that they're going to dedicate two-thirds of the fleet to guarding the jump point. How can we perform any operations if we do? That'd mean there's only the *Beijing* and the *Rubens* out there."

"Ooo," said Walker, "careful, careful. We're not meant to be talking about the *Rubens*."

Peng rolled his eyes. "Everyone knows about it," he countered. "It's not like it's a huge secret. We've had them dock here dozens of times."

"Yeah, I know, still. Orders are orders, and those orders say that there's no such thing as the *Rubens*."

"Right." Peng clicked his tongue. "We can't talk about something everybody fucking kn-"

The triple-beep of a loud alarm cut him off, followed by a cry from the radar operator.

"Incoming jump! A vessel has appeared in the Lagrange point!"

There was nothing on the schedule for that day. The station shuddered as the shockwave from the jump passed over them. The Commanding Officer, Iranian Captain Lale Harandi, stepped towards Peng's screen. "Move to condition one and sound general quarters. Report, Mister Peng."

Peng's screen flashed information at him. He scanned over what the readings were telling him.

"No IFF transponder detected, Captain. Vessel is 200,000 tonnes, bright appearance on thermals, identical in size and configuration to a Toralii cruiser. No sign of strike craft."

Harandi's response was immediate. "All reactors to full power, load missile launch tubes, and prepare to fire. Ready rail guns. Mister Kelly, signal fleet command."

Peng's fingers darted over the keyboard. "Tubes one through fifteen ready, Captain, with rail gun turrets alpha through charlie standing by." A decompression alarm at the airlock drew his attention. "Captain, the *Sydney* has disengaged from dock without authorisation. They're moving into an attack position on the contact."

Captain Harandi just nodded. "Ignore the *Sydney* for now. What's the contact doing?"

"Just sitting there, Captain. I'm reading no strike craft, no weapons fire, nothing."

"Captain," said Walker, "incoming transmission from the Toralii vessel. Coming in on 121.5 MHz. Recording."

121.5 MHz was the standard frequency the Toralii used to initiate communication with Human forces. Technically, it was a distress frequency, which also made it useful since it was almost always kept clear.

"Play it through the speakers," Captain Harandi ordered, tapping her fingers on the back of Peng's chair. "But keep a lock on them. ROE is clear; the moment they fire anything, or launch any craft, we nuke them and shut off the jump point until cleanup takes care of the wreckage."

The speakers crackled slightly and the Operations centre of the blockade was filled with a thin, robotic voice that spoke in broken, halting English as though being machine translated.

"Attention Terran type two outpost. This is Warbringer Avaran of the Toralii Alliance Vessel *Seth'arak*. Respond on frequency Four. Two. Eight. Point. Six."

The *Seth'arak*. Everyone knew the *Seth'arak* and Warbringer Avaran. It was the first real, straight out engagement between Humans and the Toralii navy. It ended with the *Tehran* being crippled and captured by the Toralii, with both other ships taking severe damage.

The message began to repeat. Captain Harandi nodded to Walker. "Open a channel on that frequency. Let's talk to them."

There was a moment's pause as the frequency was changed. "Four two eight point six, Captain. Open in three, two, one..."

Silence.

"This is Captain Harandi of Cerberus Station, acting under Task Force Resolution. You are in violation of the Sol system's sovereignty. Engage your jump drive and leave this system, or you will be destroyed. No further warnings will be issued on any frequency."

["This is Warbringer Avaran."] The voice spoke Toralii and was heavy and slow, as though burdened with some great task. ["On behalf of the Toralii Alliance, we have come to negotiate a cease-fire between our peoples."]

The Operations room was filled with a shocked silence. Harandi gestured to mute the audio and Walker tapped a key. "Audio off, Captain."

Peng turned in his chair, giving voice to what was on everyone's mind.

"Does... does this mean we win?"

*****

Broadsword Archangel
En route to the Earth-Moon L1 Lagrange point

Two hours later

Liao was glad that she finally got to catch a ride in the *Archangel*. Technically the Search and Rescue ship for the *Beijing*, the *Archangel* had performed a daring move and rescued her CAG, Alex Aharoni, from capture by the Toralii. That incident had weighed on her mind for some time. The rational thing to do would be to leave a single ejected pilot behind when the entire ship was in danger, but Ben had come up with a solution that had allowed him to be saved. Despite the fact that a few days later Ben had annihilated a colony full of unsuspecting Toralii civilians, Liao still felt a little gratitude for Ben's part in the rescue.

Ben had saved a life, then taken fifty thousand others. It seemed strange to be grateful to him.

"Do you think there was some credibility to the Toralii threat, then?"

James shrugged. "I don't know. But they knew about it well before they pulled their embassy, so... why would they wait for months then withdraw without a word?"

Liao leaned forward, putting her elbows on her knees. "I don't like it. The Kel-Voran love a fight... For them to just up and *leave* doesn't make any sense."

"They like a fight," James corrected, "but they dislike grossly unbalanced battles. They're not suicidal."

Liao snorted and ran her hands through her hair. "Great. So staying on Earth is suicidal. What a vote of confidence from our new allies."

James chuckled. "Hopefully, when we rendezvous with the Tehran, they'll have some damn answers for us."

The intercom crackled and the voice of Lieutenant First Class Medola, the navigator and radio operator of the Broadsword *Archangel*, filled the hold where they were sitting.

"Attention passengers and crew, stand by for jump."

The proliferation of the reactionless drives had proved to be revolutionary when it came to space travel. When Liao had first assumed her command, it took three days to get to Luna, Earth's moon, via conventional rocket. These days, a Broadsword could do it in a matter of hours.

She casually clipped on her seatbelt, glancing to her side to check for the fifty thousandth time that her baby was safe. She continued sleeping soundly and oblivious to the journey taking place around her. She would be the youngest Human in orbit, the youngest Human to experience microgravity, a number of firsts. But her mind was not on any of those things.

The artificial gravity switched off and Liao felt queasy. Fortunately, James rested his hand on her thigh and she immediately begun to feel a little better. The baby, meanwhile, just gurgled slightly, yawning in her sleep, but otherwise didn't react.

Without an outside perspective, the jump was imperceptible to those experiencing it aside from a faint hum of energy. Liao, whose normal post was at Operations deep within the much larger *Beijing*, rarely heard that sound. It felt good, in a way, to be closer to the ship's surface, more in touch with how it moved and sounded.

"Jump complete."

Gravity slowly began to return. There was the briefest of pauses and Liao reached down to unclasp her seatbelt, but the gunship pitched hard to port, almost throwing her across the cargo bay. She was suddenly very grateful that she hadn't removed her seatbelt. The baby began to wail, and Medola's voice returned, this time charged with energy.

"Contact, twelve o'clock level. All crew, condition one, weapons tight. Prepare for emergency jump."

Liao and James exchanged a panicked glance and undid their restraints, moving as one to free themselves. Whenever the jump drive was engaged, even a small one as found on the Broadswords, it heated up. As a ship in space was a closed system, the only way to get rid of that excess heat without boiling the crew alive was to let it slowly radiate away. An emergency jump, though, would flush coolant into the jump drive so they could get away sooner. This brute-force approach lead to the very real possibility of uneven cooling of the spherical jump drive. If it cracked, even microscopically, this could result in an imprecise jump at best and, at worst, the risk of catastrophic failure.

Being at the rear of the craft when the rearward-mounted jump drive exploded would be very bad.

Liao unclipped the baby and, together, the three of them moved forward towards the cockpit, hands on the railings in case the ship pitched again, Liao holding the infant with one arm. When they reached the thick metal hatchway, Liao heard it unlock with a faint click. She pulled it open with her free hand.

"Lieutenant Medola, what the hell is going—"

Through the perspex of the Broadsword's cockpit, she saw a Toralii cruiser, a ship she recognised as the *Seth'arak*, docked with the *Sydney* and surrounded in a swarm of strike craft.

"—... on."

The Broadsword's radio crackled faintly and an Australian accented woman's voice came over the line. "Broadsword *Archangel*, this is Cerberus Station. Transmit identification code."

Medola tapped her console. "Code as follows: bravo-zero-zero-seven-one-xray-oscar-eight-romeo-alpha."

"Confirming code, break. Confirmed."

"Cerberus Station, *Archangel*. Affirmative, break." Medola lifted the talk key, then twisted in her seat. "You want me to ask them what the hell's going on, sir?"

Both Liao and James nodded.

"Request sitrep, Cerberus Station. I'm staring at the arse end of a Toralii cruiser that's *really* not meant to be here."

"Broadsword *Archangel*, Cerberus Station, interrogative. Do you have Captain James Grégoire and Commander Melissa Liao aboard?"

"Affirmative."

"*Archangel*, confirmed. You're cleared to bring Liao and Grégoire aboard the station using the main hangar bay. Be advised, *Archangel*, situation is as follows: we're dealing with a diplomatic situation at the moment. The presence of Captain Grégoire and Commander Liao are requested in the main conference room immediately."

"Rodger, Cerberus Station. Out." Medola closed the line.

"Me?" Liao asked, staring in confusion at James. "What the hell do they want *me* for?"

Cerberus Station

Fifteen minutes later

Cerberus Station was a tiny outpost, home to only fifty souls that would take shifts between manning the blockade and the Mars colony below them. Finding the single conference room in the facility was easy; Liao and James made their way there straight from the hangar bay, taking the most direct route through cramped corridors full of people all trying to go the same way.

The arrival of the Toralii ship had caused quite a stir. Captain Harandi met them half way to the room.

"What's going on?" Asked Liao, a question that elicited a shrug from the Persian captain.

"Who knows? He came aboard with his marines. Said he wanted to speak to you and only you. He's ignored our diplomats and barely said two words to me, just that he wanted to see you."

Liao frowned. "Me?" She glanced to James. "And I thought I was just here as an adviser."

"Your reputation precedes you," said Harandi, reaching up and adjusting her green headscarf. "He's waiting in conference room two."

"Very well then. I guess we'll go see what he wants."

The way became more and more congested as they drew closer.

"Make a hole. Coming through." James lead the charge, clearing the path for Liao who clutched her baby close. The infant squealed and threatened to cry again, but a few gentle pats on her back brought her to calm once more.

A crewman pulled open the hatchway, and James and Liao stepped through, moving into the long, rectangular room filled to the brim with people.

And Toralii.

Three stood at the back of the room wearing the full-body, armoured spacesuits, with empty weapon holsters and gaps in their suits where their inbuilt energy weapons had been removed. The suits were also painted black with gold trim, a colour scheme as yet unseen by her. Normal marines wore red, their commanders, white. As with the others, though, their faces were obscured by the strange material that served as a visor, which appeared to be solid, but Liao knew was actually some form of liquid held in shape by unknown forces.

It was the seated Toralii before them, though, that immediately drew her attention. An older, white-furred Toralii with patches of black streaked with grey sat with his arms neatly resting in his lap. A thick, jagged scar ran down his face, exposing the slightly purplish Toralii skin flushed with their strange purple blood. He was wearing what Liao could only interpret as the Toralii equivalent of a dress uniform, a lavish, gold affair decorated with silver strips and multicoloured ribbons.

Liao, still cradling her child, gave him a curt nod. "Warbringer Avaran, we finally meet face to face."

A green light flashed on a metal device attached to his right ear the moment Liao spoke, ceasing when she had finished. As though understanding her completely, Avaran began to speak. ["Indeed,"] he said, ["but had I known how far your reputation would spread, Captain Liao, perhaps things may have been done differently between our people."]

Liao pulled back a seat and, somewhat awkwardly with the baby in her arms, slid into it. She was acutely aware of how ridiculous she looked; the Toralii had gone all out on the pomp and ceremony, with their most official clothes and, presumably, elite guards. She was wearing slacks and a baggy T-shirt and carrying around a gurgling infant. James, taking a seat to her left, was at least wearing his standard uniform. Harandi took the seat to her right.

She couldn't help noticing, though, despite the vast gulf between what the Toralii were wearing and her own appearance, that Warbringer Avaran regarded her with something approaching respect.

"I wish a great many things would be different between our people," Liao stated. "Although before today, I would have said that the situation had escalated well beyond the point of rational discourse, I'm glad to see that this assessment was in error."

["I fail to see how you could be surprised at this turn of events, Captain Liao, Slayer of Varsian the Immortal, when your agents have us so completely overwhelmed and your victories are so total."]

"Agents?"

Avaran's eyes narrowed slightly, betraying a hint of aggravation. ["Coy, Captain Liao, but I think at this point, candour would appear to be your best ally. I speak, of course, of your pilfered technology, the ship you stole from us, and of our own weapons turned against us."]

The *Rubens*, Liao suddenly realised, the Toralii vessel James mentioned as being captured and turned over to the Human forces.

"Well, we have been forced to this course of action by the Toralii restriction against jump drive use."

["A restriction you have flouted at every turn, to our chagrin. Had the Kel-Voran not resumed hostilities against us, we would have crushed you long ago."]

"Regrettable for you, then, that they have."

Avaran gave a terse nod. ["So it would appear, yes."] He fixed his gaze on her, lowering his voice somewhat as he spoke. ["But we are not here to discuss hypothetical situations, Commander Liao."]

"To be perfectly honest," Liao said, "I'm not sure what we *are* here to discuss, except that the operations of the *Rubens* are obviously causing you some distress. I fail to see how that's our problem."

Avaran's lips curled up in a strange kind of smile. ["I can understand that feeling, Commander Liao. But the... *inconvenience*... it has caused has been significant, including the loss of Belthas IV."]

"It is my understanding that the *Rubens* has destroyed a grand number of your ships. I am pleased that they appear to have stung you in a tender place. It is, of course, within our power to cease the attacks, but this is not something that we shall do without cost. I'm sure you understand."

["Ships?"]

Confused, Liao nodded her head. "Uhh... yes. I assume you're here to ask us to cease the attacks upon the Toralii supply lines, yes?"

Avaran regarded her, not answering right away. For a moment Liao thought that perhaps he was waiting on the translation hardware to catch up with her, or was thinking of exactly the right way to word what he was going to say. The scarred Toralii's face was unreadable as he studied her, and Liao grew uncomfortable under his continued gaze.

"We are open to negotiations," she said, trying to keep dialogue open, "and we would prefer peaceful coexistence to our current situation. But we will not surrender our jump drive technology."

["I'm not sure we are communicating accurately,"] Avaran said at last, carefully choosing his words and speaking slowly and evenly. ["Whatever operations you are running against Toralii Alliance shipping networks are of absolutely no consequence to the Alliance at all. I am not even aware of any. Between jump mishaps, defection, Kel-Voranian pirates and countless other hazards which are a part of the inherent dangers of travelling through space, ships are lost every single day. I am not concerned with... whatever schemes you may be executing against our logistical infrastructure or whatever success you may have earned there. I am primarily concerned with Belthas IV, the forge world, and the occupying force currently holding it."]

Magnet's force had taken a *planet?* James had described the repurposed *Rubens* as being the same configuration as Saara's original vessel. A small, fighter-carrying, scout ship that could hold, at most, five hundred soldiers. The likelihood of them being able to garrison an entire planet seemed extremely low. A subtle glance at James, then Captain Harandi, revealed that they wore thinly disguised expressions of confusion.

"I'm... certain we can work out some kind of arrangement. May I confer with my colleagues for a moment while we discuss the matter?"

["Of course,"] said Avaran, sitting back in his chair. ["I shall remain here."]

"Very well. Captain Harandi, Captain Grégoire."

*****

Liao, James and Harandi stood and made their way out of the room. Liao handed her baby to one of the nearby crewmen, then the marines cleared the corridor. The three of them formed a huddle and Harandi spoke first.

"Does anyone have the slightest clue what the fuck he's talking about?"

James shrugged helplessly. "None. The *Rubens*'s mission directive was solely to harass shipping and attack targets of opportunity. They have five Wasps, a minelayer Broadsword and twenty five marines. The *Rubens* docked here almost a month ago; there was no indication that they were going to attack any planetary bodies, let alone occupy one. If Magnet pulled this off, it's got to be some kind of bluff. Maybe it's a planet like Velsharn, almost entirely uninhabited."

"Well," said Liao, "as unlikely as it seems, Avaran appears to be convinced they *did* attack this 'Belthas IV' and that they're currently holding it." She looked at Harandi. "Can you get Magnet on the horn and ask him what the fuck is up? Is there a communications protocol or a way to get in contact with him?"

Harandi shook her head. "That's difficult. They're more or less autonomous; the ship jumps around, attacking where it can then retreating. They tend to hide out near busy jump points, laying mines and generally making pests of themselves. We've got no way of communicating with them, but they are supposed to report in every month. They're about due."

Liao mulled that over. When the *Beijing* was in space, it was much the same story, a fact she had relied upon at her trial. It was ironic that, now, she could see the disadvantages of being out of touch with the rest of the fleet. While it gave Magnet and his ship autonomy, it meant that coordinating their efforts was more difficult. "Well, I guess the only thing we can do is wait until the *Rubens* docks next and ask."

"I suppose so."

"Although," James said, "that doesn't exactly help us right now. Whatever's happened, it seems to have thrown Avaran and the whole Alliance off their feet. I think we should capitalise on this if we can."

The other two nodded in agreement.

"Right," said James, "well, let's see what else we can find out about this planet and what's happened to it. Maybe this could be the break we've been looking for."

"Agreed."

Liao took a breath, then looked back towards the conference room. "Let's see what we can find out."

*****

"Apologies for the delay," Liao said as she resumed her seat. "We obviously have a lot to discuss."

["Obviously,"] agreed Avaran, although to Liao, the Toralii seemed less convinced than he did just a moment ago.

"Regarding Belthas IV," James said, "we are currently out of communication with our agents there, but we can arrange for a message to be sent to them to open a communication line with the fleet. In fact, we may be able to permanently station a diplomat in the region, if this would be agreeable to you."

["A diplomatic presence would go a long way to restoring order to this system, yes. The forge world is a vital part of the Alliance's infrastructure. It is the primary manufacturing facility for the Telvan, and we rely upon it through trade. After our recent losses, we require the forges to be operational and are willing, for now, to discuss a temporary measure to allow the Humans to keep their jump technology."]

That struck a chord with Liao, something that stood out more than anything else Avaran had said so far. The Telvan that Liao had met on Velsharn seemed more than willing to ally themselves with the Humans and resist the Alliance. Saara was Telvan. It was well known that they were not part of the Alliance and were, in many respects, considered allies; even after the destruction of Velsharn, efforts had been made to try and bring the Telvan more completely into the fold. The likelihood of Magnet deliberately attacking a Telvan colony, or attacking one in error and holding it long enough for the Alliance to become worried about it, was extremely low.

"Recent losses?"

["Perhaps you have not heard,"] Avaran offered, shifting slightly on what Liao realised must be an extremely uncomfortable chair for his body shape. ["Although this is not unexpected, given the small size of your forces there. They would be, I imagine, unwilling to relinquish control of their prize, even to inform you of their victory."]

It *was* the *Rubens*. Liao kept her eyes on Avaran, forcing her composure to appear calm, but inwardly she was struggling to understand how a victory this vast could possibly have occurred.

"In the interest of disclosure, maybe you can enlighten us, then, so that our dialogue can proceed with the best possible information available to both parties."

The Toralii inhaled slightly as though admitting some great personal failure. ["Last month, the Alliance pooled our forces from many sectors and attempted to reclaim Belthas IV, an operation that failed. Your soldiers and sailors are to be commended, Commander. We have *greatly* underestimated your kind and your ability to wage war. The Toralii have not suffered a defeat of this kind in hundreds of years. A third of our fleet lies in ruins, annihilated by a single ship, and it will take us decades to rebuild... And a species with such destructive power cannot be our enemy. This is why we are offering your species this amnesty."]

The silence in the room was palpable, a thick, pervading fog that smothered rational thought. A full third of the Toralii Alliance fleet was enough force to occupy hundreds of star systems along with the spaces in-between. This was a cataclysmic disaster for them and, if true, the balance of power in the entire Milky Way galaxy was soon to shift, although in which way nobody could be certain.

That was why the Kel-Voran abandoned Earth, not because they were afraid of the Toralii attack upon her person, but because they were afraid of humans. They did not want to be anywhere near a species who could bring the greatest empire in known space to their knees with a single ship.

But how had they done it?

"Our communication with our ground forces is limited," Liao lied, "and so no, we had not received this report. The outcome, though, was what we expected."

["Of course. Possession of the experimental voidwarp devices has long been theorised to be one of the most powerful devices one can own. Their use as a weapon is undeniable. The Telvan have performed amazing advances since they turned the first prototype over to us."] Avaran gave a bitter chuckle. ["Which, I suppose, explains why you destroyed the facility after you wrestled the device from them. You are wiser and more savage than I had previously given you credit for, Commander."]

"The facility?" Liao spoke without thinking. "Are you referring to the Velsharn Research Colony?"

Avaran frowned slightly, his scarred face regarding Liao with a mix of curiosity and interest. ["That is the name the local Telvan gave it, yes. Our long-range sensors reported your ship arriving and collecting the device. Its radioactive signature was seen departing that world to test the device, but returned at a later date to destroy the facility, presumably to prevent any more of its kind from being developed. The radiation signature of the unique void was subsequently spotted at Cenar before it too was destroyed, and now at Belthas IV."]

"Yes, but that wasn't us that destroyed Velsharn. It was..." her voice faded away as the terrible realisation dawned. "... Ben."

Avaran raised a fuzzy eye-ridge in confusion. ["Yes. The commander of the vessel that assaulted Belthas IV identified himself by that name, a Human name. Our Forerunner probes intercepted the transmissions made to the surface, but since landing on the planet, we've had no contact with this 'Ben' or any other representatives of your forces."]

Realisation came to her in a sudden wave, like a floodlight being shone in her face, and Liao could think of nothing to say. When Ben had engaged the *Beijing*'s jump drive and leapt away across the stars, she fully expected that would be the last she would ever see of him. But, it seemed, Ben had somehow gathered a ship and the power to occupy a planet, all in a few short months.

She leaned across the desk, her tone becoming quiet. "Warbringer Avaran, the Toralii have a reputation for honesty and integrity, do they not?"

["You know this to be true."]

"Then hear this. I do not have a perfect understanding of what has occurred, but Ben is known to me. He is not," she clarified, "a member of our military, and we do not have any power over him." Liao leaned back, choosing her words carefully. "But he is... someone I have had significant dealings with, someone with whom I have a certain rapport. I will do whatever is in my power to investigate what has occurred on Belthas IV, and I will, if possible, attempt to find a peaceful resolution on behalf of the Alliance, and others."

Avaran started at her as though trying to pierce the veil of some elaborate deception she was setting up. To have admitted that Ben was not a part of their military, she knew, was to give away their primary bargaining chip, but she was aware of the bigger picture. Ben's possession of the jump drive had shown where the balance of power would swing to fill the void left by the decimated Toralii fleet.

Towards him.

["Why would you do this?"]

"I want my people to be left in peace. I want possession of our jump technology to be sanctioned by the Toralii Alliance. I want the hostilities between our people to end. We don't have to be friends," she said, "but we can no longer live at war."

["I can promise you none of those things,"] Avaran said, ["not in the long term. But I am empowered to offer you a period of grace where your use of the voidwarp technology is sanctioned, as is your passage through Toralii Alliance space towards Belthas IV, or anywhere your investigation may lead you aside from occupied worlds."]

Liao considered for a moment, then nodded. "Very well." She went to stand. "It is customary, as a sign of good will, to shake hands upon the reaching of an accord."

["I am familiar with the gesture. We learnt a great deal about your peoples while the crew of the ship you call the *Tehran* were... guests... at Cenar."]

James stiffened slightly beside her, and Liao quickly spoke to prevent an incident. "Then this is good." She stood, moving to the end of the table, and Avaran did the same.

She slid her hand into his massive paw, the two exchanging an amicable, if forced, shake of their hands. Liao was surprised by his size, but also by the sheer strength in his grip. Saara's hugs could crush her, but her paws were soft and cultured. Avaran's were rough and calloused. The hands of a warrior.

It seemed odd that, not so long ago, Liao, James and Avaran had been trying to kill one another in the black gulf of space, but now they were, tentatively at least, working together.

Avaran's nostrils flared slightly and Liao caught the gesture.

["You smell of blood."]

Liao retracted her hand and, as she did so, saw a red smudge on the underside of her sleeve. A spot of Tai's blood from the shooting that had somehow escaped her efforts to scrub her hands clean and had passed unnoticed on the trip to the station.

"Sorry," she said, "it's…"

Tai's death, the death of the Velsharn colonists, now the death of untold Toralii servicemen at the hands of Ben's terrible power. Her legacy seemed to be slaughter and devastation, to bury her friends and enemies alike. Now she had literal blood on her hands, a metaphorical stain turned very literal.

"It's nothing."

Act II

Chapter V

"Game Plan"
*****
Cerberus Station

The next morning

The TFR *Beijing* appeared in the Mars-Phobos Lagrange point with a flash of light and the subtle rumble of the resultant shockwave as it passed over the station, a gentle shaking that faded quickly. Liao saw her old ship through the observation portal for the first time in nearly a year, a familiar and welcoming sight that made her heart soar.

The ship was just as she'd left it—long and thin and powerful, lined with fins to dissipate heat and dotted with missile launch tubes. It was widest at the rear and came to a narrow, thin point like an arrowhead, its dull metal finish glinting slightly as the faint light of the station's floodlights illuminated it.

Liao was wearing her own uniform again, something that pleased her immensely. It felt comfortable and welcome, a return to the life that she had fought so hard to maintain. No, she was not the captain now, but in her mind, the *Beijing* would always be her ship.

She waited at the docking port for what seemed like an eternity before the seal locked and pressurised, making entry to the ship possible. She knew from experience that the crew would be eager to disembark even for a short while. She stood by in an adjacent corridor as the first wave of uniformed crew departed, laughing and joking with each other. She didn't want to be recognised, didn't want to make a scene.

None of them saw her, but as she prepared to step out and move aboard the ship, a stretcher supporting a wounded crewman was gingerly carried out of the airlock. The bearers held an IV bag aloft, walking past her with slow, careful steps. The station had no real medical facilities, so she knew they must be unloading him for transport to Mars, or even Earth. She caught a look at the wounded man's face; it wasn't one she recognised, and neither were any of the stretcher bearers. This would be a common sight, she mused, as the team walked down the corridor and turned towards the station's tiny infirmary. Unknown crew, strangers aboard her vessel.

["Commander Liao?"]

A voice startled her. Liao turned around, her face lighting up. "Saara!"

The Toralii woman stepped forward and wrapped her up in a tight, bone-crushing hug.

"Ow, ow, ow!"

["My apologies, Commander."] Saara released her but Liao still held on, squeezing the Toralii woman around her upper chest.

"It's quite okay, really. I didn't need those ribs anyway." She smiled, stepping back. "What the hell are you doing here? James said you were aboard the *Tehran*."

["I was, but of course when I heard you were here, I requested a brief leave of absence to visit you."] She smiled a wide, toothy smile. ["Given the disposition of the Commanding Officer, it was unsurprising that this request was granted. Besides, we were in the neighbourhood."]

Liao smiled. "It's wonderful to see you again."

["And I you, Captain. Thank you for showing me Earth... I have many fond memories of your planet, and I wish to return as soon as I am able."]

The thought pleased her. "Great. Let's go to Hong Kong next, okay?"

["I am unfamiliar with that location."]

"You'll love it. I promise." Liao couldn't keep the smile off her face. "So the *Tehran*'s here, huh? All three original Pillars are together again... that'll be quite the sight."

["It would appear so. Bear in mind, though, that we have had combined operations since you left."]

At the mention of that, Liao felt a faint feeling of regret in her gut. Saara's face shifted subtly, and Liao wondered if she'd picked up on her reaction, a suspicion confirmed when the topic was swiftly changed.

["And the *Madrid* will be joining us within a day."]

Liao forced her tone to remain lighthearted. "Good. We can best project our strength when we're together."

Saara nodded eagerly. ["Sound military doctrine, Commander."] Her eyes widened. ["I was almost forgetful. Commander, Captains Knight, Harandi, and Grégoire request your presence. The TFR *Washington* has been launched from its berth under the command of Captain Anderson, and after it's undertaken its first jump, it will be moving to the Cerberus Station with the *Madrid*."]

Liao frowned. "They're putting the *Washington* into action without a shakedown cruise?"

Every newly launched Pillar of the Earth had undertaken a shakedown cruise, a first journey via reactionless drive, typically out to Jupiter or Venus and back. This was seen as a good opportunity to find and solve problems with the incredibly complex machines before they were to see actual combat.

Saara's face belied her concern, too. ["Grégoire explained to me that it is the opinion of Fleet Command that the *Triumph* class vessels are now a proven platform and ready for mass production. Protocol now dictates that the shakedown cruises for current and future vessels be curtailed to one day. Construction and material issues have delayed the *Moscow* and the *Tripoli* from being able to launch with the *Washington*, regrettably, so they are still a month away."]

"Great. Don't they remember all the problems the *Sydney* had in the beginning?"

["Evidently not. Additionally, your nation of Libya's financial problems necessitated a large grant from the South Korean government. They're petitioning to have the ship renamed the *Seoul*. Meanwhile, the Brazilians, who also contributed significantly to Libya's assistance, wish the vessel to be christened the *Brasília*. As you Humans say, everything is political."]

Liao opened her mouth to say something but Saara's eyes lifted, looking over Laio's shoulder. She followed Saara's gaze until her eyes fell upon Summer Rowe.

"Hey, Cappy!" The fiery redhead skipped forward, grinning impishly. "Ya' made it!"

Liao shook her head at Rowe's exuberance. "Well, look who's still not locked up in an insane asylum yet."

"Hah. Are you fucking kidding me? Everyone *else* is the crazy one. I'm totally sane."

"I'm afraid it's relative." Liao couldn't help but feel that Summer's bubbly, energetic personality was infectious after having been without it for so long. "But anyway, it's great to see you again, but I'm not the captain anymore."

Summer blew out a loud raspberry. "Yeah, well, Commodore Wrong is a shit-eating shithead. They need to give that crotchety old fuck the boot and get you back in command, I reckon."

Liao grimaced slightly, glancing around to make sure nobody had overheard. "Commodore *Vong* is a decent Commanding Officer," she said, "based on what I hear. I have confidence in his abilities."

["I, too, preferred you in command,"] offered Saara, ["and I think your style is much more agreeable than his."]

"And I appreciate that. But for the foreseeable future, the *Beijing* is under the command of Commodore Vong, and that's all there is to say about it."

Rowe rolled her eyes in an exaggerated gesture, causing guffaws from Saara.

Liao made little 'tsk tsk' noises at them both. "What, are you two six years old?"

"Mentally? About fourteen." Rowe gave a wide, cheesy smile. "Certified, desensitised, disaffected youth."

"You're 28."

Summer looked offended. "That's still young!"

"Try joining a youth group and see what they say." Liao gave her a clap on the shoulder. "Anyway. Let's go see the captains, shall we?"

Summer gave her a strange look, half concerned, half elated. "You're acting really weird."

Liao blinked in surprise. "What? No I'm not."

"Yes, you are." Rowe leaned in towards her, almost accusingly. "You're... you're a lot less of a stick-up-your-arse, super-boring captain now. Maybe taking some time off for the first time in your work-a-holic life has done you some good!"

"I'm the same person I always was, Summer. For what it's worth, though, *you* haven't changed a bit."

"Hah, and I hope I never do." Rowe clapped her hands eagerly. "So, you want a tour of the ship?"

Liao gave her a sceptical leer. "Why? What have you changed about it?"

"Oooh, well, wouldn't you like to know."

Liao put her hands on her hips. "Summer, if you've fucked with my ship while I was away, I am going to destroy you."

["Aside from the newly installed, networked, tactical IFF computer, nothing of significance has been altered by Summer, Commander Liao. I promise you that."]

Rowe stuck out her tongue at Saara. "Spoilsport."

*****

Conference Room
Cerberus Station

Presumably because she had no actual ship to command and very little actual work to do, Liao was the first to arrive.

The conference room, only hours ago packed full of Toralii, marines, guards and observers, was now conspicuously empty. Liao spent a moment studying the seat where Avaran had sat and the occasional strand of fur left behind on the rear of the seat. It seemed impossible to believe that one so mighty had come to this room practically begging for an audience, ready to negotiate a cease fire. For all her victories and hard work, she had not accomplished anything so major in so little time.

Perhaps they didn't need her after all.

She reminded herself that Avaran didn't even know about the *Rubens* and either knew nothing of what the other ships had been up to during her time away or didn't care. Yet the attack on Kor'Vakkar, the destruction of Cenar, even the events at Velsharn, these things were all known to him. Although she had not done these things alone, her ship and her command had been the driving force behind them. Her involvement was intertwined with every part of those events to the point where, if one were to remove her, they would never have taken place at all.

Perhaps they *did* need her after all.

The hatchway swung open with a faint groan. A tall, older Chinese man with surprisingly fair skin and the shadow of a beard and moustache across his face stepped into the room. His epaulets gave his rank as a Commodore, and Liao spent a moment sizing him up.

"Commodore Vong, I presume?"

The man extended a hand, respectfully inclining his head. "Commander Liao. It is a pleasure to finally meet you in person." His tone was polite and formal, but Liao sensed a subtle underlying coldness about it and she doubted the sincerity of his words.

Still, she gave him a firm handshake. It wouldn't be the first time her reputation had preceded her. "Likewise. I hope you're taking good care of the *Beijing*, sir."

Vong moved around to the head of the table, easing himself into a seat. "She's in good hands, Commander. Don't worry about that." He pulled a small notepad out of one of his pockets and snapped off a pen clipped onto the side. "We've enjoyed a modest amount of success working alongside the *Rubens* to harass Toralii shipping lanes and the like."

Liao felt a slight pang of annoyance at the use of the word *she*, but by her own logic, she could not deny the logic behind its use. Liao had claimed, somewhat as a matter of pride, that although tradition dictated that a ship was always a woman, this was only because the captain was married to the job. When it came to the *Beijing* and its female captain, of course, that would make the ship a man.

But she was no longer in command, and to argue this fairly minor quibble would be inappropriate. She inclined her head. "Warbringer Avaran indicated that the shipping harassment was of little consequence to him, sir."

"Warbringer Avaran is entitled to his opinion, but to be frank, Commander, the opinions of Toralii mean little to me."

Liao wondered for a moment if that opinion extended to Saara. "Well, in any event, he didn't seem to care that we were doing it, sir. Are there any plans to alter the *Beijing*'s current area of operations?"

Vong jotted a few notes down on his pad, and Liao tried to read the characters upside down. "After the investigation of Belthas IV has been completed, the *Beijing* will return to assaulting the Toralii supply network. As the least capable of the four existing Pillars, this is a job well suited for it."

Liao had to remind herself that Vong was pressed into this task after retirement and probably was not as attached to the ship as she was. "The least capable, sir? The *Beijing* is identical to the other Pillars."

"Damage sustained in the engagement at Cenar has meant that the port rail gun has been rendered inoperative. It is fixable, but with the more advanced *Washington* and *Madrid* now available for combat operations, it is less critical to have all three original ships at maximum capability. Rather than spend months on the Luna dry dock repairing a single embedded system, it is better that the *Beijing* make itself useful. Even with a single rail gun and sparing use of nuclear devices, the *Beijing* has sunk considerable tonnage during your absence."

She kept her tongue and tried to keep her tone steady. "I understand, sir. And any attack on the Toralii infrastructure is a solid tactic. However, the Toralii Alliance is vast. Saara told me they have over sixty *star systems* that are directly settled and thousands that have outposts, research stations, or unmanned settlements. Even if the *Beijing* is destroying two ships a day, the amount of trade that goes on between those systems is significant. I'm sure there are better ways to harm them than destroying a few freighters, sir."

"You see, Commander Liao, that's the difference between you and I." Commodore Vong clicked his pen closed, then slowly folded both arms onto the table and leaned forward. "I'm quite content for my ship to score safe victories, reliably and evenly, without resorting to personal heroics. Under my command, the Beijing has suffered no significant damage whatsoever. We've lost no strike craft, except one which was damaged in a training mishap and returned to service, and our victories have been predictable, clean and comfortable. The worst injury we've sustained is the head of the marines pulling a muscle. We're inflicting steady damage on the Toralii, and we're doing it every single day of the week. Over the course of my command, we have sunk more estimated tonnage than the *Tehran* and the *Beijing* did *combined* at Kor'Vakkar, and we didn't have to execute a blind jump on the word of an alien, then cripple two ships and lose the lives of nearly seventy crewmen, to do so. Even setting aside the loss of life, factoring in how long the *Beijing* alone has spent in repairs, in terms of tonnage sunk per week, the ship is doing better under my command than yours."

"I wasn't aware it was a competition, sir."

Vong gave her a cool stare. "War is a game of economics. We have to make it clear to the Toralii that antagonising us will cost them, regularly and consistently. A few spectacular losses don't frighten economists as much as a steady stream of red in their ledger."

Liao didn't have anything she could contest with Vong's assertion. It was true that the *Beijing* had spent most of its operational lifetime being repaired, but the slow harassment of the Toralii shipping lanes seemed woefully ineffective to her. What was the point of it all if their presence wasn't even being felt?

They sat together in uncomfortable silence until the door swung open again. Liao was relieved to see it was James.

"Captain Grégoire," she said, keeping her tone distant.

"Commander Liao." James gave her a professional smile, but out of the corner of her eye, she could see Vong's face tighten slightly. Their relationship had been fodder for the tabloids, and it was impossible to think that Vong wouldn't know of it.

Right on James's heels came Captain Knight who took a seat on the other side of the table, giving Liao a friendly nod.

"Good evening, Captain," she said.

"It's a pleasure to see you again, Commander Liao. I hope your little rascal's doing well."

She smiled. "She's here, if you want to see her after the briefing."

"I'd like that," he replied, resting his hands on the table and closing his eyes a moment, then blinking a few times.

"Long night?" Liao asked.

"Long few months," he answered, "with more to come."

The last two people to arrive, Captain Lale Harandi and Flight Lieutenant Mike Williams, came in together. Liao had to remind herself that, certainly with Commodore Vong present, it would be inappropriate to refer to Williams as "Magnet".

"Captain Knight," said Williams, taking a seat opposite his former commanding officer.

Liao spent a moment looking at the man she'd heard a fair bit about but had not had the chance to meet personally. He was a tan-skinned Australian with heavy facial scarring, leading to a broken, uneven face that Liao couldn't even consider ruggedly handsome. That said, she knew he was one of the best pilots in the fleet; she knew, more than anyone, that although people intrinsically trusted attractive people and preferred to be around them, when the chips came down, the one single skill that mattered in war was how effectively a person could kill their enemies.

Noticing her staring, Williams gave her a curt nod. "Commander Liao, I've heard a lot about you, ma'am."

"It's a pleasure to meet you in person," she replied. "Your reputation precedes you. How fares the *Rubens*?"

"Very well. It's a Toralii ship, so we're not entirely sure we're sailing her right, but they've packed a lot of firepower into a very small space. The fact that she's got a working Toralii transponder and they don't appear to have noticed that the ship's missing has been remarkably useful. We've got intel from locations you could only *dream* of."

"Good," Liao said. In her mind, the *Rubens* was a far better fit than the *Beijing* at this task of harassing Toralii shipping lanes; the only thing the *Beijing* had going for it was its immense strength, but even at the height of its power, with both rail guns intact, it had taken all three Pillars of the Earth to make a solid stand against a single Toralii cruiser. A smaller, faster, repurposed alien vessel was much more likely to slip away unnoticed. "What are the plans for the ship's future?"

"Well, a lot of our strength comes from our covert operations. If we do too many of them, we risk blowing our cover, so we're off for a few months to lay low, rearm, refit, see if we can coax a little more power out of the Toralii systems, and let the Intel guys climb all over them for a while, then we're right back out there."

"What about the command structure?" asked Commodore Vong. "Are there any plans to rotate the crews?"

Williams shook his head. "None yet. The crew is a volunteer-only outfit taken from all over the fleet. We're a tight, cohesive unit and we're, frankly, a little nuts. If we're caught, it'll be a lifetime in whatever gulag the Toralii Alliance is using instead of Cenar, or worse. Guerrilla warfare and intelligence work is technically a mixture of spying and terrorism, and if our own cultures are anything to go by, people tend to take a dim view of both."

Liao could see he disapproved of the notion but gave Williams a reassuring nod. "I understand completely."

Vong cleared his throat. "Let's turn to business, shall we?"

Nods around the table.

"The Toralii have a problem," Liao began, "two problems, really. The first of them, the occupation of Belthas IV, is short term, but the loss of their fleet's a lot more substantial. It might be tempting to suggest that their problems are our advantage, but it's important to realise one thing; the Toralii have been in charge of all they survey for hundreds of years—it's true—but they're not the only species with a fleet of ships out there. A dramatic shift in the balance of power is not something that will favour us."

"I'm inclined to agree," said Williams. "From what I've seen of the Toralii in the field, behind their lines, it's a very disorganised but very powerful web of planets, all protected by their fleet. If they have lost one third of their naval assets and word of this spreads, strands of that web are going to be stretched. Some are going to be broken. From what we know of the Kel-Voran, they're certain to take advantage of this. If the Kel-Voran go all out on the Toralii Alliance, given their weakened state, it's unlikely they'll care about us."

Murmurs of agreement around the table.

"It seems," said Liao, "that we have a few courses of action open to us. Although they're weakened, the Toralii are still the five hundred pound gorilla when it comes to planet spanning empires. The Kel-Voran are probably more numerous, but they're so factional I doubt they could stop squabbling amongst themselves for the few years it would take to be a genuine threat to the Toralii. So one course of action we can take is to assist the Toralii Alliance if we can, with the help of whomever we can muster, and then hopefully earn amnesty regarding the use of jump technology.

"Alternatively, we can let whatever will happen play out. Let the Kel-Voran sink their teeth into the Toralii, hope it's enough to keep them distracted and their attention away from us. There's a number of advantages to this, most notably that we avoid as much combat as we can. The disadvantage, of course, is that one Toralii cruiser was a sufficient challenge for three of our ships at their prime and in a dedicated defensive posture. Avaran asked for our help; if we spurn that request, it wouldn't be out of his character to simply send three ships to completely crush us." Liao looked to Commodore Vong. "What does Fleet Command say?"

"Fleet Command is of the opinion that the Cerberus outpost gives the solar system an impressive defensive posture. With the defences at Mars being strengthened every day, and a secondary ring of satellites being installed around Earth, they are less concerned with the possibility of attack via the Lagrange points. If an all-out assault against Earth is launched, Fleet Command believes it will be launched by ships appearing at the outer edges of the solar system and travelling slowly inward. It is estimated that this will give Earth a year to prepare which should be sufficient."

Liao, having faced a Toralii cruiser and outnumbered it three to one, didn't feel as confident as Fleet Command appeared to when it came to their ability to fight off a Toralii assault. The Cerberus blockade was powerful, yes, but the *Beijing*, the *Tehran* and the *Sydney* together had stood toe to toe with just one of the alien ships and had only survived because the *Tehran* had rammed it.

"I would not be so certain," Liao said, glancing to Harandi, "of our ability to resist a determined push by the Toralii. Saara has expressed the opinion that our strength will hold, but with full respect to her and her knowledge, and also to Captain Harandi and her station, Saara is only a pilot... and she is Telvan. She may not be aware of all the Alliance's latest tricks, and there's a very real risk that our entire blockade is a facade. The Toralii Alliance have made it their business to win, completely and utterly without question, every war they've engaged in for the last few hundred years, and they've chosen to engage in many. This, if nothing else, should give us significant reason to be concerned."

"To be honest," Harandi said, "I sometimes wonder about the same thing. The French, after World War I, built the Maginot Line: a supposedly impenetrable wall of defences along the French-German and French-Italian borders to defeat further aggression from the east. The Nazis, however, simply went around it by invading Belgium."

"We didn't see that one coming," quipped Grégoire. Liao smirked at the Belgian man, then regained her composure.

Liao studied the faces around the table. "It's my opinion that if the wrath of the Toralii navy fell upon us, we'd be dogs barking at the lightning, trying to fight something we just couldn't understand." She paused for a moment. "But fortunately, we don't have to decide today. All we promised Avaran was that we would investigate, so I think our first step should be to look into what happened at Belthas IV."

"Agreed," said James.

"If we send the *Sydney*, the *Tehran* and the *Beijing*," offered Knight, "this is not only an impressive show of force, but it allows us to keep the *Madrid* and the *Washington* in reserve. With a little luck, the Toralii may not know we have two more ships."

"And the *Rubens*," added Williams.

Knight nodded. "And the *Rubens*. With all due respect to Captain Harandi, I think it's important to remember that wars aren't won with static defences. We need to reach out and touch the Toralii before they find a map of Belgium and find a way past this impressive, but stationary, blockade."

Liao cast a glance to Knight, trying to read his expression. On one hand, a strong show of force would be appropriate, and they couldn't cower behind the Cerberus station for the rest of eternity. On the other, Vong had a good point. They couldn't afford to overstretch themselves.

But how much of Knight's suggestion to leave the two newest and most advanced ships in the fleet in reserve was based upon the fact that the *Madrid* and the *Washington* had not yet seen proper combat, or even had a lengthy shakedown cruise? The *Sydney* was, of the three original Pillars, the ship most affected by teething issues. Did he fear that the *Madrid* and the *Washington* would suffer similar problems?

Liao looked to Vong. "It's your call, sir."

Commodore Vong, silent for some time now, didn't answer immediately. He sat, his hands steepled in front of him, resting his chin on the top of his fingers. "I think," he said, "there's a lot of guessing going on and not a lot of fact. It's clear we don't know enough about what's occurred on Belthas IV to make an accurate game plan, and the incident —along with the subsequent significant loss of Toralii naval assets, if confirmed—is a serious matter worthy of investigation, especially if the construct known as Ben is involved. Accordingly, I'm inclined to agree with Captain Knight. Send three ships to Belthas IV with the goal of learning what we can. One of our goals should be initiating dialogue with Ben, if such a thing is possible.

"The *Rubens*, I feel, needs to spend some time lying low. What Lieutenant Williams proposed is an excellent plan of action. The *Rubens*'s crew have earned some leave, Flight Lieutenant; make sure they enjoy it."

Williams's scarred face lit up. "I will, sir."

"May I make a suggestion, sir?" asked Liao.

"Proceed," said Vong.

"We found Ben on the wreckage of the *Giralan* on Karathi, deep within Toralii space. We didn't spend a great deal of time exploring the derelict, but there may be some intel to be found there if we sent down a team to investigate. Avaran gave us permission to enter Toralii Alliance space for the purposes of gathering information about Ben, so I suggest we use this offer to the best of our ability. When the *Washington* arrives, sir, perhaps they can be sent to see what their crew can pick from the bones. It would be a useful pseudo-shakedown cruise and a good test of their jump drive, too."

Liao could see Vong didn't approve, but he didn't immediately say no. After some consideration, he folded his hands. "I think we should, instead, send just the *Beijing* to talk to Ben and send the *Sydney* to Karathi. Ben destroyed a staggering number of Toralii Alliance ships without breaking a sweat, a 'show of force' of just three of our ships isn't going to matter one bit. Sending just the *Beijing* will show we're there to talk. I'm not comfortable sending the *Washington* so far away, and possibly into danger, when she's still unproven. The *Sydney* can handle that task. We'll keep the battle-proven *Tehran* here with the *Washington* and the *Madrid*. Anything else?"

It was a sound line of reason, and Liao found herself agreeing with Vong. "No, sir."

Vong returned his pen to his pocket. "Very well, then. Commander Liao, I'd like to request your presence aboard the *Beijing* for this mission. You know Ben better than any of us."

The idea of being sent on a mission on her original ship, even if she wasn't in command anymore, excited her. "Very good, sir."

Vong looked around the table. "If there's nothing else, dismissed."

*****

Corridor
Cerberus Station

Spotting Williams in a corridor, Liao power-walked to catch up to him, moving through the corridor and excusing herself whenever she had to push past someone.

"Sorry, Lieutenant Williams?"

He turned, giving a lopsided smile with his strange, heavily scarred face. He had a half-dozen thick, wide scars running from his forehead to his chin at a forty-five degree angle, with numerous smaller scars where stitches and corrective surgeries had obviously taken place. The effect was a face that was thick, leathery and uneven.

"Yes, ma'am?"

Liao inhaled slightly, steadying herself. "They call you Magnet, don't they?"

"That's my call sign, ma'am."

"On the *Rubens*, too?"

He raised a scarred eyebrow. "Pilots are a strange breed, and the *Rubens*'s an even stranger beast. We run with a small crew on a smaller ship, performing highly risky feats of derring-do well beyond enemy lines." He glanced over his shoulder for a moment, then back to Liao. "Don't tell Commodore Vong, but although I'm in command, rank matters little on my ship. It's mostly pilots or crew from the *Sydney* anyway, so we run things pretty informally. Why?"

Liao grinned. "Well, for the longest time, we thought that, when Avaran was talking about this 'lone, stolen ship', he was talking about the *Rubens*."

Magnet laughed, shaking his head. *"Really?"*

"Yeah. You should have seen our faces, I guess. We were all trying to understand how you'd taken a *planet*... much less held it against a third of the Toralii fleet." She gave a cheesy smile. "You'd be more famous than me, and you wouldn't even have to sleep with Captain Grégoire."

Magnet smirked. "He's a bit out of my league. Besides, I got a nice girl back home."

"Great. Want a free piece of advice? Use a condom."

He looked, strangely, distinctly uncomfortable at that suggestion, and Liao for a second wondered why.

"So, I'm Magnet, the planet conquerer, huh?"

"That's what we thought, yeah."

"I'm struggling to understand how a victory of that—ahem, *magnitude*—could have been accomplished."

She laughed. "Yeah, yeah. So were we. We still are, I suppose, but don't worry. We're going to find out." Liao paused. "In the meantime, I have a favour to ask you."

He tilted his head. "Sure."

"James and I weren't expecting to be recalled so we brought our child. There was some personal threat against me, so we didn't feel safe leaving her on Earth without us. But now that we know nobody's going to knife me in the dark, I think she's safer there, really. There's a very good chance these ships are going to see combat again, and she's just a baby. So... when you head back on leave, can you take her with you? There's a babysitter in New York who's basically a full time house-sitter now, and I'll happily reimburse you for any costs—"

He held up his hand to stop her. "She can stay with us, if you like. Penny will love her," he said. "She's always adored kids, and a trip to New York sounds perfect. Believe me; it would be my privilege."

Relieved, Liao nodded. "Great. Just pick her up from Ensign Mohammadi's quarters before you leave. I'll let her know you're coming."

"Will do, Captain. Good hunting."

She smiled. "Enjoy your leave."

Magnet turned and left, and Liao stared at his back until he turned down a corridor and disappeared. She began walking back the way she had come, but Rowe appeared through the crowd of people.

"Hey Cappy, off to see the CO of the *Madrid*?"

Liao blinked. "I thought they weren't due in for a day."

"Nah, they came in earlier, while you were at the meeting. I figured you'd wanna know."

Liao smiled. "Thanks for the heads up, Summer. Walk with me; we might as well see if we can meet him together."

Rowe fell into step with her and together the two made their way forward towards the docking ring. When they arrived, it was a buzz of activity; the Cerberus station was not a large outpost, and Liao could guess that the number of people who were arriving was probably beginning to exceed the comfort level for the existing crew.

The *Madrid*, as the name implied, was primarily crewed by elements from the various EU member states. Liao scanned the sea of heads trying to find anyone of suitable rank.

"Melissa Liao," said a man wearing captain's epaulets and moving out from the crowd, "as I live and breathe. Heard you might be here."

The voice triggered a memory. The name 'de Lugo' had been rattling around in her head ever since James had mentioned it, but now, seeing his face and hearing his voice, Liao's eyes widened and she felt herself flush. "Alano?"

Alano de Lugo stepped within handshaking distance, reached out, and smiled widely. "It's a pleasure to see you again. It's been a while."

The first night Liao and James had slept together, they had consumed an excessive amount of strong alcohol. Amongst the various conversation topics—Saara and what to do with her, Spanish as the language of 'sexy space lust', and others—Liao had insisted she'd never have sex with another officer. However, almost in the same breath, she'd drunkenly confessed that, during officer candidate school, a "sculpted Adonis" from Spain had visited her co-ed boot camp. Specifically, she'd said he was gorgeous, with a chest that looked like it was carved from marble, and that during his stay, Liao and he had engaged in some 'interoffice networking'.

And Alano had barely changed a bit, despite being over fifteen years older.

She awkwardly extended her hand. "It has been a while, yeah. How are you?"

"I'm well, thank you," he said, taking her hand and giving it a firm squeeze.

Liao had no idea what to say. "So, that's your ship, huh?"

"That's my ship."

"How'd you swing that command?"

"It's fairly simple, really," de Lugo said with his heavy Spanish accent. "The physical demands on a spacefaring captain are much harsher than those of an ocean going one, so the military is looking for fitter, healthier, younger officers for command positions."

Fit he was, too. Liao nodded politely. "Right. Well, congratulations. You earned it." She pointed down the corridor. "We just had the mission brief. In short, the *Madrid* is staying in town while we go out and have some fun."

de Lugo smiled his wide, perfect smile. "Have fun. We'll mind the fort while you're gone."

Liao nodded in agreement as one of de Lugo's crewmen approached bearing a manila folder.

"That'll be orders from the Commodore," she noted as he took the folder and flipped it open. "I'll leave you to it."

de Lugo nodded politely and with that, Liao and Rowe stepped away, walking away from the large crowd of disembarked crew towards the more empty and quieter corridors of the ship.

"You're drooling, Summer," Liao observed.

"Fucking oath I'm drooling." Rowe craned her neck, looking over her shoulder and trying to spy more of the Spanish captain. "Where the fuck do I get one of those?"

"Spain."

"Can we go to Spain?"

"No, Summer. We have aliens to blow up."

"Fuck aliens. I want a piece of *that*."

"Thank you, Summer. Enough."

"Bet he's got a great big fucking cock, too. I bet he has."

"I suppose it's okay."

Rowe laughed, reaching over and clapping Liao on the shoulder. "Yeah, like *you'd* know."

There was an awkward silence. Rowe's eyes widened. "Oh shit. No way. No fucking *way*. You've never been to Spain!"

She felt a warm flush creep up her neck and frowned at her friend. "It was an officer exchange program—"

"No *fucking way!*"

"—it was a long time ago—"

"No. Fucking. Way."

"It was just a *thing*. We were young. I had no idea he was going to—"

Rowe burst out laughing, a loud, barking laugh that caused eyes to turn upon them.

"Quiet!" she hissed. "This is embarrassing enough as it is!"

Rowe leaned closer, grinning impishly. "I know." Rowe clicked her tongue. "So, tell me; is there a captain in the Task Force you *haven't* slept with yet?"

Liao, completely struck dumb, had nothing to say. Rowe laughed like a lunatic and wandered off down the corridor, leaving her standing around like a lost child. She gathered her wits and stormed off down the passage in the other direction, almost running into Saara.

"Saara, thank God." Liao gave an exasperated sigh. "Please tell me you're not going to make my day any worse than it already is."

Liao expected levity, but she could see that Saara's face was clouded with anger. ["Reluctantly, I can make no promises about that, Commander."]

Frowning, Melissa reached out for Saara's arm, but the Toralii pulled back. "What's wrong?"

["Is it true that you had a meeting with Captain Harandi, Captain Grégoire, Captain Knight and Commodore Vong?"]

Liao inclined her head. "Yes," she said, "it was called by Vong. It finished about ten minutes ago or so. Why?"

Saara's dark gaze fixed on her, and Liao felt distinctly uncomfortable. She was reminded of how Saara had seen her during their early days, when she was a prisoner aboard the *Beijing*, an enemy kept captive and not a friend.

["Why did you bring me here?"]

"I'm... sorry?"

["Why did you bring me to this station? Why do your people have me here?"]

Liao stammered in confusion. "Y-You're my friend, but you're also very knowledgeable about the Toralii, and so much more than that. It's a huge galaxy out there, and we've only begun to understand a tiny bit of it. Your advice has been completely invaluable."

["So they tell me. Why, then, was I not invited to the briefing? Why do you spurn my council?"]

Liao frowned. "I'm sorry," she said. "There's so much going on, and it was Vong's meeting. I just didn't think to invite you."

["You are correct,"] Saara growled. ["You did *not* think. What else am I to do on this station? I am the de facto Telvan representative for your species. I am trying to help you, to guide your species away from the path mine took. Of becoming warmongers, murderers, hoarders of technology, a broken species without a homeworld due to our folly. I had to learn what transpired from James, and quite a shock it was to hear that you are making plans without me."]

Liao blinked in surprise. "I assumed James would have asked you there if he wanted you. He's your CO now; I thought that was the most appropriate course of action!"

["Melissa, you are my friend. This fact transcends command structure."] Saara's judging gaze burned into her. ["I expected better from you."]

Liao inhaled, closing her eyes and bringing her emotions under control. When she opened them, she had to fight to keep her breathing steady. "I'm very sorry," Liao said. "Everything you've said is true. I've... I've been away from this for so long; it will take me some time to get back into the swing of things. I'm sorry we didn't invite you, and we'll make sure you are there the next time we have a briefing. I promise."

Saara seemed reluctant, as though she had more to say, but eventually she nodded. ["Very well, Liao. I accept your apology and will attempt to move past this."]

Liao sighed in relief, managing a soft smile. "Thank you, Saara."

The Toralii did not smile in return, but turned and left, leaving Liao to watch her friend's back as she walked away.

Chapter VI

Operations Room
TFR Sydney
Karathi L1 Lagrange point

One day later

The TFR *Sydney* appeared in the jump point without incident, and Captain Matthew Knight withdrew his key from the jump system, returning it to his breast pocket. His XO, Commander Peter Baker, did the same.

"Jump complete," came the call from navigation. "We are in position at the Karathi L1 Lagrange point."

Knight moved from the jump console to navigation, observing on the large monitors what the ship's myriad of sensors were telling them. An image of the red ball of Karathi floated below them, a barren desert wasteland with very little life, high heat, and no significant resources, geological features or points of interest.

Nothing showed itself except the wreckage of the *Giralan*, once home to Ben, now a rusting wreck almost completely buried in sand.

"Launch surface teams," he said, "and have them report in on the hour. Mister Baker, deploy strike craft in a standard seven point CAP. Navigation, clear the jump point."

The Operations room lit up in a flurry of activity. Two Broadswords were launched, tiny ships sailing out through the void, hurtling silently towards Karathi. A flight of Wasp fighters launched from the hangar bay and began a wide arc, a standard patrol, and the ship slowly sailed out of the well of extreme microgravity, gently drifting through space towards the giant red planet. It was a standard deployment for a jump and, so far, everything had been moving smoothly.

A flashing light, red and urgent, on the communication officer's console stole his attention. Almost immediately, the crewman at that station called out. "Captain, incoming transmission. We're receiving a signal from..." The slightest pause, and then, "from a nearby asteroid belt, Captain."

"What's the nature of the transmission?"

"Unsure," said the communications officer, a fresh faced midshipman named Finnis. "It's a repeating signal, no discernible message. Looks to be a beacon of some description."

Knight made his way over to the man's console. "Any record of any beacons in this area when the *Beijing* was here last?"

"No, Captain. This one's new."

Knight considered, for a moment, then turned to his XO. "Sound general quarters, Mister Baker, and launch the remaining strike craft and gunships. Recall the patrol and charge hull plating. Marines to their stations. Let's head into that asteroid field and see what we can find. Mister Cruden, set a course for that beacon."

Baker moved over to Knight. "Did you want me to recall the ground team, sir?"

He shook his head, and together the two of them moved back to the command console. "No. It's going to take us hours to get there and we need the intel from the ground. Keep the CAP centred on us, but let the ground team do their work. This could turn out to be nothing. Maybe Liao and her people just missed it or didn't think to include it in their report."

"Probably the latter, sir. You know how she is with paperwork." Baker pulled up the long-range thermal camera output on the command console. "What the hell do you think is going on?"

Knight narrowed his eyes, looking at the radar output which showed tens of thousands of the rocky asteroids floating in space, vast expanses of nothing between them, then focusing on the optical camera pointed at the same region, a black blanket dotted with a faint sea of stars.

"I don't know, but I have a feeling I'm not going to like it."

*****

Captain Knight's Office
TFR Sydney

Later

Knight finished the last of the incident log, then set his pen down on the heavy oak desk.

He trusted Baker implicitly. The man had been his right hand throughout almost all of his career, always giving him good advice and keeping him focused on his job. Baker was much more cautious than him, a quality that served him well as the ship's XO.

Perhaps caution could be wisely applied here.

As Knight always did when he wanted to think, he reached out for a memento on his desk, a full-sized Australian Football League ball, a Sherrin, oval shaped and elongated like an egg. He stood, standing over by the wall, bouncing it against the ground.

Bouncing an oval-shaped ball was a particular skill unique to Australians who had played the local brand of football, the AFL, as the ball had to be bounced much like in basketball. Typically performed while running, it could also be done while standing—not straight up and down like a basketball, but forward, using the oval shape to return it to one's hand. A much more challenging task than the American version, but one that focused his mind and allowed him to think.

Knight had played on a team once as a reserve for the Geelong Cats during his teenage years before enlistment. No star of the track and field, his position was brief and unmentionable, almost entirely spent warming a bench, but it was a stint he had always treasured. He'd played a grand total of eight minutes on the field, but those eight minutes were some of his fondest memories.

No longer a member of the club and those days far behind him, Knight had kept his jersey safely stored in his home on Earth, and he took the ball with him when he was away. It was a useful thing to remind him. Once a Cat, always a Cat, he liked to think.

Thump, thump, thump went the ball and his mind turned over. What was the signal, and what was it doing there? What was transmitting it?

He didn't like this. It was a simple beacon floating out in the middle of the asteroid belt, but for some reason, it nagged at him. He tried to rationally explain it: a warning against a navigation hazard, perhaps, or even a Forerunner probe that had malfunctioned or was transmitting some kind of alert.

But alerting what?

The door to his office creaked and opened, so Knight caught the ball and stepped back to his desk. Commander Peter Baker stepped inside, a folder in hand.

"Playing footy in your head again?"

Knight gave his old friend a smile, cracking open the fridge. A bottle of the famous scotch each of the Pillars of the Earth carried was resting on a shelf, an option briefly considered but ultimately passed up. They were, after all, still on duty. Instead, he withdrew a tray of ice cubes, a container of water, and a pair of chilled glasses. "You caught me." Setting them out on his desk, Knight twisted the tray, dropping a heaping of ice into each container.

"If the crew knew you did that, they'd think you're mental."

Knight poured out water from the steel container, the ice clinking as it filled. "Good thing nobody tells them then." He picked up a glass, offering it to his XO with his left hand, the scar from a surfing accident years ago giving it a rough, calloused surface. His tone became more formal, and it was down to business. "So Peter, I heard the report came in. What did our teams find on the *Giralan*?"

Commander Peter Baker took his glass. The two men clinked their drinks together, then both sipped at the cool, icy water. "Nothing," Baker answered, "absolutely nothing. The coordinates the *Beijing* gave us were accurate, but when our marines arrived, there was just this great big hole in the ground. The whole ship appears to have been taken."

"The whole ship?"

"Yes, sir. There was plenty of debris still around, buried in the sand, but the body of the ship appears to have just been taken away. That area gets quite bad dust storms, apparently, so don't read too much into this, but we couldn't find any evidence of salvage equipment or cutting tools or anything like that. To be honest, Captain, it's like the ship just lifted straight out of the ground in one piece."

"But Liao described that vessel as a derelict, almost rusted through. Apart from the information in its datacore, I can't imagine there'd be anything of any value remaining."

"Me neither. It's a mystery for Fleet Command, I'm afraid." Baker sipped at his drink again. "What's the word on the beacon?"

Knight put his glass down on the desk, inhaling. "Not a lot, to be honest. It just appears to be a repeating, long-range signal sitting out there in the middle of nowhere."

"You seem worried," said Baker. "I would probably have just left the thing alone."

"Yeah, well, my mum always used to say I was a curious one."

"You know what they say about curiosity and cats, sir."

"I've heard that one before." Knight tapped a finger on his desk. "I hate to say it, but I've felt very strongly that, ever since the attacks on Earth, we haven't known enough about our enemies or our friends. We're going into this blind, stumbling through the dark, and so far things have turned out pretty good for us more or less. The problem is that the floor is covered in razor sharp glass, and just because we can't see it, and just because we haven't stepped on any, doesn't mean it won't cut us."

"So you're saying," Baker said, "that we need to shed some light on this situation."

"Correct. Even if it hurts our eyes, we have to see the universe as it really is. Otherwise, we're just going to continue to stumble and eventually we're going to cut our feet up. We're going to fall." Knight deliberated for a moment. "But for now, though, have our men continue to comb through the debris of the *Giralan*. Let's see what else we can find."

*****

Operations
TFR Sydney

Later

"We're entering the outer regions of the asteroid belt now, Captain. Distance to the beacon, ten minutes."

Knight studied the radar screen closely. "Very good. Start decelerating; we don't want to overshoot."

"Confirmed all engines reversed, Captain. We should pull up right beside it."

He could feel the shift in the gravity as inertia pulled him backward, the reactionless drives unable to fully correct for such a high amount of decelerationHe and Baker leaned forward slightly to compensate. "Good," he said, "make sure we get as close as possible. We'll be doing an EVA to study it."

"Did you want to bring it on board, Captain?" asked Baker.

"Depends on what we find," Knight answered. "I'm definitely not ruling out that possibility, though."

"I'll set up Engineering Bay One as quarantine then, along with a clean room path directly to it. As a precaution."

"Agreed, quarantining this thing, if we do bring it aboard, would make total sense." Knight smiled thankfully. "That's what I pay you the big bucks for, right?"

"You'd be lost without me, sir."

"That I would." Knight tapped at his command console. "How long until we can see this thing on radar?"

"Two minutes, Captain. We should be able to get a simple reading now, but the asteroids are interfering with our long-range radar."

That was to be expected. "What about thermals?"

The tactical officer considered. "Something so small won't appear very hot on our cameras, but it might help us figure out what kind of power source it's using."

Knight mulled this over. "Works for me. Let's bring up a fisheye thermal view, see what we can see."

His screen on the command console changed to a black and white image, a sea of white streaked with occasional darker spots. He switched it to white-hot, frowning in confusion at a tiny white dot sitting to their port. It was warmer than the other asteroids and far too large to be a probe. He zoomed in on that spot, tapping at the touch-responsive screen several times. It was hard to see from the artefacts and corruption, but all around the hotspot, billowing black clouds slowly expanded out. It looked, to him, like steam rising from a boiling pot of water, or the cold gasses billowing out from a pot of liquid nitrogen.

"Mister Baker, what do you make of this?"

His XO moved beside him, looking over his shoulder. "No idea, sir. It could be friction from a recent impact between two asteroids."

The density of an asteroid belt was significantly lower than most people thought it would be, their perceptions informed by Hollywood movies. Most asteroids were hundreds of thousands of kilometres apart, with the total mass of the belt being less than a fraction of most moons. The likelihood of witnessing a collision between two objects was extraordinarily low.

"I doubt it," Knight said. "It's too hot for that, and the heat dispersion is far too even." He considered. "It would explain the gas, though. Mister Weeder, can you focus the long-range radar on it, see what we can determine about its composition?"

"Aye aye, Captain. One moment."

He stared at the white dot, barely a few pixels wide, then the radar operator spoke again.

"It's about fifty thousand kilometres from the signal's origin point. It appears to be hollow, so it could be a fractured asteroid. It's hard to determine size at this distance... Something is scattering our radar pulses, but it's pretty large. It might be a chemical reaction within the exposed layers, perhaps some kind of massive geological anomaly."

"Subterranean nitrogen pockets?" Knight scowled at his monitor, the dot looming larger and larger as they grew closer. "Yeah, I don't think so. I don't like this thing, whatever it is. Can we stop before we get there?"

"Sorry, Captain. We're already decelerating at the maximum safe rate the reactionless engines can compensate for. We *could* try an emergency reversal and exceed that, but I wouldn't recommend going higher than half a G. It will make a mess, but it'll slow us down a lot faster."

Machines could typically output far more stress than a body could handle.

Weeder spoke again. "Captain, the spectroscope's returning data. Hang on one moment. Strange... very strange." he paused. "The spectrometer suggests that the nearby gas appears to be nitrogen and is significantly cooler than the hotspot itself."

"It's not a geological anomaly," Knight said. "It's *coolant*. It's a ship trying to mask its heat signature. We're stepping into a trap."

"Emergency break?" asked Baker.

"Do it," Knight said, "on my mark."

Baker grabbed the intercom headset. "All hands, emergency brace for impact. This is not a drill. I say again, brace, brace, brace."

Knight gripped the console tightly, spreading his feet to steady himself. He gave the crew an extra few seconds, then looked to Cruden, the helmsman. "Three, two, one, mark."

The ship lurched like a car swerving around a corner, the force of half the Earth's gravity almost knocking him off his feet. The fittest, absolute best aircraft pilots could, with the aid of G-suits and other devices, sustain nine-G turns, but they were strapped firmly into their seats. A full one-G turn would be the equivalent of hanging straight off his console on Earth. As it was, a half-G was like trying to ride a rollercoaster by simply hanging on.

Nobody said anything, being far too busy trying to keep their footing as the ship slowed and alarms rang out through the ship's Operations room. After a period of time that seemed to last forever but couldn't have been more than ten or fifteen seconds, the feeling eased, and the only sound he could hear aside from the alarms was the retching noise of one of the Operations crew emptying his stomach's contents onto the metal deck This was followed by the faint smell of vomit.

He could hardly blame him. "Report!"

"We've slowed, Captain. Full deceleration imminent."

Baker grabbed him by the shoulder, ashen faced. Knight wondered for a moment if it had been he who had lost his breakfast. "Casualty reports coming in, Captain. Multiple injuries over all decks."

Knight heard Finnis's voice cut over the din. "Captain, priority alert. The Broadsword *Paladin* is reporting they're under attack!"

"What?!"

"A wing of Toralii strike fighters were hiding on the surface! Their escorts are down. They're cut off!"

Knight gave a wide-eyed stare to Baker, the man returning it, then looked back to Finnis. "Get them out of there. Order the ship to make a run for the L2 jump point and escape. In the meantime—"

"Captain!" Weeder, the radar operator, said as he swivelled in his chair. "The contact, it's moving!"

Knight felt the sickening feeling in his stomach, the same feeling he had before a big game. "Damnit." Knight grabbed the intercom. "All hands, general quarters. This is not a drill." He tossed the device onto his keyboard. "Mister Baker, charge the hull plating and prepare the ship to escape. Head for the nearest jump point and execute an emergency jump. Have our strike craft execute a defensive screen."

"Aye aye, Captain!"

Turning back to the thermal camera, Knight could see the silhouette of the contact becoming clear now, a familiar sight, one he'd seen before, on the exact same screen he was looking at now, in the exact same hostile, aggressive attack position.

The *Seth'arak*, pride of the Toralii Alliance.

"Fuck! They're meant to be our allies!" He reached for the headset. "Mister Finnis, broadcast to that ship. All frequencies, no encryption."

"Channel open, Captain!"

"*Seth'arak*, this is the TFR *Sydney*, of Task Force Resolution. We are authorised by your own words to be here. Cease fire on our Broadsword *immediately*. I say again: Cease. Fire."

His answer came not in words, but in the twinkle of weapons fire on the thermal camera. "Incoming!" called his tactical officer right as a shudder ran through the length of his ship, the energy weapons splashing against their hull. Like an angry hornet's nest, tiny specks flew out of the *Seth'arak*'s belly as it disgorged wings of strike fighters.

The ship's glow on the thermal camera spiked, signalling what was happening before his tactical officer even spoke.

"Captain, they're charging their worldshatter device!"

"Evasive manoeuvres; get us out of here! Full power to the hull plating!"

No sooner had the words left his lips than a powerful impact tore through the *Sydney*, tearing the Operations crew from their seats and flinging them violently across the room to the impossibly loud roar of tearing metal and snapping bulkheads. The intense blast caused the very rivets of the ship's structure to pop, sending them screaming into computers, consoles and flesh.

Baker and Knight, who were standing together by the command console, both crashed in a heap at the base of the radar operator's console nearly ten metres away. Black smoke poured from the air vents, and the wailing of alarms increased in pitch and volume, coupled by another sound, far more ominous and summoning in him the instinctive fear of all who worked in space.

The hiss of escaping air and the scream of the decompression alarm.

"GAS, GAS, GAS!" came a cry from across Operations. "Decompression alert!"

Knight struggled to stand, but Baker's heavy body pinned him down. The damage to their ship must have been massive if it was causing a decompression alarm this far inside the armoured heart of the *Triumph* class vessel. Baker wasn't moving, but Knight managed to push him away, checking the man.

Baker's neck was bent at a strange, impossible angle, and blood poured from his nose. His eyes rolled back in his head. Knight could see immediately that he was dead. Pulling his bruised body up to his feet, he coughed out a lungful of acrid smoke and shouted out over the howl of air as it rushed out of the room.

"Report!"

Nobody answered immediately, save for the groaning of the wounded, but Finnis, the midshipman, pulled himself up and back onto his chair. "Direct hit to our starboard side! The superstructure's cracked; we have a *massive* decompression along the length of the ship! Eighteen sections are holed, and there are fragmentary decompressions reported on numerous decks! The hull armour is sixty percent ineffective, with large gaps, and fires are reported throughout the ship." He turned and looked squarely at Knight, and he could see the fear in his eyes. "They broke our back, Captain."

"Signal the Toralii!" he gasped, a hacking cough interrupting him. "Tell them we surrender!"

"They're not answering."

Knight watched the short-range radar, the tiny dots of his strike craft winking out one by one as the vast tide of Toralii ships engulfed them. In the long-range communications headset, he could hear increasingly frantic Israeli voices, but one by one, they went silent until there was nothing but the faint hiss of static. The strike craft turned to the *Sydney* now, like a rain of arrows falling on a medieval battlefield, and the *Seth'arak* glowed warm in the thermal camera.

Another explosion, this one louder and more intense than the last, tossed the ship on its axis and threw the crew into the ceiling. Knight felt his ribs bruise at the impact, then again as he fell down and struck the deck. For a stunned moment, the only sounds on the bridge of the *Sydney* were the wails of klaxons, the dull roar of escaping air, and the groan of stressed, breaking metal.

Knight knew he was concussed. The pain of his injuries seemed so distant, as though he were watching himself through another's eyes. With unsteady hands he pulled himself up to the command console, his right arm broken and hanging limply by his side. The red tinge of emergency lighting cast the console readings in a strange light. In a daze, he examined the output.

... breach on deck A. Hull breach on deck J. Hull b...

... ary coolant failure in reactor containment. Restore...

... on deck B. Fire on deck C. Reactor overload in se...

Knight could feel blood running down his forehead. He reached up and wiped it with the back of his left hand, the one with the scar, fresh blood staining the old wound. He opened his mouth to speak but inhaled a lungful of roiling smoke. Overcome by coughing, his lungs trying to breathe the thin, smoke-filled air, he doubled over again.

Seconds later, he almost tried again, but just closed his mouth and rested, half standing and half kneeling, against the command console. There was nobody to hear his orders, or able to respond if they could. Instead, he simply watched the few remaining active consoles, staring at them with an odd calm.

The deck below him trembled, shaking slightly but with a growing force. A dull explosion, distant but coming from within the ship, caused a vibration to run through his whole body.

He'd lived for nearly two years on board the *Sydney* and had come to know it intimately, like a child. Just like any parent, he could tell when she cried, and somehow, instinctively rather than logically, know where the pain was coming from and the source of its distress.

The reactor cores, lodged deep in the heart of the ship, the source of their power, contained nuclear fire, bottled and harnessed for electrical power. Eight of them in all... stored behind strong walls and multiple redundant systems, but any one of them holding more than enough force to turn his ship to ashes. Now, with the ship bleeding and broken, that fire wanted to be free.

Another rumble confirmed the suspicions of his dazed mind. The ship's containment was breached, and that nuclear fire was soon to spill out and engulf them all in its heat, as though they were unleashing a tiny piece of the heart of the sun. His ship was mortally wounded.

He didn't need to make a general announcement, either. The crew knew what was happening. The collision avoidance radar showed the ship's escape pods launching, little life rafts breaking free from the sinking ship, ferrying his crew to safety in tiny capsules with white-hot exhaust trails to mark their flight.

The arrowheads of the Toralii strike fighters turned like a pack of hounds after rabbits, closing with the speed of hungry predators, and in brief flashes of weapons fire, the life rafts were annihilated.

The pain in his body grew fainter, more distant, and Knight slumped forward on the deck, the concussion and blood loss taking their toll.

His mind drifted back, for some strange reason, to his days playing for the Geelong Football Club. Of the roar of the crowd that one single time he'd stepped onto the playing field of the MCG as a midfielder, taking the place of a much more skilled player with a torn hamstring. He'd never even touched the ball, nor gotten close, and very few people knew of his one single glorious day, but he'd treasured it for all his life.

Once a Cat, always a Cat, he liked to think.

The *Sydney's* reactors could no longer contain the pressure within and exploded, the thermal reaction consuming the ship in a vast, silent fireball It blew scorched chunks of debris out in every direction, fading a slowly expanding ball of white hot gas in the Karathi asteroid belt, a second sun for the system that slowly faded away to leave nothing but a spherical debris field. The wreckage, its course set by the atomic blast, was slowly pulled by gravity's inexorable tug into the same elliptical path as the asteroid field, the pieces of wreckage floating forever amongst the stars.

Chapter VII

"Plan A"
*****

Operations
TFR Beijing

Meanwhile

Liao felt strange to be in Operations with another person in command, but in every other way, it was exactly as she had remembered it.

Commodore Vong had, thankfully, permitted her to stay in Operations with the rest of the command staff despite her role as observer. It was a little move of solidarity which, she felt, helped mend the harsh words Vong had for her during the briefing. She suspected that Vong had meant what he had said, but also had a little bit of respect for her. It was a strange feeling and hard to articulate, but she did feel that, while he may have disagreed with her command style and with many of the decisions she made when she was in command of the *Beijing*, Commodore Vong meant her no ill will.

It was nice to be back in Operations.

The *Beijing* floated in the Lagrange point Cerberus guarded. The coordinates Avaran had programmed into their computer would take them to the L1 Lagrange point of Belthas IV, the same place the Alliance fleet had jumped to. Liao watched as Kamal removed the small key from his chest pocket and Vong did the same. The keys were inserted and turned, a procedure she had performed dozens of times herself, and the ship jumped.

It was normally a completely imperceptible thing that, apart from a few blinking lights that lit up on consoles scattered around the dimly lit Operations room, passed by without incident.

Not this time.

There was a terrific scraping noise as though long fingernails were being dragged at high speed across a chalkboard. Immediately, proximity alarms and thermal warnings began sounding. The crew reacted quickly.

"Jump complete, Captain!" came the call from Lieutenant Dao, the navigator. Instinctively, Liao turned her eyes towards the man and opened her mouth to reply, but forced it to close. "We have arrived at the Belthas system!"

The new chief of engineering, a short, stocky man with a completely shaved head named Au, called out as well. "Jump drive status nominal. The device is cooling. Hull temperature has increased by four hundred kelvin but is falling."

"What the hell happened?" asked Vong, leaning up against the command console in almost exactly the same manner Liao expected she had once done. Was this what it looked like to be one of the crew? Liao tried to imagine herself in that role, seeing it through another's eyes.

"Captain?" Ling, the radar operator, stared at his radar screen. "Captain, we appear to be in the middle of a debris field. I'm reading almost... It must be *ten million* tonnes of debris spread out over a spherical region approximately four thousand kilometres, but very little beyond that. We appear to be in the exact epicentre of the debris field. Various metals and alloys, dense materials. It's not rock or asteroids. I've never seen anything like it."

Ten million tonnes was a lot of material.

"It's a graveyard," Liao said to nobody, "the ruins of the Toralii ships. Whatever happened to that fleet, it happened fast. They were probably destroyed as they were jumping in, one by one, and it happened so quickly they couldn't even jump away."

Vong strode over to Lieutenant Dao's chair. "Well, let's ensure we don't meet the same fate. Move us away from the jump point. Make best speed away from our point of origin straight down, avoiding any obstacles if you could. Jiang, charge the hull plating."

She felt the ship move, descending, a familiar feeling. She had served as a submariner before her time in space, and it felt just like the descent of a *Han* class submarine, despite the efforts of the ship's complex antigravity systems to compensate. The ship moved forward slightly, then back.

"Sorry, Captain, there's a lot of debris."

Vong gave a wet cough, thumping his chest. Liao watched the gesture with concern, de Lugo's words coming back to her. Perhaps the highly oxygenated air really wasn't good for men Vong's age.

Recovering quickly, the Commodore looked to the engineer. "Mister Au, what was the nature of the disturbance we experienced on jump-in?"

"Captain, it appears we displaced a small amount of debris when we jumped in. There wasn't enough to disable the jump point, but since the displacement occurred at a significant fraction of C, friction on the hull has caused moderate damage to the outer plating."

"Can it still be charged?"

"I believe so. There's a good chance it should only have a small effect on the performance of the hull plating, but we're definitely going to need a new coat of paint."

They scratched my ship, thought Liao, even though her aggravation at the situation was completely unreasonable as she would have ended up in the same predicament.

Vong nodded. "Good. Lieutenant Jiang, what's our tactical situation?"

"Autocannon turrets are reporting damage from the debris, Captain. I wouldn't fire them under these conditions unless we absolutely had to. Rail gun two is offline, naturally, but our missile launch tubes should still function."

Liao wished that the rail guns had been fixed. Not that it mattered; there was nothing they could do about it now.

"Mister Ling, what's the status of the long-range radar?"

Liao could hear the frustration in Ling's voice. "The debris is screwing everything up. I'm plotting a course and feeding it to Navigation, but radar is soup. There's a lot of small dust and fine particles, and that's obscuring the bigger picture here, but by and large, there doesn't appear to be a great deal of larger pieces. Whatever happened here, the large majority of the debris is dust."

"What kind of weapon could do that?" Vong asked, and this time, he looked directly at Liao as he said it.

"Absolutely no idea," Liao answered honestly. "The Toralii used their worldshatter devices on our ships at the battle of Kor'Vakkar to devastating effect, but it was always limited, three or four shots, maximum five... It caused too much heat buildup to be used regularly. And even then, the *Sydney* took a direct hit and was still able to return fire. To turn a Toralii cruiser to *dust*, let alone dozens of them... it doesn't make any sense."

Ling spoke. "Captain, I'm detecting an active radar."

"Distance?"

He tapped on his keyboard. "One moment, Commodore. I'll find out. Application of the inverse squared law to previously observed Toralii radar signatures gives a distance of approximately 400,000 kilometres. Inverse Doppler effect suggests that the emitter is stationary." He pointed at his monitor. "It's coming from Belthas IV."

Vong nodded his agreement. "We don't have a lot of time then. Assuming they can see through the debris cloud, it's likely they can see us. Mister Dao, are we clear of the Lagrange point?"

"Two minutes, Captain."

Liao saw Hsin, the communications officer, cup his headset, then turn around in his seat. "Captain, we're receiving an automated request to open communication from Belthas IV."

"A beacon?"

"The request is for a two-way channel, sir. No idea what it could mean."

Vong nodded. "Open it. Find out what they want. And put it on speaker."

Technically, Vong was following protocol, but Liao usually preferred to take important calls one on one using her headset. As an observer though, she was grateful she would have both sides of the conversation.

Hsin touched the talk key. "Unidentified contact, this is the TFR *Beijing*. Communications open, over."

Immediately, a thin, low voice filled the Operations Room, speaking with a crisp English accent, the same voice that had called her phone, unprompted, the night Tai had arrived. It was flawless in the way it articulated every word as though it were a living creature, but Liao knew better.

Ben was not a living creature at all.

"Good morning, Melissa Liao. It is a pleasure to see you again... I was wondering when you would finally show yourself. I do trust that your arrival was not significantly hampered by my redecoration of the jump point?"

Liao felt as though there were cold water running down her spine. The flawless way Ben was able to mimic the vocalisations of biological organisms seemed to have improved since she last heard his voice, and it was rich in tone and texture, playful and energetic.

"Belthas IV, *Beijing*. We're investigating the nature of what's transpired here."

"Oh come now, Melissa. That's not your style... having your lackeys speak for you. Tsk, tsk, tsk. You're surely not still angry about Velsharn, are you?"

"Let me talk to him, sir," Liao asked Vong, but the man shook his head.

"I think it's important that we keep our distance, Commander. It would be unwise to bring excessive emotion into this."

Liao grit her teeth subtly, but nodded. "Of course."

Hsin continued. "Belthas IV, we're requesting a liaison to try and talk through this situation. If we could meet at a neutral location, or if you would accept an ambassador, we could begin negotiations. We would prefer a peaceful outcome."

A low, amused chuckle echoed through Operations. "So you *are* angry. Believe me; I can understand why. I am, of course, speaking to Mister Hsin, aren't I?"

"Belthas IV, that's correct," said Hsin.

Vong shot Liao a confused look.

"Ben copied our entire computer's records," Liao explained, "including crew manifest."

"Very well," said Ben, his voice decreasing in pitch slightly, "make your way through the debris field and open communications with me when you have. I know what sticklers you military types are for protocol, so here is my offer: I'll permit your commanding officer to come aboard for negotiations. No diplomats, I haven't time for the petty lies of talking men."

Hsin looked to Vong for confirmation, which was given.

"Very well, Belthas IV, we'll radio when we're clear."

A faint buzz of static, then the line closed.

"Mister Dao," Vong said, "plot us a course through this junk."

*****

Later

It took the *Beijing* hours to clear the ever expanding debris field. The dust was too fine to consider moving it by any means the crew possessed, so Vong had them charge the hull plating, and the ship ploughed through the cloud using its thin bow to cut through the mess, until the cloud of pulverised metal finally began to thin and Dao announced that the particles per cubic metre had reached a sufficiently low volume that they could call Ben.

"TFR *Beijing* to Belthas IV, we're clear of the debris field."

Only a moment after Hsin took his finger from the transmit key, Ling spoke up.

"Radar contact, Captain. A ship has appeared, bearing zero-zero, a hundred kilometres distant. It appears to be... an unknown configuration, 200,000 tones." He frowned, glancing at the thermal cameras. "Almost no heat on thermals, Captain. It looks like most of its systems are offline."

"Bring up the optical camera," Vong ordered. "I want to see what this thing looks like."

A monitor on the command console lit up. Liao, without asking permission, walked over beside Vong and watched over his shoulder.

It was the *Giralan*, ripped from the sands of Karathi and thrown back into orbit. Liao drank in its mismatched composition, a disorganised, horrific disagreement of freshly installed parts grafted onto the rusted hulk of a starship that had been bent and warped from its impact on the unforgiving desert sand. Under normal circumstances, a ship like this would never be spaceworthy; even through the low-resolution, blocky monitor output, Liao could see the holes in its hull, some patched with heavy metal sheets or weapons, others exposed to the void like the rot of a living creature.

This was the ship that had destroyed a third of the Toralii fleet and conquered one of their worlds single-handedly. This was the ship that had the Toralii Alliance quivering in their boots, willing to come crawling to the lesser species for a cease-fire, willing to negotiate with those they saw as criminals. For all the rust and corrosion and impact damage Liao could see on the *Giralan*'s hull, there wasn't a single impact that looked like weapon damage.

They hadn't even touched it.

From the base of the vast, dead ship a tiny vessel slipped from a hangar bay, a shining light against the black fabric of space and crowned with a faint blue light, the illumination waxing and waning on a steady frequency as it slowly floated, clearly under power, towards the *Beijing*.

"Captain, incoming transmission."

"Put it through," said Vong.

Ben's voice filled Operations once again. "Your chariot to my home has arrived, Captain. Come, let us discuss matters like civilised people."

The line crackled and went silent. Liao gave Vong a subtle nod, glad, for the first time since coming aboard, that the title of captain did not refer to her.

*****

Hangerbay
TFR Beijing

Lieutenant Yanmei Cheung watched with some degree of hesitation as the depressurisation of the hangar bay completed its cycle and the large double doors that lead to the launch bay opened, granting entrance to the ship's large flight deck.

She didn't trust things she couldn't see, and that included the thick perspex that separated her face from the airless nothing on the other side. Her work as a marine often took her places that she felt uncomfortable, including the inside of pressurised spacesuits and alien spacecraft that any sane operator would have long ago consigned to the scrapheap, but she always swallowed her fear. She was able to control her mind's protests and focus on her duty, but although the perspex was hardened and specifically designed to resist the forces of the void, it seemed so frail and humble to have something invisible separating one from nothing.

Cheung focused on the small ship as it drifted through the doors to the hangar bay, holding her high-powered rifle comfortably in both hands. Bug-like and fat, rusted and decrepit, the transport appeared almost inert except for a single blinking blue light fixed on top. The tiny ship, seemingly under power, came to rest on the metal of the landing deck, balancing precariously upon thin, spindly metal legs. A long ramp ominously descended from the mouth of the ship, silently beckoning the two of them to enter.

Her suit's radio crackled in her ear, and Commodore Vong spoke. "That really doesn't look safe."

She smiled slightly at that. "No, sir, I have to admit it doesn't. Still, if Ben was trying to get us killed, I think he'd have a better way to dispose of us than letting us die a rusty ship-related death." She wiggled a hand. "Spacesuits protect from tetanus, too."

They walked together towards the ramp, Cheung moving in front of Vong, the classic bodyguard position.

"I'm not sure how things were with Commander Liao, Lieutenant, but I think it's important we maintain a professional distance."

Cheung nodded her head, exaggerating the gesture slightly so that he could see her suit move. "As you wish, sir." She moved into the maw of the small vessel, surveying the surroundings. It was dark, and none of the internal lights seemed to be active. Then, with a slight vibration, the ramp began to close. Several bright, white lights flickered as they sprung to life. The door sealed and locked, and all around her Cheung heard the faint hiss of air filling the compartment.

"Permission to remove my helmet, sir?"

Vong shook his head, looking around for a seat. There wasn't one. "I don't think we should," he said. "We don't know what kind of atmosphere is here, nor what kind of contaminants are in these metals."

Cheung knew that Ben had full knowledge of what life support requirements Humans had but said nothing. She let her rifle hang by the strap, glancing at her arm-mounted O2 sensor. It was safe for her to remove her helmet, but orders were orders, and it made sense.

She barely felt the ship move at all as it lifted off, turning with barely a hint of momentum. The Toralii version of the reactionless drive that cancelled out the ship's inertia was clearly more powerful and accurate than their own, even in such an ancient, decrepit ship.

The trip was conducted in silence aside from the faint hissing of air circulating within her suit. With no outside perspective and very little in the way of inertial shifts to give them any kind of direction, it was only when the hatchway began to open with a loud creak-groan that Cheung realised they had arrived.

The shriek of metal-on-metal was loud, even muffled by her suit, and she almost wished Ben had not pressurised the ship so she would not be subjected to the noise. When it finally ended, the ramp striking the deck with a loud clang, Cheung shouldered her rifle and slowly made her way down.

They were inside a place that bore a remarkable similarity to the hangar bay of the *Beijing*, a wide open space with a high ceiling, packed full of corroded hulks of vessels, some with their landing struts partially buried in the sand that covered the metal deck in large patches. It seemed so odd to find the natural desert joined with the ship, to see it almost entirely indistinguishable from her previous visit when it lay beneath the surface of Karathi.

Waiting for them near the base of the ramp were a number of small, spider-like robotic creatures that Cheung recognised. Bevra defence drones, automated weapons which automatically attacked and destroyed non-Toralii life. Unlike the decaying, rotten corpse of the ship, these robots were chromed and sleek, giant cockroaches with glowing blue eyes and delicate, articulate legs. Two powerful energy weapons were built into their foreclaws. Saara had indicated that they had a range of seven kilometres, something their research had confirmed. A rusted, ruined model from the wreck of the *Giralan* had been brought aboard the *Beijing* during their salvage of the ship. The Humans had studied the Bevra drone's weapons but had not yet been able to successfully reverse engineer it.

They looked at her, their myriad of sensors tracking her movements, but made no attempt to raise their weapons or threaten her in any way. Reaching the bottom of the ramp, she hesitated slightly, then waved for Vong to follow her.

When they both stood shoulder to shoulder, one of the machines stepped forward.

"Follow," it intoned, a flat, synthetic voice that reeked of the artificial. "The master will see you now."

Cheung gave a polite nod of her head. "Lead the way."

Immediately, the machines turned and strode towards a gaping hexagonal exit, their metal legs skittering across the rusted deck as the constructs lead the pair of Humans into the gloom.

The skittering robots, ignoring the sand and the occasional corroded hole in the deck, took Cheung and Vong further into the heart of the ship. There, the corrosion became less intense, and the sand gave way to metal.

It was just as she remembered it, but different. Every now and then, a brand new, shining plate was welded into place over what was obviously a gaping hole. Thick bundles of cables ran along the corners of the corridor, occasionally ducking and weaving through the corridor's supporting frames, disappearing into the bulkhead to reappear later. Clumps of thin, pale, blue lights flickered along the length of the cable, occasionally pulsing and flickering, casting a strange light along the entire corridor.

"This place is more than a little creepy, sir," Cheung observed.

Vong nodded in agreement, despite his request to remain professional. She knew that the Commodore was an experienced commander, someone who had seen a great many things over the years, and although she could not see his face, his body language, his defensive posture, told her that he was more than a little apprehensive. Cheung was sure he had never experienced anything like this. No one had.

The robots guided them to a large, open-mouthed staircase that descended down to the next level, then the constructs moved to either side of the entrance. The construct that spoke first gestured down the stairway with a metallic claw.

"I'll check it first, sir," she offered, and Vong nodded again. Cheung carefully moved down, her rifle snug up against her shoulder, the barrel pointed down towards the ground.

The stairway lead to a wide open room with a raised ceiling that was covered in computer screens, consoles and electronics. The majority of them, in contrast to the silent, dark screens found dotted throughout the rest of the ship, were active; they displayed innumerable graphics, displays and readouts in the Toralii language, the text scrolling past so fast Cheung had no hope of reading it. The ceiling, braced by struts and supports, was almost completely covered by an image of outside space, a field of untwinkling stars on a sea of black. Judging by the distance they had travelled and the gradual disappearance of the otherwise ever present sand, Cheung knew that this room was deep within the heart of the ship. The roof was no window; it was a full projection, detailed and perfect.

On a raised dais in the centre of the room, the focal point of the entire area, was a large metal chair. Within it sat a metal ball, roughly spherical and similar in appearance to the jump drive on the *Beijing* but capped in a large, twin-linked turret. A river of cables flowed into the large dais below it, the various threads converging into a giant vein linked into what she presumed was a giant computer, the living heart of the ship.

More of the same Bevra robots scurried around near her, indifferent to her presence, like a swarm of oversized bugs feasting on a corpse.

"It's clear, Captain," she called over her shoulder, "more or less."

She heard Vong's footsteps behind her, then out of the corner of her eye, saw him move up to her side.

"This must be the ship's bridge," Cheung remarked, "but I don't see Ben."

"Then," came a deep, booming voice, "you are not looking hard enough."

The sphere slowly uncurled revealing six elongated legs, two claws, and a large head, twin blue lights mounted in recessed sockets like a ghostly man peering out of an ancient Greek helmet. Gracefully and delicately, the metal insect rose up on its legs, stretching itself above the ruined chair to an imposing height, the top of his head almost touching the ceiling.

This was a new look for Ben. Cheung knew that the construct could control his 'body' remotely, taking and using whatever form he desired, his mind safely housed within a featureless hexagonal datacore. Whereas his previous preferred appearance was a maintenance drone, working futilely and endlessly to repair the destroyed guts of the *Giralan*, this body seemed much more hostile, aggressive and, most notably, armed. The turret moved independently of the body, swivelling around with a faint whir before sitting still upon his back.

"Good evening, Commander Liao."

Vong stepped forward, hands by his sides. "Com—"

Ben jerked forward, his eyes flashing a bright cyan, and raised his claws in anger. The turret spun faster than Cheung could see, its twin barrels focused ominously on Vong.

"Liao dares to send a minion in her stead?"

Cheung raised her rifle and levelled it at Ben, but he either did not notice or did not care.

"Commander Liao is no longer in command of the TFR *Beijing*," Commodore Vong offered. "I am Commodore Wei Vong, of the People's Republic of China. I speak for our people."

Ben skittered forward, his thin claws grasping the rusted metal of the floor. He moved off the raised dais, claws clacking together eagerly.

"I thought I had expressed myself clearly and was confident that it was not unreasonable to expect that Commander Melissa Liao would be the one to come aboard my vessel to see my triumph. I have no interest in you, nor your people, and you have absolutely nothing you can offer me but your swift departure to fetch Commander Liao so I may converse with her and her alone." The sky-blue lights that served as Ben's eyes flared dangerously as he spoke. "Where is she?"

"She is aboard my ship," Vong admitted. "She has accompanied us as a consultant."

"A consultant." Ben's British accented tone dripped with sardonic mockery. "Commander Liao, the fearless Valkyrie who brought fear to the hearts of the fearless, she who broke the back of Kor'Vakkar and inspired the Kel-Voran to seek alliance with your pitiful race, the slayer, the bringer of death, she whose very name now inspires *fear* throughout the known galaxy... the Human who dares to defy the most powerful empire this section of the galaxy has ever seen and gets away with it... is now a *consultant* to some snivelling word-man in way, way over his depth." Amplified by some unseen source, Ben's voice suddenly increased in volume as he gave a booming, mocking laugh that echoed as the sound bounced down the empty, hollow corridors of the dead ship. "*You waste my time.*"

"You speak highly of Commander Liao, but I assure you she is human, Ben, not a God, just a Human who's doing well for herself, might I add. While she's no longer the commanding officer, she is now serving in a much—"

"Enough! Return from where you came, then send Commander Liao to me."

Cheung looked at Vong but was unable to see his face through the reflective visor. She lowered her rifle. If Ben didn't fear her weapon at all, it was likely utterly useless.

"Very well, Ben. I will return with her."

Ben slowly raised a claw, pointing it directly at Vong's face. Her fingers closed around the pistol grip of her rifle, feeling her muscles tense involuntarily, but she kept her weapon down.

"Be advised, Commodore Vong, that machines have a different perspective on time than you Humans do. In the time it takes my audio system to produce a single word, my processors perform billions of operations on thousands of threads of thought. Every second we stand here is an eternity to me, and while I am synthetic and do not age as you do, my patience is not unlimited, and it wears dangerously thin. I will tolerate no duplicity on this matter and expect Commander Liao, and absolutely nobody else, to come to this chamber. If she is not brought before me, wrath beyond your wildest imagination will be visited upon you. Am I absolutely, perfectly clear?"

Commodore Vong straightened his back, hands steady by his sides. "I understand. I will return to my ship, and I will send Commander Liao to you." The man turned away slightly, as though preparing to leave.

"Only she is permitted to come aboard my vessel," warned Ben, "a restriction I take extremely seriously."

"Yes, Commander Liao will not be accompanied. Is that all?"

For a moment Ben said nothing, appearing to stare, motionless, at the pair of them, and then he bobbed his mechanical head with a faint whir. "Go."

Vong began to walk, motioning for Cheung to follow. She subconsciously moved to stand in front of him, but when she drew shoulder to shoulder with Vong, Ben spoke again.

"Lieutenant Yanmei Cheung?"

With a glance at Vong for permission, which was granted with a subtle nod of his head, Cheung turned to face Ben once again. "Yes?"

"The copy of the *Beijing*'s records I have in my datacore show that you joined the *Beijing*'s crew as a Warrant Officer. Is this correct?"

Cheung frowned slightly in confusion, nodding. "Yes, that's correct. Commander Liao gave me a field commission after I supported her against Sheng's mutiny."

The construct traced a digit of his left claw along his chromed chin, drawing a faint metal-on-metal scraping sound as it brushed across the surface. "The records concur with this assessment. So you would say you are a loyal person who dislikes deception?"

Uncertain of how to respond, Cheung merely nodded. "I'd like to think that is so."

Ben shuffled forward, his metal legs clinking on the raised steps that lead to the broken remains of the chair. "This is excellent. Regrettably, I do not feel that Commodore Vong takes my warning with the gravity it is intended."

Cheung looked at Vong in confusion, then back to Ben. "Warning?"

"My insistence that Commander Liao is to come alone."

"Ben, I'm sure he wants to make sure that diplomatic relations are as comfortable as they can possibly be. Why would you think he doesn't?"

Ben's eyes glowed a fierce blue, casting a pallid light over the entire bridge. Around him the tiny army of robots turned to face them as one, clicking their claws in anticipation. Cheung subconsciously tightened her grip on her rifle, stealing a glance towards the exit out of the corner of her eye.

"Lieutenant Cheung, I posses a great deal more sensory capability than you humans, and once I discovered it was not her within that suit, I chose to use this capability. I can see each of your frail, fleshy forms through those suits as though they were not even there. When I gave my warning, Commander Vong's body language shifted slightly. His eyes flicked slightly to the left as he spoke, which indicated that he was accessing the creative section of his brain rather than the logical section. His speech was slightly stilted, slower, outside of the standard deviations for his previously observed vocal patterns when claiming things I could confirm were true, such as when he gave his name. When Commodore Vong answered my question, his fingers drew closer together, signalling a rise in the adrenaline content of his blood; his heart rate increased and the temperature of his skin increased by a quarter of a degree. Further, my neurological pattern analysis confirmed that the synapses in the creative section of his brain, rather than the logical, fact-based sections, were the most active while he answered."

Cheung heard Vong shuffle uncomfortably beside her, but she kept her gaze on Ben. "So?"

A faint, barely audible hum filled the room. "So," answered Ben, "to prevent further misunderstandings, I feel I must encourage you to remember how important it is that Liao, and Liao *alone*, is the next and only Human to set foot on my ship."

*****

Hangerbay
TFR Beijing

One of the advantages of not being in command was that Liao could be somewhere other than Operations. Protocol had called for Cheung and Vong's radios to be patched into the *Bejing*'s systems so they could monitor their progress, but it appeared that Ben took some exception to this. The moment the two had entered the strange, bug-like shuttle in the Beijing's hangar bay, the communications line returned only static.

She waited, standing in the decompressed open area, arms patiently folded as the minutes ticked away. Soon the sight she expected to see arrived; a faint glint against the starfield as a banking ship caught Belthas's light and reflected it. Soon the ship, silent and dark, slid into the *Beijing's* hangar bay and settled upon the deck. Liao stepped up to the ramp as it lowered, trying her radio.

"Commodore Vong?"

"Vong's not coming." Cheung stepped down the ramp, rifle hanging limply on its sash. Her spacesuit was covered in a spray of dark blood, drawing a stark contrast to the otherwise pristine white of the mylar and perspex.

"Cheung?" Liao, knowing that the Operations room was listening in, spoke to them. "Medical emergency in the hangar bay, Cheung's suit breached!"

Liao stepped forward, grabbing hold of Cheung's shoulders and looking her over, searching for where she had been wounded.

Cheung held up her blood-splattered hands. "I'm fine," she said, her voice quivering slightly over the radio. "It's not me."

"What the hell happened?"

"Vong's dead," Cheung said simply, "and Ben is mad, furious even, insane. Even more so than the last time we saw him. He wants to see you, and only you, *right now*."

Liao felt her chest tighten. "Vong's dead? Are you sure?"

Cheung's tone wavered slightly. *"Very."*

Hesitating, then giving a firm nod, Liao moved past her, moving up the ramp.

"Good luck, Captain," Cheung said, turning to face her, looking up to her as she stood at the bottom of the ramp.

"I'm not the captain anymore," Liao replied. "You know that."

The ramp began to rise. From behind Cheung's blood-splattered form, Liao could see suited figures bearing the red cross of the medical team running out to meet them.

Cheung seemed to hesitate as though about to argue the point, but instead, she just unslung her rifle and let it drop to the floor. "Don't lie to him," she said, and then the door sealed, and Liao could hear nothing but the faint hiss of static as the ship lifted off the deck.

Chapter VIII

"Plan B"
*****

Hangerbay
Inside the Giralan

Stepping out of the tiny shuttle into the vast hangar bay, Liao moved over to the airlock. She watched her wrist mounted oxygen indicator with a wary eye, but the tiny LED glowed a bright green as the last of the air filled the airlock to the hangar bay. She reached up and unclipped her helmet, sliding it off her head.

The air in the tiny shuttle was dry, cool and surprisingly earthy, even though the soil that dotted the floor of the airlock was more sand than soil. Liao cast a wary eye at some of the patches made on the metal hull, given the ship's composition, but eventually put her concerns beside her. Ben had been fixing the *Giralan* for many years and knew his craft well.

She placed the helmet on the ground and wiggled out of her suit, discarding the heavy, bulky protection, except for the boots. She strapped her pistol's holster to her hip, then waited.

The airlock door to the rest of the ship, adorned with a simple square window, had a flashing, red light embedded directly underneath the thick, foggy, smeared glass. It blinked on and off hypnotically, bathing the entire room in a strange crimson glow.

Why did Ben want to see her so badly? Why her, specifically?

The light turned green and the door opened, presenting a pair of Bevra drones, their chromed bodies glinting in the faint light.

"The master will see you now," intoned the lead drone and Liao followed the pair of robots down the long corridor into the dark heart of the ship.

The long, winding corridors seemed endless to her, but the time passed quickly. She remembered Cheung's blood-splattered suit, suddenly cursing herself for not bringing a medical kit. If Vong was severely wounded, which he undoubtedly was given how much blood was splashed all over Cheung, there was little hope she could save him without specialised equipment.

Tai's injuries floated into her mind, her bare hands trying to keep his blood within his body, all to no avail. She pushed those thoughts out of her head.

The drones lead her to the centre of the ship. Liao stepped cautiously down the stairwell, her pistol cupped comfortably in her hands, and the heavy spacesuit boots clunking on each step until she reached the bottom. As she did, she felt her foot slide forward, and it was only her training, and the fact that she had her finger off the trigger, that kept her from firing in surprise. Keeping her footing, Liao lifted her boot, looking for what she'd stepped on.

A brass shell casing from a standard QBZ-99.

The vast open area, the equivalent of her Operations room, was stretched out before her and was crawling with robots. The thing that drew her immediate attention, though, was the large, dark, rust coloured smear near the base of the stairwell that stretched out almost two metres long. Nearly a dozen spent brass cartridge casings lay scattered haphazardly over the ground, the entire area smelling of cordite and smoke. Faint drops of blood covered nearby surfaces, and it did not take Liao long to realise exactly what she was looking at.

"So good of you to come, Commander Liao. I'm glad my message was finally communicated accurately." Ben's robot body crawled up atop the central dais, his six long legs skittering delicately as he took purchase upon the large computer core. "And so good of you to remove your helmet to prevent further… misunderstandings."

Liao stared at him coldly. "Where is Commodore Vong?"

"Commodore Vong will not be joining us."

Liao's gaze flicked to the rusty stain, then back to Ben. "Why have you done this? Why have you attacked this planet?"

"You have questions. I have questions. We are both on a journey of discovery. I eagerly seek answers from you, but I am patient, so I will explain my words first. The sun is, in almost all myths and legends, a source of strength and power to your species. It was Ra to the ancient Egyptians, Apollo to the Greeks of ages past, Tonatiuh for the Aztecs. The sun features prominently in your people's recorded religions as a God. As your societies evolved and grew beyond superstition, you began to embrace the laws of physics and nature as your guiding principles, but you still do not ask *why*: why do such things as the forces of nature exist, why do they do the things they do, why the universe works according to mathematics and numbers."

"Poetic but meaningless," said Liao. "Ancient Humans worshipped whatever damn thing they felt was powerful enough to destroy them in hopes of appeasing the supernatural powers, therefore surviving and prospering. As our people grew, we found we no longer needed such things."

"I agree. I believe this is the biological creature's gift," Ben said, casually extending a claw to give one of his robots a gentle pat on its chromed head, "the ability to be wrong. Powerfully, totally in error. Wrong in conclusion, methods and assumptions. Wrong in every way that someone can be wrong. But then, you tread down this path of wrongness, embracing it utterly in a way my kind never could."

"I'm not here to debate philosophy with you." Liao slipped her pistol into her holster. Ben didn't appear damaged at all, but Cheung had, seemingly, fired nearly half her magazine. If a high powered rifle was of no effect, her little pea-shooter would be even less so. "I just want to know what the hell's going on here."

"Do you ever question why the sun sets?" asked Ben. "Do you ask why the moon's lesser light conjures such mystery and reverence amongst the humans?"

"Mystery and, what...?" Liao blinked and shook her head. "I have no idea what you're talking about. I just want to know why you've attacked these Toralii. Haven't you quenched your bloodlust with what you did at Velsharn?"

"Velsharn was just the beginning." Ben clacked his claws together eagerly. "Just the beginning. Although I will admit, I regret what I did."

Liao narrowed her eyes. "You do? When I spoke to you afterwards, you said you had no regrets, that you had planned out all the consequences of your actions and, therefore, if you had your time over, you wouldn't have done anything differently. What's changed?" Her tone became acidic. "Has the Grinch's iron heart grown three sizes today?"

"You misunderstand," Ben said. "I do not feel sorrow as you might. Instead, I merely feel that my course of action was not optimal. It was a waste of resources."

"Stop speaking in riddles." Liao felt her blood rise. "Just tell me what you're getting at."

Ben's robotic face broadened into a wide smile. "Direct as always, Liao. I like that." He skittered down, coming face to face with her, his head stooped to be at her level. Liao held her ground. "What I mean is what I said before," he said, "and that is to say that the reason behind *why* our universe is the way it is, is now of great interest to me. I intend to answer these questions, but unfortunately, in my current state, I cannot."

Liao didn't flinch, looking Ben directly in his giant eyes. "So you intend to... change your state?" She waved a hand at him. "Is this what your new body is meant to represent?"

Ben laughed, bobbing his head as he did so, a gesture Liao found remarkably natural. "No. This form is merely a means to an end. Instead, I intend to introduce errors into my system. I intend to inject chaos, entropy, as your species is gifted with. I intend to become more... human."

Liao raised an eyebrow, folding her arms. "And how, exactly, do you propose to do that?"

Ben raised his head, moving back from her and retreating up the dais. "It came to me as I was rebuilding the *Giralan*. A species known as the Iilan developed voidwarp technology and subsequently had its homeworld consumed in Toralii fire. They are masters of bio-mechanical and genetic engineering. They tinker with their own DNA, those that remain, changing and evolving constantly. I sought out their great spherical ship, and I bartered my knowledge of the Toralii for their secrets."

"To what end?" Liao asked. "You're a machine. What possible use would this knowledge be for you? Tools for developing biological weapons?"

"You think in such destructive terms. I plan not to destroy; I plan to create." Ben waved a claw to the side, and the wall on the far side of the room slowly hissed and began to slide open. The room was bathed in a bright green glow from the other side, and Liao could see that the long, thick cable that lead into the central dais emerged on the other side of the wall, branching into eight forks. Each fork linked up to a tank full of bubbling liquid, each tank dark and unlit.

There were forms in the tanks. Humanoid forms, small and stunted, blurry and indistinct behind the semi-opaque glass.

"Ben," Liao said, her tone slow and deliberate, "what in God's name have you done?"

"The Toralii created me," Ben said. "I am their child. I only want to be more like them. To be like them, I must have children of my own."

She turned back to the construct, eyes wide. "What does that even mean?"

["Perhaps it would be better if *I* explained,"] came a voice from beside her, speaking the Toralii tongue. Liao whirled around, emitting an audible gasp.

A grey-furred Toralii male, naked and with thin, sickly limbs, stood on the rusted deck of the *Giralan*. He had an oddly neutral smile on his face, as though not quite looking at Liao but looking past her. His pale, ghoulishly white skin showed through in patches where his fur had been shaved off, and Liao could see the razor-thin lines of surgical scars, with the occasional glint of metal below.

But that was not what caused Liao to recoil in horror, or for her to instinctively reach for her pistol.

She recognised him. The Toralii was Leader Qadan from the Velsharn research colony. He was someone who had shown her great kindness, but one she had seen baked to a charred crisp by her ship's nuclear weapons. There was no way this man could be him.

"What the *fuck* are you?"

The faux-Qadan's mouth split into a wide, unnatural smile. ["Don't you recognise me, dear Liao?"]

"I know who you look like, but you aren't Qadan. That man is dead. I saw his body."

["Of course, but his DNA lives on, along with the DNA of every Toralii who lived on that world, in the backups of their computers, which I recovered from the ruins of the colony. I only chose him because he was the one you were most familiar with. I thought it would engender... familiarity."]

"Go fuck yourself," she spat, unholstering her pistol and raising it at the Toralii man's face. "You're a monster."

["Go ahead; shoot. You should know by now that I can communicate with any of the drones around me. Now, with the help of the bioneural implants, I can even control biological forms. Soon I will perfect the necessary process to upload my consciousness to this form, and then I'll be just like you."]

Liao stared at the mindless, remote-controlled Toralii as though it were the living dead. It wasn't life as she saw it; it was a perversion of life, a twisted and warped mirror of the Toralii she'd known. She backed away, slowly moving up the stairway, unable to look at the horrid creature.

"You'll never be like us," Liao spat, "even with flesh and blood. What makes us Human isn't the structure of our atoms; it's something more than that, some deeper connection to each other that can't be quantified. A Human is more than an individual... We're a *collective*. We're a social animal, and it's how we treat our fellow Humans that makes us what we are." She stabbed a finger at the dark stain on the deck of the *Giralan*, taking another step away further up the hexagonal entranceway. "Humans kill, but Humans kill to protect ourselves individually or collectively. We kill those who harm us, threaten us, not men coming to negotiate. It's not what you do; it's why you do it." She sneered slightly, curling back her upper lip. "If you think you're one of us just because you want to be, I'm afraid you're tragically mistaken."

["This body's heart beats, and I give it a mind. I fail to see the difference between the Qadan that stands before you and the Qadan you saw on Velsharn. Even his voice is the same, his mannerisms taken from his video logs."] The Toralii smiled. ["I am just as much Qadan as he was."]

Her hand trembled. "You're not," she said. "You're a pretender, a ghost, just a corpse that hasn't lain down and died yet." Liao lined up the sights on her pistol to Qadan's forehead. "Lemme help you with that."

She squeezed the trigger. Her pistol roared in the highly oxygenated atmosphere of the *Giralan*, the heavy round from her Type 54 blowing out the back of the clone of Qadan's head in a spray of purple blood.

Ben didn't react as the corpse slumped in a heap. "Interesting," he said. "Violence is the solution here. That was not what I considered the most likely outcome."

"What the hell did you think I might do?"

The light snapped on, illuminating the centre tank, the large liquid vat bathed in a strange, light green glow as though the liquid were luminescent. Inside was a Human female, naked and floating in the tub, a series of metal breathing tubes inserted into her chest and down her throat. Liao stared at the person, horror filling her as she slowly realised who she was looking at.

Herself.

"To be honest," said Ben, "I expected violence at *this* revelation."

Liao turned and ran, the heavy boots of her spacesuit clunking on the rotting metal deck as she sprinted down the unlit corridor, away from the image of herself and the corpse of the Toralii she'd known.

As she ran, she could feel the optics of the construct she had once called her friend watching her with cool indifference.

*****

She ran until her lungs hurt, until she finally collapsed onto her knees in one of the many hexagonal corridors. Her chest heaved as she forced air into her lungs, gasping and panting, forcing her body to recover.

She had recently become a mother. She had created life, just as Ben had done, but that was different. She couldn't quite quantify exactly how, but something seemed intrinsically wrong with what Ben had done. Even if it was only a clone, bringing a dead man back to life and using his body as a puppet, especially when it was someone Liao had known in life, struck her as terribly wrong. Then there was the image of her own face, flesh and blood, but many years younger. She didn't even want to think about that just yet.

She couldn't stand to be in the same room as Ben. She couldn't even stand to be on the same ship as him.

Although her body ached and her uniform was soaked in sweat, Liao wasn't done yet. The moment her legs would carry her again, she pushed herself back to standing and ran. She liked the pain, liked the burning feeling in her limbs, the protests of a body that had spent nearly a year caring for a baby and eating New York pizza, a body that had spent nearly a year neglecting its fitness.

When she was younger, a junior officer in the service, she had run often, especially during her sea-going time as a navigator on the Chinese navy's *Han* class nuclear attack submarines. She would jog from stem to stern and back again over and over, a perilous obstacle course but one she would relish. It felt good to run: to push one's body beyond comfort, to improve it, to weaken it so it could grow again, stronger than before.

The hangar bay loomed ahead of her, light pouring in through the hexagonal entrance to the twin doors leading to the airlock of the vast open cavern. She stumbled through the first door, gasping for air and peering through the tiny glass window to the hangar bay beyond. The little ship was gone, as she expected, but her discarded spacesuit at her feet remained. She kicked off her boots and stepped into the legs of the suit, pulling it up over her uniform. She squirmed into the suit, then reached for the helmet.

A voice from the discarded headset stopped her.

"How far do you think you can run in this place?"

She pulled up the spherical dome, bringing it close to her head and touching the talk key dangling down from the helmet. "I don't care what you have to say," she said. "We're done. We're done. What you're doing is *sick*. It's not right, and I don't want to help you. I don't want to talk to you. I just want you, your ship and your experiments to be flaming debris."

There was a brief pause, uncharacteristic for the construct who usually began speaking immediately. "I'm not sure I was clear. I'm not looking for the meaning of life, or anything more than the simple experience of being alive."

"Listen, you fucked up Pinocchio wannabe, you have a lot to learn about us 'biologicals' if you really think that by putting a fleshy mask over your datacore you can conceal what you are."

Another pause. "Do you think of your privileges, Liao? The precious gifts you enjoy as part of your existence—to breathe, to live, to die. How strange it is, don't you think, to want those things? To want to die if I am, for but a few minutes, deprived of oxygen. To live in one body, one form, with an organic mind, giving away my perfect intellect. To die, eventually, as all biological creatures die."

"Yeah, well, you know what we have? A *conscience*."

"One step at a time, Liao. One step at a time."

Liao wanted to say more, but another voice came over the line. Kamal Iraj. "Commander Liao, this is TFR *Beijing* actual. Report status."

Ben answered, his British accented tone clipped and annoyed. "The good Commander is busy, Commander Iraj."

She squeezed the transmit key. "Kamal, I want you to lock everything you have on this ship and blow it to atoms. Full spread, maximum yield, rail guns target centre of mass. Fire for effect." There was no answer except a faint hiss over the line. "Kamal?"

Liao turned at the faint sound of metal feet on the deck behind her. Two drones, identical to those that had escorted her to Ben, slowly strode down the corridor towards her, their weapons raised.

"The master will see you now," the lead drone intoned.

"Tell the master I don't give a shit what he wants."

"The master will see you now."

Liao drew her pistol, lining it up to the spider-like head of the Bevra drone. She squeezed the trigger, the round screaming as it ricocheted off the drone's metal head and embedded itself against the deck. The finish wasn't even scratched. She fired again and again, each round having as little effect as the first until the slide locked back and her ammunition was exhausted.

"You will be brought before him by force if you do not comply."

She ejected the empty magazine and reached for her spare, jamming it in the base of her pistol. "And what if I don't want to?"

"You will be—"

Liao clicked the slide closed and pressed the weapon to her temple. "And what if I *really* don't want to?"

There was a tense delay as the robot silently regarded her, then the drone spoke with Ben's voice. "Last time I saw you, your biometric data indicated that you were pregnant. You are no longer pregnant. There was a high probability of that foetus being carried to term, so I can only assume you have a child now. All my data regarding Humans suggests that you treasure your children and that before a child reaches their first decade, they are essentially relying on their parents to sustain them. You will not terminate your life while that child needs you."

She idly flicked her fingernail over the trigger, dragging it across the plastic. A faint clicking noise echoed around the airlock. "Oh, I don't know. I'm feeling pretty impulsive right now. Don't know what I might do. Open the airlock door, Ben."

"I'm afraid I can't do that, Liao."

Liao snorted with sardonic laughter. "Oh, if only Summer were here to hear you say that." She used her thumb to pull back the hammer, readying the pistol to fire with even the lightest pull of the trigger. "You went to a great deal of trouble to bring me here, to show me these... these *things* you've created, and I really don't think you're going to be willing to let me blow my brains out all over this airlock."

Ben's tone carried an edge of quiet malice that Liao had never heard in his voice before, a subtle change that carried through the drone's tiny speaker. "You'd be surprised what I'd be willing to do."

Liao would not be cowed so easily. "Me too."

"Well then, I guess we're at an impasse," Ben admitted, "since I control the airlock door and you control the trigger on your pistol. This will end exactly one of two ways. Either you shoot yourself, or I back down."

"Seems that way. But I'm not as patient as you. Maybe I'll just get bored and do it right now."

"Or maybe," said Ben, "I'll do what I did to the Toralii fleet—engage this vessel's voidwarp device and jump to a location within the space currently occupied by the *Beijing*, displacing an area the volume of my ship at the speed of light, vaporising the majority of the *Beijing*'s mass instantly. An ignoble end to a vessel that has accomplished so much."

Liao thought of the expanding debris field. The Toralii had been killed instantly, far too quickly to escape or warn the other ships. "Why do you even want me to stay anyway?"

The drone chuckled in Ben's voice. "Oh, don't worry about that, Commander. Besides, I don't have time to explain it before the *Beijing*'s marines blow down the door and give you your heroic escape."

"What?"

There was a dull, muted explosion that vibrated through the metal of the deck. Liao twisted her neck, looking out the thick perspex window to the hangar bay. A Broadsword gunship barrelled into the large open space, landing skids extended as it slid at reckless speed onto the deck. Before it had even stopped, the large mouth of the loading ramp began to extend, and Liao could see helmeted figures beyond carrying the heavy automatic grenade launcher developed specifically for ship-boarding operations. The Bearded Dragon, they called it.

Liao turned back to the drone. "You knew they were coming the whole time?"

"Of course. I see using the ship's eyes. My ability to multitask far outpaces your own. I'm performing thousands of tasks at this moment, including monitoring your ship and its useless flailing."

She imagined the outside of the ship, rotten and covered in weapons. "You could have stopped them at any time. You could have fired on them with your new little toys, or you could have just, as you said, jumped right on them. Yet you let them through." She took the pistol away from her head, casually clicking on the safety and holstering it. "I'm not going to play your games, Ben."

Through the window, Liao saw the marines tap a blowtorch against the glass. Liao clipped the helmet on, her suit swelling as air filled it. A high pitched whine filled the airlock as the marines began to cut through the airlock door.

"Ben," Liao said, "I'm leaving now."

"If you say so," said the drone, its voice muffled by her helmet.

Her radio hissed, and through the heavy static came a voice she recognised.

"Commander Liao, this is Lieutenant Medola of the Broadsword *Archangel*. Stand by for extraction. Get away from the outside door. The decompression is going to be nasty."

The inside door silently slid shut, cutting her off from the drones and preventing the whole ship from decompressing. With a roar and a woosh of air, the hatchway covering the exit to the hangar bay blew out, silently flying across the room and striking the opposite wall. Liao was pulled off her feet by the force of the air vacating the small airlock, but strong arms grabbed her, preventing her from flying out into empty space.

She and the marines made a clumsy, low gravity run towards the hangar bay, their magnetic boots thunking on the deck as they moved. Together they bundled themselves into the ship. The Broadsword lurched as its pilot wheeled her around and tore out of the hangar bay, the ramp closing as it cleared the mouth of the launch area and flew out into the void, banking towards the *Beijing*.

The ship's cargo hold repressurised and the marines, one by one, pulled off their helmets. Liao's eyes met Cheung's, her spacesuit still bloodied, and she nodded appreciatively.

"Thanks for coming back for me."

"Nobody gets left behind, Commander," Cheung said, smiling as she crouched in front of her, "not even officers."

Liao managed to return the smile. "You're going to have to stow that attitude now you have your commission, you know."

"It's not possible to change my mind now, is it?"

"Considering the effort I went through to give it to you, no. Sorry."

Cheung laughed and stood. "Okay, let me go check on the Broadsword crew. I'll have a report for you in ten."

Liao nodded, watching Cheung depart. The rest of the marines chatted amongst themselves and otherwise ignored her, which suited her fine. She digested what she'd seen, turning the scene over and over in her head and trying to commit as many details as possible to memory. She knew that the *Beijing* and the rest of the fleet would want answers, and she needed to provide as many as she could.

A daunting task.

As she sat there, her hands shaking slightly from the fading rush of adrenaline and from the memories, Liao's helmet once again filled with Ben's voice.

"Goodbye, Commander," he said. "I'll see you again soon."

Act III

Chapter IX

"Bayonets and Brave Soldiers"
*****

Outside Saara's Quarters
Cerberus Station
Sol System

Two days later

Ben had let them go.

Liao had always been independent and had treasured her ability to do things for herself. It irked her, on some level, to know that, despite everything that had happened on that ruined ship, it had all come down to Ben's generosity, Ben's willingness to let her live for reasons that she really did not want to spend too much time thinking about. Yet as the days passed and the fleet readied themselves for their next move, she couldn't shake off the feeling that they, despite their allies and considerable advantage in terms of numbers, were in well over their depth.

The images of Qadan, and of her own face, haunted her. That was another image she didn't want to dwell on.

With Vong confirmed dead, the command of the *Beijing* had fallen to Kamal. However, Liao had petitioned Fleet Command to reinstate her for a period of two months, until this issue had been resolved and her leave was technically over.

To her palpable relief, they had approved the motion, a decision made significantly easier by Kamal's unsolicited endorsement. She owed that man one hell of a Christmas present.

They had a lot to discuss in today's briefing, but first, Liao had an obligation to her friend. She pressed on the door chime of Saara's quarters.

["Enter."]

Liao did so, turning the metal handle on the hatchway and pushing open the door. "Saara?"

She was crouched over a laptop with extra large keys Liao had made especially for her. Liao stepped through the door, closing it behind her. "We were having a briefing today," she said. "I was hoping you could attend."

Saara's head appeared over the laptop, and Liao could see the profound sadness on her face. The sadness she had earlier had returned. ["Captain, I am sorry. I cannot attend the briefing."]

Frowning, Liao moved closer. "Is something wrong?" she asked. "You wanted to be a part of these things, and I'm specifically asking you..."

["Nalu has offered me a position aboard her vessel."]

Liao stared for a moment. "I'm sorry?"

Saara turned the laptop around so she could see. On the LCD screen was a copy of the station's email client. Open was a transcription of a message they had received.

"It says here that the Telvan have located your mother, alive..." she looked up. "In a psychiatric hospital."

["That is an imprecise translation, but I understand what they mean. They refer to retreats for those with the khala worm, those with broken minds."]

Liao sat opposite her, folding her hands in front of her. "The khala worm?"

["A sickness,"] Saara explained, ["that took my parents. It affects the mind. A tiny parasite, literally a worm, that bores its way into the brains of Toralii, secreting a chemical that suppresses the survival instinct. Those who suffer feel not the desire to eat, sleep... to *not* do things like stride off cliffs or, as my father did, open airlocks aboard transport vessels and decompress the ship for reasons that will never be understood but were not malicious. The khala worm was reported lost with all hands, but apparently those reports were in error."]

"I'm sorry," was all Liao could say. "But she's alive, right?"

Saara's gaze returned to the screen. ["Biologically speaking, yes, but with an infection that has lasted this long, I very much doubt she is herself anymore."]

"What can I do to help?"

["The Telvan have pledged to send an ambassador to discuss the matter of Belthas IV. That ambassador has offered to return me to my people so I may investigate what has transpired with her."]

Liao's heart clenched. "You're... leaving?"

["I am afraid that I feel compelled to go."]

Liao stiffened slightly. "I... I do understand," she said. "I know this must be hard for you, shocking even. But these are tumultuous times for our people. For me, too."

A shadow passed over Saara's face, so sudden and swift Liao almost didn't see her expression change. ["You would deny me this opportunity to be reunited with my mother, long thought dead?"]

"I'm not denying you anything," Liao said, suddenly defensive. "I'm simply saying that perhaps *right now* is not the best—"

["You disregard my council when it is inconvenient, but press me to stay when I have urgent personal matters happening elsewhere?"] The Toralii's voice rose. ["You deny me access to your briefings, then slap me when I ask to leave? Am I your pet-beast now?"]

"Saara, listen—"

With a roar, Saara upended the table and knocked Liao onto her back, the laptop clattering to the ground. Liao landed hard, the wind knocked out of her as the table's hard edge slammed into her abdomen, pinning her to the metal deck.

["Perhaps it is *you*, Commander Melissa Liao, collector of titles, WHOM SHOULD LISTEN!"]

Liao couldn't breathe, couldn't get air to her throat to speak. Instead, she wheezed and scratched at the table, trying to lift it off her body. Saara lifted her foot, pressing it to the table's lower leg to it down harder.

["You disregard my words at every turn! Who told you not to trust the construct with the *Beijing*'s computers? It was I! Words imparted from wisdom earned by experience, disregarded by a childish member of a childish species, your infantile selves taking foolish risk after foolish risk! Have you heard not a word I say? You provoke the Toralii Alliance at every turn, *deliberately*, as though ignorant of what they shall do!"] Saara pressed down harder, and Liao felt the metal crushing her body. ["They will burn your worlds, child, they will sear the very flesh from your bones for defying them! They have done so a hundred times over and they will do so again; here I am, giving my time, my words, to you, and you spit in my face!"]

Her vision began to tunnel, the lack of air crushing the life out of her. She scrabbled feebly at the metal, but Saara's massive foot-paw kept her securely pinned.

["You and I, right at this moment, we represent the Humans and the Alliance,"] Saara said. ["For while you wear your uniforms and collect your titles as though you think that gives you power over them, at any point they could simply reach out and crush you like an insect."] Saara leaned over the table, putting her face within a foot of Liao's. ["Do you feel death's cold breath on your neck, Commander? The crushing despair that comes from knowing all your strength, all your courage, is insufficient to weather the storm?"]

Her dying body surged with adrenaline and, somehow, she managed enough to gasp out. "Saara... please..."

["If you continue down this course,"] Saara said, her tone careful and deliberate, ["this moment will not be the last time you beg a Toralii warrior for your life."]

The inky blackness around her became total, and her arms lost all strength, sinking slowly to the deck, her mind starved of oxygen and her lungs empty. As her consciousness faded away, she stared directly into Saara's large, yellow eyes, so full of anger and sadness, of rage and despair.

*****

Later

She awoke with a coughing jerk, her body numb.

Everything was as it was when she had entered. The table, now resting on all four legs again, stood where it had stood previously, the laptop resting atop it with its lid closed. She lay on the couch in the quarters, a blanket draped over her, as though nothing had happened at all.

She tried to sit up, and her abdominal muscles lit up in agony, an instant, painful reminder that the events really had taken place. Gingerly, she peeled back her uniform, revealing the ugly stain of a bruise the size of a bottle of water laid horizontally across her belly, where the table's blunt edge had crushed the air out of her.

Somehow, she managed to walk all the way down to the *Beijing's* docking port, taking things slowly and walking with a casual, relaxed gait despite every step sending rivers of pain up her body. She passed through the threshold between ships and into the heart of the *Beijing*, walking down to the infirmary.

Doctor Saeed, the Iranian man who had treated her for the early part of her pregnancy and had even saved the life of her unborn child, smiled as she came in.

"Well, well, well. I was not sure I'd ever see that face again. It's very good to see you again, Capta-... Liao. How's the little one?"

"It's good to see you, too," Liao said through clenched teeth, aware there were nurses nearby, "and she's very healthy, thanks to you. Can I have a word in your office?"

He gave a nod of approval, and together the two walked into the locked, soundproofed room that Saeed used as part quiet work area, part consultation room.

"Certainly, Commander. What's on your mind?"

Liao lifted her jacket and showed him.

"What the hell have you done to yourself?" he said, reaching down, peering at her bruise, and touching the injured area gently. "This is a serious injury..."

"Going to be totally honest. I bumped into a table."

Saeed straightened up, affixing an incredulous stare on her. "Was the table shot out of the rail guns, perchance?"

She laughed, then grimaced. "Ow, ow, ow. No jokes, please." She eased herself down into a chair, groaning. "Ship-wide standing order: nobody is allowed to tell jokes."

"You're going to have to extend that order out a few weeks," Saeed said. "This is a serious piece of damage. Two weeks in bed, no excuses."

Liao shook her head. "Can't do it, Doctor. We're about to launch an operation. You got two days to fix me."

"The body needs time to heal," Saeed said. "I can't just wave a dermal regenerator over you to fix it."

She gave him a blank stare.

"Sorry," Saeed said, a cheesy smile on his face. "Summer organised a *Star Trek* marathon."

"Even when she's not here, that woman manages to cause me problems. Besides, why would you want to watch that? You live on a spaceship."

Saeed smiled, then crouched beside her on the chair. "You can tell me what happened," he said, his tone becoming serious. "I'm joking around, but there's bruising to the muscle. You're going to be in a fair bit of pain for some time, and there's not a lot I can do about it except dope you up a bit."

"Great," she said, "so dope me up."

"That depends," Saeed said. "I'm concerned about this, and I'm concerned about why you don't want to discuss it."

Liao grimaced. "I've always told you everything, but I can't. This time it's kind of personal, and it's still something I'm trying to fix..."

"If James is hurting you, you need to—"

She shot out of the chair, wincing again at the pain in her abdomen. "It is *not* James!"

"Then what?"

So she told him, in full and complete detail, what had happened. Saeed listened intently, nodding occasionally, but didn't say anything until she'd finished.

"Sounds like she has a point," he said, "and it also sounds like she's a young woman who's discovered something intensely personal and who might need a little bit of space for a moment."

"Well... yeah. I'm happy to give her some space, but her timing *sucks*."

Saeed smiled. "You'll just have to deal with that, unfortunately."

Liao nodded, closing her eyes a moment. "I know," she said. "I just want her to be okay. I hope she comes back."

"I hope so, too," Saeed said, patting her on the shoulder. "Now, let's get you nice and drugged up, but once this operation is complete, I want you to rest. I can order you to, you know."

"I've been resting for almost a year," Liao said. "It's high time I finally got moving."

Outside the Conference Room
Cerberus Station
Sol System

Two days later

The days passed and she did not see Saara at all. Wherever the Toralii was hiding, impossible as it seemed as she was the only alien on such a tiny space station, Liao saw neither hide nor hair of her. With the help of drugs and time, the pain of the bruise on her body began to fade, but the ugly black stain remained, a reminder of what had happened.

But she could no longer dwell on Saara's anger, or if her indignation was legitimate or not. There was work to do, and they had allies to meet, including the ambassador who would, presumably, be shortly taking Saara away.

She could not think on that, either. Liao spent a moment composing herself outside the conference room, strengthening her resolve and fiercely promising herself to keep focused on her duties, before finally stepping inside.

Avaran, Harandi, James and de Lugo had already arrived and taken their seats, sitting in silence as they politely awaited the remainder of the committee. Captain Anderson of the *Washington* was expected momentarily, as were two dignitaries, Vrald the Blood-Soaked of the Kel-Voran Imperium and Leader Nalu of the Telvan. This would be the first time that representatives of all four factions had sat in one room.

The subject of their discussion was war. Not the hit-and-run, cold war, guerrilla style fighting that they had been a part of until the arrival of Ben, but full, total war against a powerful enemy.

It was decided that, by the combined efforts of the Toralii Alliance, the Telvan, the Kel-Voran and Task Force Resolution's Fleet Command, Ben's grip on the planet had to be broken. Each had been conducting their own operations until this point, and this meeting was an attempt to pool their knowledge and resources to better combat their common enemy.

The door swung open, the heavy decompression hatchway groaning softly as the marines on the other side opened it, permitting the first of their visitors to enter: Vrald. He was a short, squat and stocky Kel-Voran who stood at just over four and a half feet, his reptilian body covered in scars and tattoos. He wore a brightly coloured, almost lurid vestment which was adorned with various bone slivers. Tiny vials of blood, a dozen or more, hung around his neck on a chain. His cold, emotionless eyes scanned the room, lingering on Avaran, and the two exchanged a leer. Liao and the others said nothing, the marines closing the door with a faint clang.

Finally, Vrald took his seat, fixing his gaze on Liao and speaking in the archaic version of the Telvan dialect they used.

["It warms my heart to finally meet thee, The Butcher of Kor'Vakkar, The Bringer of Terror, Slayer of Varsian the Immortal. Thy strength in battle and indomitable courage will be assets in this coming struggle."]

The mention of the full list of her accomplishments caused her grief as she thought of what Saara had called her. Collector of titles...

Avaran leaned forward, scowling darkly. ["Accolades earned by the slaughter of my people. Varsian was the head of my assault troops, and I knew him personally. Daily, his widow and children mourn his loss."]

["We honour the strength of the living, Toralii, not the dead. And word that thy brethren's blood spills into space brings me great joy. Too long hast thy species held fast to power, ignorant of the burning sting of defeat."]

Avaran snarled and went to speak, but Liao held up a hand. To her surprise, the Toralii fell silent, and Vrald turned to her expectedly.

"We're not here to talk about the battles of the past," she said, "only to solve the single pressing issue that has brought us together: Ben and the situation on Belthas IV."

["Yes,"] said Vrald, his reptilian features lighting up at the mention of Ben. ["A truly glorious battle stands before us. Our intelligence operatives noticed the movement of numerous Toralii ships—far too many for any routine operation. We had feared, initially, that thy species had angered them and that their fleets were embarking on the destruction of thy worlds. Relieved were we, indeed, to find their fire and fury turned on another. Now we sit in eager anticipation of the coming struggle!"] The Kel-Voran slammed his scaled fist onto the table. ["Against a foe powerful enough to lay waste to the Toralii fleets!"]

Avaran looked as though he might explode, so Liao spoke quickly.

"Yes, a very powerful foe. I agree and wish to—"

The door opened again, held by a marine. A grey haired Human in the uniform of the United States Navy stepped over the lip of the door and into the room, giving a polite nod to those present. Despite the colour of his hair, the man was younger than Liao expected, shorter too, with a slight build and tan skin that indicated mixed Latino heritage. He immediately turned, gesturing in welcome to a person Liao could not yet see.

"Leader Nalu," the man said, his accent softened with a thick Southern drawl, "like I told you at the docking ring, it's a genuine pleasure to have you aboard. Your presence is most welcome."

A slender, frail looking, grey-furred Toralii woman dressed in simple brown robes came into the room, reaching up and pulling back her hood while giving a polite nod to all present. ["On behalf of the Telvan, I thank you for inviting me,"] she said. ["It is a privilege to be here."]

Liao locked eyes with the Toralii who was going to take Saara away. Nalu held her stare and, for a very brief moment, some unspoken communication occurred between them. Liao knew that Saara had spoken to Nalu, but the Toralii's eyes held no anger, only a slight sadness that mimicked that which she had seen in Saara.

["Hah,"] said Avaran, ["They sent *Nalu*. Do the Telvan not even care about the fate of their own worlds?"]

Nalu didn't respond to Avaran's jibe. Instead, she simply took her seat.

"Avaran," Liao warned, "we're here to work together."

He sneered at Nalu, but blinked rapidly, a gesture Liao knew to be the equivalent of a shrug. ["As you wish."]

"With everyone here," Captain Anderson said, "let's get started. I assume you all received the dossier of information we prepared?"

Liao had written down everything she had seen, every word she and Ben had exchanged, to the very best of her memory, along with every scrap of data they had acquired about Ben, his possible motives, technology in his possession and anything else they could think of.

The delegates each signalled that they had.

"That's basically all we know."

Vrald scowled. ["Then thy species knows little indeed, Liao. Your entries seemed more concerned with speculation regarding *intent* and *psychological profiles*, whereas the Kel-Voran intelligence network hath not been idle at all. We have operatives on the planet who hath been feeding us solid information for weeks. Tactical information."]

That drew stares from around the table.

"How did you get these assets in place?" asked James.

["That is classified."]

Nalu straightened her back. ["Ben's blockade has been total. We know that. Our forerunner probes have found no evidence of any ship entering the system except the Alliance vessels which were destroyed with all hands. You must have had those agents in place *before* the invasion..."]

Vrald gave a wide, wicked grin, revealing a long row of serrated teeth. ["Oh tiny Toralii girl, the weakest of your kind, thy expression brings a smile to this scarred face. Thy nature is too trusting, thy hearts too soft, and of all the Toralii factions, the Telvan are the easiest to infiltrate due to thy trusting hearts and weak minds."]

["Pah,"] said Avaran, ["Kel-Voran *intelligence*. What an oxymoron. You beasts are barely sentient, little more than unthinking animals, a dangerous but ultimately stupid predator far too dull to ever rise above us. Even after centuries of 'war' with us, you do little more than annoy us with your pointless folly."]

Vrald's claws dug three long gouges in the plastic of the table. ["Ahh, well, if thy frail bones could find the strength, thou might draw iron with me, dog! But I warn thee, after I stand victorious on the field of bloody battle, thy final, mewling words shall be inscribed on thy grave!"]

Avaran laughed, a loud, raucous sound that shook the walls of the conference room. ["A *sword*? He has a *sword*?"]

["Blades are more than enough of a match for thy puny—"]

"ENOUGH." Liao stood, pressing her fingertips to the table and leaning over to face the delegation. "We don't have time for this. If we don't focus, *now*, I'm going to have my marines throw you all back on your ships. I haven't the patience for the squabbling of small-minded idiots and the bickering over who's going to inscribe what on who's grave. If you travelled to our solar system to do that, you can just piss off back to where you came from, because I don't care." She steadied herself, slowly drawing her hands together and standing straight. "We're here to talk about Ben. So..." She unclasped a hand, extending it towards Vrald. "Please, Vrald, share with us what you've learnt."

For a moment, it seemed as though the Kel-Voran was going to turn on her, his dark, emotionless gaze fixed on her. Liao stared him down, keeping her expression neutral but unyielding.

["Thou art every bit as courageous as whispers say you are, to speak to me so."]

"Thank you."

Vrald glared at her for a moment longer, then gave a low, amused chuckle. ["Indeed."] The Kel-Voran reached to his belt, producing a small, flat, circular device which he tossed onto the table. It immediately lit up, and the space above the table was filled with a representation of Belthas IV, hovering in the air. Vrald stood and poked at an area with his claw.

["The main settlement and factory buildings are here, and here. Ben hath seized them all, the population kept under curfew by a small but growing army of newly forged constructs. According to our operatives, he hath repurposed the foundries. Originally, only one facility produced constructs, but now they are all involved in the process. His army grows by the day."]

"Where is the civilian population kept?" asked James. "Hiding out in the settlement?"

["Correct."] Vrald inclined his head. ["Why?"]

"If we're going to attack this planet, we have to keep in mind that the civilians of the planet aren't allies of Ben. They're his prisoners."

["So?"]

Nalu spoke up. ["So, *obviously*, we will have to avoid civilian casualties if at all possible."]

Vrald gave her a toothy, eager grin. ["Will we, now?"]

"Yes," said Liao, looking to Nalu meaningfully, "we will. With the civilian population being held in the settlement, and with no military targets in that area, fortunately this should be an easy task."

"Correct," said Anderson, "but I think we're getting a little ahead of ourselves here. We still don't have a way to deal with Ben directly, or his ship."

Avaran looked at him in confusion. ["We don't?"] Then to James. ["Haven't you discussed our proposal with them?"]

"We haven't," said Liao, "although we were hoping both of you may have some ideas."

["You were aboard Ben's ship,"] said Nalu. ["What did you see there?"]

"Nothing of any strategic importance," Liao offered diplomatically, "but it was... disturbing. It's best we don't dwell on it."

Vrald and Nalu seemed distinctly unhappy with this, exchanging a glance, but they turned back to the table. ["Pah, keep thy secrets then,"] said Vrald. ["Ultimately, they are just dust in your mouth."]

Nalu turned back to Liao. ["I am less concerned with what we don't know than with what we do. The point Captain Anderson has made, though, is a good one. We still do not have any way of dealing with Ben's ship. He was able to handily destroy a third of the Toralii Alliance fleet by himself. We would do poorly if we underestimated him, and I have no desire to send fleets of my ships to their doom."] Nalu folded her hands. ["While I am content to discuss hypothetical invasion plans, I think we should work through this problem in a logical, linear fashion, starting from the earliest, most significant problems and working our way down."]

"Agreed," said Liao. "I'm open to any suggestion regarding Ben's ship."

Silence.

"That's depressing," commented James.

Avaran chuckled. ["I agree, Captain Grégoire."]

Nalu looked to Liao. ["Commander, I am curious about one thing, if we may deviate for a moment."] Nalu looked to James and Anderson, then back to her. ["Our intelligence sources say that you have one more vessel, the *Sydney* by designation. Where is that ship's commanding officer?"]

Vrald snarled. ["We expect that the coward hath fled, Nalu, and ask not such quivering, whining questions that hath small bearing to our situation. We fight with the army we have, and fruitless questions about the location of a coward too weak to fight his battles are a pointless waste of time."]

"The *Sydney* is overdue from Karathi," Harandi said. "They were due back two days ago. We dispatched a Broadsword from the station to investigate a day ago, but they have not returned. We're not concerned at this point; each vessel is allowed significant autonomy, and such overstays are normal."

["I will have one of our scout vessels search the Karathi system for the *Sydney*,"] offered Avaran. ["You do not need to dedicate your already thin resources to this."]

Liao looked at him curiously. It was true that the Task Force possessed far fewer ships than the mighty Toralii Alliance, but something about Avaran's tone and his phrasing gave her pause. The Toralii Alliance had never struck her to be the charitable type, especially when it came to fleet resources. One of the Pillars of the Earth carried roughly a third the firepower of a Toralii cruiser, were less reliable, had thinner armour, and were larger targets in combat. The Alliance may have lost a third of their fleet, but even now, Avaran had a half-dozen ships at his disposal. If the *Sydney* had not returned by the time of the battle, its presence would barely be missed.

So why did Avaran want them to stay away from Karathi? Why did he not want them to look for the *Sydney*?

["Regarding Ben's ship,"] said Nalu, "perhaps there *is* an option we could explore."] She rested her paws on the table. ["I have been giving some thought to this problem, although I had hoped that there might be a more concrete solution available. There is one avenue we may try, though, if none can offer an alternative."]

"What's that?" asked James.

["I might suggest that we approach the Iilan. They are very secretive, but they are, above all else, scientists and researchers. The Telvan sought out one of their ships many years ago, and after some trade, we came to a mutually beneficial arrangement."]

["The Iilan spoke to you?"] Avaran peered at Nalu, scepticism painted on his face. ["They fire on our ships when we approach Majevtor or flee."]

["A somewhat unsurprising reaction given what you did to their homeworld."] Nalu turned to face Liao. ["But yes, we have achieved a somewhat tenuous, but agreeable, rapport, when we can find them."]

"You think they might be willing to help us against Ben?" Liao grimaced slightly. "They were also willing to help *him*. Ben told me that he traded with the Iilan, gaining knowledge of bioengineering. That's how he made his clones."

["Yes,"] said Nalu, ["we read your report. In fact, it was that section that made me think that the Iilan might help us. They are... apolitical. They would not feel a philosophical alignment with what Ben has done, merely that their trade was successful and fair."]

"So they care about fairness, huh?"

"Can't complain about that," said de Lugo, and Liao felt as though she had to deliberately look at him, over her instinct to avoid it. Summer's words resonated in her head.

"Right," she said. "So if we approach them, they're likely to help us?"

["I believe so," Nalu said, ["and I will accompany you, if you feel it will help."]

Liao nodded. "Look," she said, gesturing to the holographic planet, "how about you boys stay here and plot your little war while the girls go shopping at Majev-tor and try to get you some new toys to play with, huh?"

*****

Later

Liao arranged quarters for Nalu, safe ones deep within the ship, and then when she was comfortable, sought her out. She took several breaths, steadying herself, then casually rang the door chime.

["Hello?"]

"Nalu? It's Commander Liao. I was hoping to speak to you privately about a personal matter."

There was a faint groan of metal as the door opened. ["I assume you are here regarding Saara,"] said Nalu, leaning up against the side of the doorframe.

"Yes. She and I quarrelled before she left, and I want to make things right by her."

["I'm afraid I cannot help you. Saara is an adult and can make her own choices."] Nalu gave Liao a stern look. ["Unless you are considering detaining her by force..."]

She shook her head emphatically. "No, nothing like that. I won't stop her leaving if she wants to leave. I just want to apologise for what I said." Liao paused, locking gazes with the Toralii woman. "And to say that I hope she finds her mother."

Nalu considered for a moment, then slowly nodded her grey head. ["I will pass along that message,"] she said. ["Is there anything else?"]

"No," said Liao, "and thank you for your time. We leave in four hours, so be ready, but for now, I have to go yell at the most frustrating woman in the universe."

*****

Engineering Bay One
TFR Beijing

Later

To find Summer Rowe, Liao just followed the sound of Australian-accented swearing.

"Ahhrgh, you piece of fucking shitty piece of shitty fucking *shit*. What the fuck is wrong with you?!"

Engineering was, rather than one section, a number of interlinked sections called 'bays' that were the playgrounds of the Engineering crew. The whole Engineering team, a figurative and literal well-oiled machine, was controlled from Operations. The Engineering console spoke to every part of the ship down here: power regulation, damage control, jump drive operation. If Operations was the beating heart of the ship, the very centre of its being, then the Engineering team was its veins and its nervous system, pulsing vital information and power to every corner of the ship, managing every system, and ensuring that it functioned. A simple order from Liao became a hundred smaller instructions, broken down and distributed throughout the ship.

Liao went to significant effort to ensure that the rest of the crew was more than invisible cogs in the vast machine that was the *Beijing*, but the reality was that she just didn't have time enough to see the whole crew in a day and still get any work done. Accordingly, she'd barely had time to share two words with Rowe since coming aboard.

In the past, when she was the chief of engineering, Rowe's presence aboard the ship had been something of a nuisance to Liao. Rowe was rude, abrasive and she had an almost complete disregard for military protocol and discipline. She caused problems with her lack of interpersonal skills, but her absence from the Operations room had been a distinct void in Liao's working life. The new engineer appeared to be competent, but despite Rowe's stunning lack of professionalism, it was clear that Au wasn't working on her level.

Liao had said it in her trial. She needed the best.

"You're in a fine form today," Liao said, stepping up to Rowe. The redheaded Australian was crouched over a work bench, tinkering with one of their Dragon's Breath rifles. The weapon's guts were scattered everywhere, and Liao had no idea how Rowe was keeping track of the multitude of tiny screws that seemed to be scattered everywhere in no discernible pattern or order.

"Yeah, well, if those fucking retards in Melbourne spent a few moments to retract their heads from their own arses then maybe, just maybe, I could get some work done around here."

Liao leaned over to inspect the device, careful not to tread on any of the parts that littered the metal deck. "What's the problem?"

"The problem is that this weapon's bullshit."

"A little more specific, if you please, Miss Rowe."

Rowe stabbed a finger towards what Liao could only guess to be the firing mechanism. "The problem," she said, "is that the damn thing's *too* finely well made. The firing pin, the ejection mechanism, it's all very precise. Too precise. Everything's got no margin for error, no wiggle room. It means that if a little speck of dirt gets in the bitch, it can't fire at all. It jams up, fails to properly eject the shell casing requiring a manual cycle, or worse, blows itself and its operator sky high."

"It can explode?"

Rowe nodded. "Yeah. You remember that breaching charge that we recovered from the wreckage of Saara's ship?"

"I do, yes."

"Well," said Rowe, "the warhead in the shells are based on that technology, shrunk down. That's how we're able to pack so much boom into them. Well, it turns out that one of the properties of that material is that if you squeeze it, which is exactly what happens when you have contaminants in the barrel, it explodes."

"Okay," said Liao, "so how do we fix it?"

"We make it shittier."

Liao stared down at the weapon. "I'm going to be honest, Summer; I'm not a big fan of this course of action in general."

"No, no, no. I mean, we loosen the bolts a little. Sand it down a bit to make it fit together a little *less* perfectly. Especially since this Belthas planet is covered in sand, I figured this is going to be a pretty important modification."

"Okay, so do it. What's the problem?"

Rowe threw her hands in the air in frustration. "The problem is that if I adjust the tolerances, it's not as accurate and, of course, introduces more problems. This isn't exactly what I do. What I do is software, systems, programming and design. I'm a theoretical person, not a fucking wrench monkey down here in the lower decks. I program things. I run things. I design things. This kind of work, really close in shit with tools and lathes, is what Au does."

"I'm inclined to agree." Liao straightened her back. "What does Au say about it?"

"How the hell should I know?"

Liao pursed her lips in thought.

*****

Liao's Office
TFR Beijing

Later

"Mister Au, it's good to finally meet you in person."

Au gave a crisp salute. He was a short, stockily built man with fair skin for someone from central China, something which made Liao suspect he had southern Russian heritage. His head was completely shaved and he had youthful, childlike features that contrasted with the formalness of his uniform. He would be quite cute if he were a few years older, but Liao couldn't help but notice just how tired he looked.

"Thank you, ma'am. It's good to be here."

Liao said nothing for a time, just looking at him, her hands folded in front of her as she sat behind her desk.

"Ma'am?"

"I'm just wondering," said Liao, "if you're happy here."

"Of course," Au answered immediately, "this is my dream post. Everyone in the People's Army Navy wants to be a part of the Pillars project, even if they can't get a posting aboard the *Beijing* itself. For me to be here is everything I've ever wanted in a post, ma'am."

"I meant, actually, your position in Operations, as the chief of engineering."

"I do miss working down in the bays," Au admitted, "but with Miss Rowe being reassigned after what she said to Commodore Vong, I was the next most qualified. I was the natural choice to put up in Operations."

She nodded. "Regrettably, Commodore Vong is no longer with us. While I want to honour his memory by honouring the decisions he made while in command of this ship, I also feel compelled to give my ship the best crew I can, in the best positions they can be. I want my crew to work where they're comfortable and in positions where their skills are best put to use."

"I see, Captain."

"I suppose I'm asking you if you would prefer a move back to the Engineering Bays, to exchange positions with Miss Rowe." She smiled. "You'd probably get a bit more sleep, but I can't promise there'll be an abundance of that for any of us in the days ahead."

Au's face seemed to brighten somewhat. "Although I'm very fond of the title, I think that'd be good."

"Summer doesn't seem to care about titles. I'm sure we can keep you on the books as the chief of engineering, but just have her up in Ops."

"Sounds perfect to me, ma'am."

Liao smiled widely. "Right. Well, dismissed then."

*****

Operations
TFR Beijing

Walking out of her adjoining office, she stepped back into Operations.

"Welcome back, Captain."

It felt good to hear that, and Liao couldn't fight the huge, proud grin creeping over her face as she stepped into the command centre. She nodded to Lieutenant Jiang at Tactical. "Thank you," she said, "it's good to be back."

Rowe spoke up. "Captain, we're ready to launch."

"Good," said Liao. She could tell right away that Rowe was much happier back at Operations. Hopefully, that happiness would translate into a more productive, tighter crew. "Then let's make it happen. Decouple from the Cerberus station and move to the Lagrange point."

There was a faint groan as the ship detached from the station, and the Operations room filled with chatter.

"Reactor level nominal, Captain."

"Ahead one eighth. Reactionless drive engaged."

"ETA to Lagrange point, two minutes."

She tapped keys at her command console, examining the ship's systems. Every display, every light and switch and bulb was intimately familiar to her. It was as though she had never left.

Sometimes, during her time on Earth, she would dream that she was back here, back in Operations. Some people dreamed that they were still in high school, or university, but Liao's dreams were always here, in the central core of her ship, surrounded by 200,000 tonnes of metal and composite materials. Sometimes, the cry of her infant would stir her from her sleep, and for a few moments, her brain would think she was still at her post and the sound was the General Quarters klaxon.

Now her dreams were the reality.

The plans for war were still being sorted, but already she could feel what was coming, like the smell of sweet air before a storm, the distant rumble of thunder on the horizon. After two years of fighting and running, of struggling to survive, of staking out a little bit of space for their species to live upon, now they were doing more. They were attacking a Toralii world defended by a construct who had laid waste to the best of the Toralii Alliance, and they were doing it with a host of allies.

A host they planned to expand with their visit to the Iilan. She knew that this mysterious species held, potentially, the key to disabling Ben's trump card. If they had a solution for them, then the fight was on. If they didn't, it was already lost. All the bayonets and brave soldiers on the ground, all the guns and missiles in space, would be absolutely worthless if Ben's jump device remained in operation.

"We're at the Lagrange point, Captain."

It was time. The jump coordinates were locked in and the ship's crew stood by to jump. Now they had to trust Nalu, trust that the Telvan woman would lead them to the Iilan and their salvation.

Liao reached into the pocket of her jacket, retrieving the small metal key that activated the jump drive, then nodded to Iraj. "Good, charge the jump drive and prepare to jump the ship."

Chapter X

"The Iilan"
*****

Operations
TFR Beijing
Near the great singularity Majev-tor

Liao withdrew the key and replaced it in her pocket.

"Jump complete, Captain."

She nodded, walking back to her command console, leaning over it, and studying it intently. "Good. Are we in position?"

"Absolutely no way to tell," said Dao. "We're seeing further out than any Human has ever seen before. As far as I can tell, based on the information we were given, we are in position."

"Captain," called Ling, "our radar is currently showing..." he paused, "absolutely nothing, except one contact approximately 400,000 kilometres away. 200,000 tonnes."

"Nothing?" Liao asked.

"Nothing. No planets, no solar bodies of any kind." Dao frowned slightly. "We're in the void, Captain."

The distances between solar systems were vast, almost unimaginable. Seeing the solar system as a whole meant that even the largest planets, such as Jupiter and Saturn, were just tiny specks in the vast black ocean, where the distance between the planets was measured in how many minutes it took the light to travel that distance. But the distance between stars was measured in light-years, a vastly larger distance.

And in that great, empty space between solar systems was nothing. Radiation, some dust, very rarely rogue comets and even rogue planets, but otherwise nothing. The universe, conceptually, was essentially empty, the vast majority of its area being the featureless nothings between worlds. She had known this, logically and intellectually, but it was suddenly, only now as the *Beijing* floated in the great empty nothingness on the other side of the Milky Way galaxy, that she came to truly *know* this fact and understand its implications.

She felt very small indeed.

"Let's see if we can get in contact with that ship," she said, "and find out how far away we are from the singularity."

"Captain," said Ling, "we have a *massive* distortion, bearing 20 by 270, three quarters of an AU from our current position."

"Is it Majev-tor? Show me."

A few taps of Ling's keyboard sent the radar data to her console, and she stared at the readout.

The radar screen showed the vast sea of nothing stretching out on all sides of the ship, with the tiny blue dot of the unknown contact floating some distance away. The radar waves, moving at the speed of light, were still coming back to them; the view slowly shrunk as more and more of the surrounding space was recorded and the lack of returning radar pulses was marked as empty.

Beyond a certain point, though, a large wall existed below them, sealing off a part of the universe. She knew it to be a hyper-massive sphere, colossal beyond any of her experience, so to her, it appeared to be a featureless flat wall.

On their side of the wall was essentially nothing. Dust. Comets. The other ship. Readouts filled one side of her screen, conveying all manner of information. The spectroscope showed a certain concentration of hydrogen atoms per cubic metre, the projected flight path of a small comet, the local ionising radiation levels: small things that occupied the vacant spaces in the universe.

But beyond that wall, that line she could see so clearly on the radar screen, there was nothing of a different sort, a complete, total emptiness that was something else entirely. It was the complete, total, utter absence of all things. No radiation at all. No dust. No hydrogen atoms. There was a complete, absolute emptiness there that rendered her speechless.

At high school, her favourite subject was Greek history and philosophy. It was from those studies that she had picked her own name, Melissa, a gentle goddess who discovered honey. She knew that the Greeks who followed Epicurus, a group of materialists and scholars who existed around 300 BCE, were the first to derive the notion that atoms of matter existed in a featureless void. Epicurus proposed the idea of *the space between worlds*, a concept he called *metakosmia,* the relatively empty spaces in the infinite void where worlds had not been formed by the joining together of the atoms through their endless motion.

The translation she had read compared the Epicurean philosophy to that of pages on a manuscript. Where the words and letters were the atoms and the gaps between them, the *lacuna*, represented the *metakosmia*.

The lacuna, 空白 in Chinese. The absolute, complete nothing, devoid of meaning and substance.

The thought suddenly leapt into her mind as clear as bright day. That was what the singularities were. The lacuna, the gaps of the manuscript of the universe, the holes where nothing was and nothing should be.

"Captain?" said Iraj, over her shoulder.

She realised she'd been staring at her monitor. Liao straightened her back, nodding to her XO. "Yes?"

Iraj looked to Ling, then back to Liao. "Mister Ling reports that the Iilan are attempting to open communications with us." He frowned ever so slightly, his tan face wrinkling. "Are you... okay?"

"I'm fine," she said, reaching up and adjusting her hat. "Sorry. I was just... looking at that great bit of nothing and getting all philosophical inside."

"Well, be careful with that. Remember what Nietzsche said, *When you stare into the abyss, the abyss stares back at you.*"

Liao returned her gaze to the radar screen, to that vast, slowly expanding field of nothing, then reached for her headset.

"I think I understand what he meant." Liao adjusted the headset, watching as Iraj put his on as well. "Patch in Nalu," she said to Hsin, their communications officer. "She will be in her quarters."

Hsin tapped some keys, spoke words into his headset, then turned to Liao. "She's ready and standing by."

"Good." Liao took a breath. "Open the channel."

["Who comes to the graveyard of the Iilan?"] came a voice, low and echoing in her ears, speaking the Toralii dialect. She had been told that the Iilan were birdlike and had, subconsciously, expected a chirping, high-pitched voice, but this was different.

["I am Leader Nalu of the Telvan. We have had dealings before, fair Iilan."]

["That we have, Leader Nalu, but your current vessel does not match the schematics of your previous visits. We are wary. What species do you travel with?"]

Liao looked to Kamal. A lot hinged on their introduction and the first impression they made.

["They are called humans,"] said Nalu, her voice quiet and respectful. ["And their ship is called the *Beijing*."]

["This is worldship eight. I am Paar, the speaker for this vessel."]

Liao looked to Kamal. "Worldship?"

He shrugged, then Nalu continued. ["Have you heard of the events that transpired at Kor-Vakkar?"]

["We have indeed, and we are pleased. Word of the deeds of the humans, and of the great Wrathbringer who broke Kor-Vakkar's back has reached even us, the ghosts of those who once lived within the great void."] There was a pause. ["We have obtained their language data files in a recent transaction. Is she with you?"]

Liao touched the talk key on her headset. "This is Commander Melissa Liao of the TFR *Beijing*. It's a pleasure to finally hear your voice. We've heard a lot about your species of late."

The response, now in English, was low and curious, somewhat emotionless but tinged with energy. "Have you, indeed? Strange words to come from the lips of one so famous so quickly, Commander Liao. You surprise us with your humility."

The voice spoke perfect English with a British accent. The same accent Ben spoke with.

"It's a quality I find myself with from time to time," Liao said.

"Very well, foe of the Toralii Alliance, Spear of Earth, what brings you to the ruins of our home?"

Liao took a deep breath to steady herself. "We need your help."

"Many come to us for aid: individuals, ships, countries, planets, systems, species, alliances. All want their chance to pick the bones of the dead Iilan empire, to feast on our remains, to gorge themselves on our technology and grow ever more powerful. We weary of those who take our power, wielding it as though they, themselves, forged it. Those who offer us baubles for gold."

"We're not here to offer you anything more than a fair deal," said Liao, "and we don't know if you have what we need, anyway."

"We have a great many things," came the reply, "of great power, or great curiosity, or great artistic value. We value all. Some we share; some we do not. Some we deny the very existence of. You have impressed us already with your deeds, human, so tell us what it is you seek."

"The construct known as Ben. He has taken a world in Toralii space, Belthas IV. We need your help defeating one of his technologies."

Soft, deep laughter came over the line. "We have knowledge of the construct Ben, and we supported his efforts at a vast discount. He has been in contact with us, reporting on his success, and we are *most* pleased. The destruction of so many ships of the Alliance makes our hearts sing, Commander Liao. The enemies of the Alliance are our friends, and we shall celebrate their victories whenever they can be had."

"I know the Alliance did terrible things to your people," Liao said. "I'm not unsympathetic. I know you must be pleased that he used his device to destroy many Alliance ships. And believe me; that's been quite a boon to us as well, but Ben won't stop until he's had his revenge, and I don't think he can ever be convinced that whatever slight he's endured has been repaid in full. Ben wants to be human; he wants to be a real boy, but there are no fairy godmothers in the real world. There's no ending for Ben that doesn't involve either his destruction or genocide."

"Genocide. Such as the act the Toralii Alliance perpetuated on us? Forgive me for being heartless, Commander, but there is no sympathy left in our hearts for the butchers of our forefathers, no matter how pained their plight may be."

She closed her eyes a moment. Then they were back to square one. Without the Iilan's assistance, there could be no way to defeat Ben.

"May I ask... do you know of Ben's jump technology, the device that allows him to activate it outside of jump points?"

"We are aware of it."

The response, Liao thought, was guarded. Whereas before the Iilan seemed eager to discuss the topics Liao brought up, now they seemed hesitant, reluctant.

"Do you possess similar technology?"

Another laugh, this one fainter and more strained. "If you have come to barter for a similar device, you are wasting both our time. We possess no such technology. In fact, Ben has pledged to turn his device over to us once the campaign at Belthas IV has been completed, to be documented and studied, the information stored in our archives."

Liao tapped her headset, thinking quickly. "No, we're not seeking one of our own, but... Excuse me; hold on one moment." She turned to Rowe. "Miss Rowe, what do we know about that device?"

Rowe rolled her shoulders. "Nothing. It's basically a separate co-processor that can be patched into a standard jump drive. It works like magic; you put in the coordinates, anywhere, and it takes you there."

"What did we learn about it when we had it? Any key piece of knowledge we could tell them?"

Rowe stared at her as though she had a spider crawling all over her face. "You... didn't read my report?"

"No." She blinked. "Should I have?"

"I sent it to you, like, months after the trial! It took me *weeks* to write, and I hate writing shit! You know I suck at that kind of stuff, but I did it!"

"Months? Summer... Summer, I wasn't even in the service at that point. How could I have possibly read it?"

Rowe stared again, then looked away. "Well, I wrote it," she said, her tone grumpy.

"Good. We're now all very glad you did. How long is it?"

"Long. Real long, like, two hundred pages. It has X-rays of the jump drive, spectronomical analysis, chemical analysis, a bunch of bullshit I copied and pasted in."

Liao nodded thoughtfully. "Sounds promising." She touched the talk key. "Sorry for the delay. We were in possession of the jump device for an extended period of time, and we have compiled an extensive report of its contents. We were unable to reverse-engineer its technology, but this may be of interest to you."

There was a long pause. For a time, Liao thought the Iilan had stopped responding to them, but then came the voice again.

"Prepare for docking."

*****

The view on the monitor was an odd one.

The Iilan ship was a perfectly spherical, golden ball that floated towards their vessel silently, ominously, the colours shimmering slightly in the faint light of the *Beijing*'s spotlight. As they drew closer, the details on the hull became more obvious; small grooves ran over the whole device, and it seemed to be a mesh of interlocking gears, twisting and turning, constantly working.

When it drew close enough to dock, a metal tube extended from the side of the Iilan hull as though it were alive; it contorted itself, twisting around until it latched onto the *Beijing*'s docking port, fluid and undulating as though filled with flowing water.

Liao left Kamal in charge and moved out of Operations to the docking port, a briefcase in one hand. She met Cheung and a team of her marines on the way, forming up ceremoniously near the entrance. With a final nod to Cheung, the door was opened, and Liao stared down the long corridor.

It appeared to be full of the same light green liquid as the tank on the *Giralan*. The fluid seemed to be held in place by some invisible force, undulating slightly as small changes in the air pressure of the *Beijing* pushed the wall of liquid back and forth. Just beyond the wall, floating half way up the passage, was a black mask similar to an industrial breathing mask or a gas mask.

"Please don the mask and come aboard," came a voice, distorted as it filtered through the liquid. "We cannot survive in your atmosphere."

"Can I survive in that?"

"With the mask to assist breathing, you can."

She set down her case and stepped closer, leaning forward and gingerly extending a hand. She pushed her hand into the liquid, finding a surprising lack of resistance, then retrieved the mask. The metal was surprisingly cool as though it had been sitting in ice for a time.

Pulling back what functioned as the head strap, Liao pulled the device over her head. With a faint hiss, the device molded to her skin, creating a tight seal. The cold was uncomfortable for a moment, but she soon became accustomed to it.

Liao did not want to enter that liquid, to become the image of herself submerged in the tank, but there was no other option. There was nothing else she could do since they needed the Iilan's help and she feared offending them. With a glance behind her to Cheung, Liao picked up the briefcase and stepped past the invisible wall that separated air from fluid.

She immediately felt the effects of zero gravity, although there was, for once, a complete lack of the usual nausea that accompanied it. Instead, Liao floated in the cool liquid, feeling comfortable and suddenly at ease. With barely a slosh of her hands, she found herself gliding effortlessly through the stuff, floating towards the inside of the sphere.

The entire ship was laid out before her. There appeared to be no rooms of any kind within the sphere, completely full of the green fluid, and Liao could see hundreds—if not thousands—of figures moving around within the liquid. A metal ball in the centre of the vessel, covered in protrusions, was the only visible mechanics or hardware in the entire ship.

One of the figures drifted close to her. The creature, completely covered in dark brown feathers, had wings for arms and tiny, clawed feet. It had a large, long, hooked beak that was entirely unprotected by any kind of breathing apparatus.

"Commander Liao, I presume?" the Iilan said. It was the same voice she had heard over the radio. When it spoke, its beak clacked slightly, but its tongue was articulate and complete. Somehow, despite the large barriers between their physiology, it could speak English like a native.

"That's correct." Liao's voice was muffled by the mask, but she could hear herself well. "You are Paar the Speaker, correct?"

"That is I."

Liao felt herself slowly turning, floating upside down. She struggled to right herself to no avail. "I'm sorry, I'm just not used to being under water."

The Iilan didn't seem bothered by Liao being inverted relative to him. She assumed that, in a direction-less sphere, this would happen often. "Many are not. This particular fluid is a technology of ours; it dissolves waste matter, sweat, excretions, dead skin and dead feathers. Additionally, it is highly resistant to radiation, heat, poisons and toxins, along with inertia. Our systems are built around it and it is one of our greatest possessions."

Liao was not entirely comfortable with the idea of swimming in dissolved excrement, but she remained diplomatic. "I've seen it before," Liao said, "in the tanks on Ben's ship. He was growing... humanoids. He was growing a clone of me."

"I cannot discuss previous clients' exchanges." The Iilan inclined his head. "I am sorry, though, if the idea has caused you any distress. We use cloning technology to preserve our species, although many find it unnatural."

Liao, somewhat uncertainly, nodded her head, finally managing to right herself. "Many among our kind would consider it unnatural, too."

"When you are desperate to just survive, there's no line you won't cross, no threshold you'll be bound to. Every member of every species says that they would hold to their principles to death, but so few of them do. The survival instinct is strong, and it keeps you going, even when there's no hope left. When there's nothing left but ashes in your present and a cold, empty death in your future, you keep going. Some call it hope. Some call it perseverance, but to us, it is merely the existence of day to day."

"I'll keep that in mind."

"Actually," said Paar, "I sincerely hope you forget it, that this matter never crosses your mind again, and you never feel those words apply to you or your kind. I hope you can avoid our fate and that you can be spared the loss and pain of your planet. I hope you do, sincerely and genuinely, but I fear for your planet, Earth. I hope it should never come to pass, but perhaps the loss of one's homeworld is the baptism of fire all species must endure, the toll they pay for a life amongst the stars."

"We have put a lot of effort into defending Earth," Liao said, "but I thank you for your concern."

The Iilan regarded her with sad eyes. "I fear that whatever preparations you have made will be insufficient. You are a young species, fit and eager, and you display great promise. I simply pray that you are not too eager and too strong, and that you do not reach beyond your limits. The Toralii Alliance may seem to be working with you, but I assure you, they always—*always*—keep their own desires, and their own goals, closest to their hearts. This is their way, their nature. You cannot change it."

Liao did not know what to say. "I will try to remember your advice."

"Thank you." The Iilan gave a polite nod. "To business, then?"

"Yes, to business. I have a copy of the report in my briefcase, but I'm afraid it will not survive the liquid, as it is written on a material that is severely weakened by contact with water."

"We can generate a synthetic atmosphere later to open your case." Paar clicked his beak. "But I know that you will be unwilling to give up the full report for nothing in exchange. So please, what is it you desire in exchange for your information?"

Liao was struck knowing this was the second time she had bartered for technology using information. Perhaps, she mused, she would have Rowe install a larger database on the *Beijing* to store more of Earth's media.

"We need a way to disable Ben's jump device, temporarily at least, so we can assault his vessel."

"We have several ways of doing this. However, they are valuable technology, since we use them to escape Toralii Alliance ambushes."

Liao felt an itching under her mask but fought the urge to scratch. "As a show of good faith, we are happy to let you read the full report before you make your decision."

Paar regarded her curiously. "A very interesting show of faith, Captain, to surrender your bargaining chip with nothing in return."

"Nalu tells us that the Iilan are reclusive, but fair. My reputation as a warbringer has spread to even your ears, Speaker Paar, but I am like you. I would trade everything I've done for a reputation as a fair, just leader who keeps to her word. I would prefer that over all the adulation of the Kel-Voran, of the Toralii, and of the other warlike species in the galaxy. That is not who I am."

Paar, strangely, seemed to smile with his eyes, rather than his beak. "Very well, Captain. If that is your desire, I can assure you that we will evaluate your report and derive a conclusion. Please, you can remain here, if you wish, while we confer and evaluate the information for ourselves."

*****

Liao floated in the strange fluid for what seemed like an hour. In a ship with no walls, the Iilan floated away with her briefcase, and Liao, out of politeness, didn't follow him. Soon he was lost in the sea of Iilan, the closest ones giving her curious looks but saying nothing to her.

Finally the Iilan returned, floating towards her in the faintly glowing green fluid.

"We evaluated your report," Paar said, his tone slightly hesitant and reluctant.

Not a good sign.

"I see," Liao answered. "It contains all we know. I'm sorry if it was insufficient."

"It was... primitive," Paar answered, "with numerous misspellings and poor grammar, but it also contained a surprising amount of information as well."

Damn that woman, Liao thought. She could at least have used a spell checker.

"Accordingly," Paar said, "while the information is not of insignificant value to us, it is not, on its own, worth one of our more treasured secrets, although the speculation side of the report was informative. Whoever wrote it seemed to have a great love for the technical and an affinity for understanding things on a basic level."

Liao felt a clenching in her chest but nodded diplomatically. "I see."

"However, it is also the opinion of our leaders that yours is an honest species. Strong and impulsive, yes, but those feelings can be tempered out of you in time. We see much promise in you, and we see little future in our continued research here at Majev-tor. We will move on to the other singularities in a generation or two, but we wish to do some good before we do. We have decided," he said, "to grant you the least of the technologies you can use to accomplish your goals; we will grant you one single device, with a single use, in exchange for the report, despite the significant discount this would present... on certain conditions."

Liao released a breath she didn't realise she was holding. "Conditions. Go on."

"The device will be returned to us, and it will be returned unopened and unexamined. Analysis of your report has given us insight into the methods you use to study things. We will take precautions against such attempts. They will not be pleasant for you."

Liao nodded. "We won't peek inside Pandora's Box." She held up a hand to mollify Paar's confusion. "A Human legend. I'll throw in the story for your personal reading; don't worry. Please, go on."

"We want Ben's jump drive intact, if possible, or full salvage rights if it is not. Additionally, we want any data acquired during the battle, or any other information about this technology you find."

"Agreed. We'll give you whatever is left, and whatever we know about the jump drive, we'll share with you when we return your device." She reached up and adjusted the mask slightly. "Is there anything else?"

"Not at this moment."

The wall of the ship behind her extended out, reaching for the *Beijing*.

"Then you may return to your vessel. We will send through the device within an hour, along with instructions to employ it."

Liao's Office
TFR Beijing

"They fucking call this a *weapon?*" Rowe upended the tiny package onto Liao's desk. A small circular device with a button on top clattered to her desk, along with a six inch square sheet of some rubbery material that bounced when it hit the wood. "I think you got robbed, Captain."

"Well, let's not be hasty. What is it?"

Rowe picked up the rubbery slip, holding it up to the light. "Nothing, it's blank."

Liao could see writing on the opposite side. "Turn it around."

"Oh, wait, it says, 'Please see other side.'" Rowe flipped it in her hand and began to read. "Measure the distance between your ship, currently, and the edge of Majev-tor. Be within half that distance, and push the button. All jump drives within the area will be disabled for a period of six times the time you spent aboard our vessel." Rowe turned it over, then again. "That's all it says."

"Well, they seem to like their technology simple, just like the Toralii."

Rowe made a disgusted face. "Simple? Those Iilan fuckers are serious chowderbuckets. If it doesn't take a doctorate to operate it, I couldn't give a fuck about it."

"Tell me something I don't know."

The redhead's face lit up. "Did you know the defibrillator was invented before CPR?"

"I hate you, Summer."

Rowe leaned forward, reaching out and pinching Liao's cheek. "I know you do, Cappy-Cap." She smiled and withdrew her hand. "Anyway, let's teleport across the galaxy and blow up a robot, okay?"

"Sure." She took a breath. "Let's go do that."

"We are ready to jump, Captain."

Floating beside the jump console, Liao gave one last look at the Iilan ship, then reached for her key. Before she could withdraw it, however, alarms blared around them, and the Operations room was illuminated by emergency lighting.

Rowe called over the din. "Captain! The jump drive has activated!"

"What?!" Liao glanced at Kamal, who looked similarly confused, his key still in his hand. The jump drive should not have been active.

"Restoring gravity," said Jiang, tapping at her keyboard.

Liao felt gravity return, using the console to steady herself as she floated back down. "Report! Jump drive status?" Her tone conveyed her displeasure, her gaze locked on Rowe, the grip on her console as tight as iron.

"Cooling, Captain. It got a little heated, but it should be ready to jump again shortly. Eight hundred degrees Kelvin... seven hundred, dropping." Summer pushed back her seat, giving a loud, relieved sigh. "Whatever happened, it looks like it was just a temporary glitch. It was probably the alien thingy, or maybe the damn thing just wanted to go somewhere, then changed its mind. The *Sydney* had a similar issue during their shakedown cruise... It could be a glitch in the system that we're only just now starting to see. Maybe it's the new jump drive or some manufacturing flaw."

Closing her eyes a moment, Liao reached up and dragged her hand down her face. "Find out what the hell happened," she ordered, straightening her back and folding her arms in front of her chest. "If my ship is going to spontaneously start to jump without my express authorisation, then just as spontaneously *stop*, I want to know *exactly* what's going on. Disassemble the whole jump assembly and examine it piece by piece. Audit the system code line-by-line if you have to. I want answers, and I want them as soon as you can get them to me."

Rowe gave a nod. "Aye aye, Captain. We'll start looking into it immediately."

Liao stepped over to Rowe's engineering workstation, leaning over the woman's shoulder. The two read the scrolling text on the computer monitor which Liao only understood a fraction of but which Summer seemed to comprehend, nodding occasionally in thought.

The incident nagged at her. It felt wrong, and she knew—somehow knew—that this was no ordinary system glitch. Jump drives didn't just spin up, then just as suddenly power down. A million possibilities swirled through her mind. Was it Ben's influence, or the Iilan, or their strange device, or interference from Majev-tor? Or was it just, as Summer said, some kind of glitch?

But perhaps that wasn't it. Yes, the events were suspicious, but that wasn't it. There was something else that was eating at her, gnawing at the back of her mind, drawing her attention away from the scrolling diagnostic text and forcing her mind to other things. It was like having the name of a song on the tip of her tongue, hearing its melody in her head and reproducing its tune, but being unable to articulate its name.

Then the question and the answer jumped into her head, fully formed.

"Allison," she murmured.

Summer twisted in her seat, raising a curious eyebrow. "Hmm?"

Liao smiled down to her chief engineer. "Sorry, just thinking aloud." She paused. "Do you like that name? Allison?"

The redhead stared at her as though she were crazy. "Sure, it's nice I, uhh, I guess... Why?"

Liao's smile grew, and she slid one hand to Rowe's shoulder, the other gently resting by her side, the tips of her fingers playing with the fabric of her uniform. "For my girl," she answered, "I think I've picked out her name. I'll have to check with James first, of course, but..."

Rowe shrugged and went back to work while Liao felt her eyes drawn to the external monitoring viewer which displayed an image of the stars outside. She had seen such a view countless times, of course, but for some reason at this particular moment, she felt drawn to it.

She stared at the view, her warm smile remaining, as though some missing piece of the puzzle that was her life had just slotted into place. The nagging feeling immediately faded away to nothing, leaving her with a sense of completeness and serenity that outstripped any comparable feeling she'd had in her lifetime.

Allison. She would name her child Allison.

*****

Operations

One hour later

"We figured out what it was." Rowe jabbed a finger down at the box. "The device. It emits the same kind of radiation that our jump drive does, but much, much stronger. It's like shining a floodlight on a shadow puppet show—the device's radiation blocks the way the jump drive works at a fundamental level that I could explain, but I know you'd just get mad and yell at me if I tried."

Liao listened as Rowe spoke. "Correct. How did you discover it was the device?"

"Basically, we found fluctuations in the jump drive's power consumption. The closer we brought it to the jump drive, the worse the fluctuations got. So we figure it's screwing it up."

"Okay," said Liao, "how do we fix it?"

"We can't," Summer replied, "but we *can* move it to the bow of the ship and stick it in a Faraday cage. That should keep its influence on the jump drive to a minimum."

Liao considered. "Do it," she said, "and make sure we get the jump drive working as soon as possible. The Iilan will be wondering why we haven't jumped out yet."

"Well, that, or they're chuckling to themselves, knowing that our jump drive will be screwed up." Rowe tapped her finger on her console. "Guess we know it works though."

"Yeah, a little *too* well if you ask me." Liao looked to the door. "Go. Fix my ship."

Summer grinned and skipped out of Operations, and Liao was left to her command console, left to the huge wall of nothing that ever so slowly grew out to meet them.

Allison...

She was aware of Iraj looking over her shoulder, but she didn't say anything, the two of them staring at the monitor intently.

*****

Operations
TFR Beijing

A day later

Everything was ready. The plans were made, the pieces in place. The *Beijing* hovered in the Mars-Phobos L1 Lagrange point waiting for the very last signal to be given so their operation could begin.

Liao hadn't discussed the name with James, so focused was she on the upcoming battle, but she would talk to him the moment they had some free time.

The *Sydney* had not reappeared. This fact, now of growing concern to Liao, caused her some degree of worry. They had agreed to wait until the final jump preparations to discount the ship's presence, a time which had now arrived.

"Ready to jump the ship. Artificial gravity coming off in three, two, one... mark."

Liao gripped the jump console tightly, using it to steady herself as the gravity faded away. She felt her feet float off the floor, the old familiar feeling of sickness in her gut as her body protested the lack of familiar gravity keeping it down. "Mister Hsin, inform the fleet that we're about to jump and confirm the jump order."

"Aye aye, Captain." Hsin spoke into his headset, making several rapid calls, then turned back to her. "The *Tehran* confirms that, immediately following our jump, they're going to be right behind us, so we need to vacate that jump point as quickly as possible. Receiving word from the Kel-Voran; they're ready for their jump, the Telvan for theirs, and... the Toralii Alliance ships also report that the way is clear. Once we've disabled Ben's ship, the route to Belthas IV will be clear."

Liao repositioned herself, using her grip to keep her position as level as possible. "Very good. Let's do it then."

Iraj floated next to her, his own key in hand. He leaned in to speak, his voice quiet so nobody would hear him above the murmur of the Operations crew. "I didn't get a chance to say so before, but... it's good to have you back, Captain."

She gave him a relieved smile. "It's good to be back. And... it's good to have your support, Kamal. Thank you."

"You know I've got your back, Captain. Besides, in my mind, this is your ship, your first child. Nobody should take it from you."

"Thank you."

She took a breath, then the two inserted their twin keys into the jump console, a large black board covered in a variety of blue lights. Liao stuck her key in the left hand slot and Kamal inserted his to the right.

"Executing jump."

She turned the key with a satisfying click, and the ship leapt across the stars, to war.

Chapter XI

"Murphy's Law"
*****

Operations
TFR Beijing
Belthas system

The *Beijing* appeared in open space at the Belthas IV L1 Lagrange point surrounded by the dust of the Toralii Alliance fleet, the ghosts of so many ships ground up and distributed in an ever-expanding sphere. The dust had mostly dissipated from the jump point, so their arrival was as ghostly and quiet as typical jump arrivals, with no indication from Operations that anything had happened at all.

Liao's feet kissed the ground as the gravity was restored. "Report," she said, glancing to Ling expectedly.

"Jump complete, Captain. No vessels in our immediate vicinity. Launching strike craft and gunships."

"Good," she said, "now get us the hell out of here. Clear the jump point so the *Tehran* can come in behind us."

Dao was already on it, his fingers working over his console before Liao had finished speaking. Immediately, the ship moved forward, sliding out of the jump point and into the faint dust of the Toralii fleet's remains.

Liao watched the waves of the radar system slowly reach out over the planet, its moon, the debris field of the best of the Toralii Alliance which was reduced to powder.

The radar found nothing bigger than wreckage the size of a car.

"Captain," said Ling, "the *Tehran* has appeared in the jump point. They're clearing the jump point now. Still no contacts."

"Any sign of the *Sydney*?"

It was hoped, somewhat fruitlessly, that the *Sydney* would be waiting for them in the Belthas system.

"Negative, Captain. No sign of the *Sydney* in radar range."

Liao nodded to Ling. "Very well, looks like we're doing this one on our own. Keep an eye out for them. If Ben doesn't want to show his face, I guess we'll press on to Belthas IV and wait. He's bound to appear at some point." Liao tapped her foot impatiently. Where the hell was Ben?

The radar waves moved beyond the planetary system. Nothing bounced back at them except the Kel-Voran fleet appearing at the L2 Lagrange point, and the Telvan fleet at L4.

The L5 Lagrange point, where the Toralii Alliance fleet was expected to appear, was completely empty.

"Mister Ling, confirm that there are no contacts at L5."

"Confirming that, Captain. Nothing at all."

The worried feeling she had in the pit of her stomach grew stronger. "Well, there goes over half of our attacking force, straight off the bat."

Iraj frowned, looking at his monitors. "Maybe they are just delayed."

"They were supposed to jump out right after us, what could be keeping them?"

He shrugged. "We won't know; let's just hope they show up."

Liao frowned darkly, looking back to her own set of monitors. "We're doing far too much of that for my liking."

The ships journeyed on, and Liao continued to study the long-range radar. After a time, Jiang glanced over her shoulder, catching Liao's attention.

"Captain, I was thinking. It's possible the *Giralan*'s hiding in the shadow of the planet, or possibly behind the moon."

"Then it's a double blind situation. We can't see him but he can't see us." It was a pretty large assumption, but Humans were a species evolved to find patterns in everything: a tiger in the bush, causes of rain, causes of natural disasters, why the sun rose every day. It was this pattern recognition device that allowed Humans to see patterns in things that were difficult to otherwise spot, but it was a flawed device. The rate of false positives was absurdly high, because the penalty for incorrectly identifying a pattern, such as tiger stripes against bamboo, wasn't high... but a false negative meant that you died. So there was an incentive to favour false positives over false negatives.

Liao suddenly remembered what Ben had told her, how he valued this mechanism, the one that allowed Humans to be wrong, to error, and through their mistakes discover something new.

Was there a pattern she had missed here?

The *Tehran* and the *Beijing* ships moved into formation, side by side, moving across the empty void towards Belthas IV.

"Mister Hsin, patch me into the strike fleet."

A few taps of a keyboard and it was done.

"This is Captain Liao. Status reports as follows: the *Beijing* and the *Tehran* have arrived and are en-route to Belthas IV. No sign of the *Sydney* as of this time."

There as a significant delay as the message was relayed to the L4 Lagrange point and back. ["This is Nalu. Captain, we see no sign of the Toralii Alliance. The L5 is clear."]

"Perhaps the Alliance ships misjumped. Can you relay a message to Vrald's ship, see if they can see them?"

The Kel-Voranians were out of direct communication with a planet between them. After some time, Vrald snarled into the line. ["More likely those cowards turned tail and ran!"] He bellowed with laughter, the noise loud enough that Liao's ears hurt. ["Magnificent! More for us!"]

"Has anyone made contact with Ben's ship? Our scope is clean."

["We have not,"] said Nalu. ["We thought he may be using the mass of the planet to conceal his presence. But if you cannot see him, it is unlikely he is there."]

"Maybe Ben has disabled the L5 jump point and is using it to hide out there. There's a significant amount of debris in that region from the Toralii Alliance fleet. It's not much, but it *might* be enough to throw our long-range radar for a loop." She glanced to Iraj, releasing the talk key. "We can't use the device until we see him. If he's not near Belthas IV, we'll waste our shot."

"Agreed," he answered, "press on to the planet. Murphy's Law applies. Besides, no good plan survives contact with the enemy."

"Well, we haven't even seen the enemy yet."

Iraj folded his arm. "Yeah, well, Murphy was a grunt. What the hell did he know?"

The pair of ships sailed towards Belthas IV, enclosing on the planet in three ways, the Humans on one side, the Kel-Voran on the other, and the Telvan coming in on their flank.

*****

"I am so bored; you have *no* idea. None. I feel like I'm being sucked into a boredom black hole, only to be crushed to the size of a boredom atom in a massive outpouring of cosmic boredom energy."

Liao didn't even look at Rowe. "You've made your entertainment situation perfectly clear, Miss Rowe. Please just... *try* to focus on the ship's systems. We'll be there in an hour."

"An hour is, like, way too long." Rowe folded her arms and pushed back her chair. "I just wish Ben would show up and kill us. Getting blown to atoms would make a nice change."

Liao reached upward, stretching her arms. "Master at Arms?"

The marine guard stepped forward from the door. "Captain?"

"If I took my pistol and shot Miss Rowe in the head, would you tell anyone?"

"Hey!" said Rowe, scowling.

He snorted slightly. "No, Captain."

"Noted. Thank you."

Rowe grudgingly turned back to her console. "Yeah, you wouldn't shoot me."

"Probably not," admitted Liao. "It'd be a waste of a perfectly good bullet. That's what we have airlocks for."

The time passed, and the spectre of Belthas IV loomed larger and larger in their monitors. Their ships, two of the three original Pillars of the Earth, were filled to the brim with the devices of war. The major powers of Earth had all contributed, in some way. They had German special operations units, South Korean marines, American Rangers, soldiers from the People's Republic of China and the Islamic Republic of Iran, all fighting together.

It was a heartening sight, seeing the armies of the world united under one banner, fighting together to preserve their species. National boundaries still existed, and old hatreds still burned strong, but this was a step, one of many tiny steps to try and shift the identity of people from nationalities and towards a species, to truly become the Human race. Liao felt intensely proud of this moment, even as she worried for the outcome. No sign of Ben, no sign of the Toralii Alliance...

Finally, the two ship drew close enough to the planet to form up with the rest of the fleet, moving together as a massive wedge in low orbit of Belthas IV's gravity well. Ling, Dao and Jiang coordinated the fleet's combined sensor network while Iraj pulled up the tactical overview.

"Captain, the fleet is commencing long-range scans of the surface."

Liao touched her own screen, overlaying the data the Telvan had provided on the planet. "Excellent. Coordinate with the maps we have. See what we can determine are the key areas we need to take."

"Very good, Captain." Iraj gave her a meaningful look. "Still no signs of hostile ships."

"I don't like that either," Liao said, "but it's possible he's just watching us for now, seeing what our plans are before he makes his move. But rest assured, Commander... Ben is out there."

They spent a moment examining their maps.

"This facility," said Iraj as he pointed to a white hot spot on the thermal camera, "is marked by the Telvan as being the main factory complex. It's almost certainly where the majority of the drones Ben's been making have been created. Irrespective of if Ben shows up or not, if we take that facility, there's no way he can grow his army anymore."

"There's a lot of heat in that area," Liao observed thoughtfully. "How's it getting power?"

"Built in reactor. The Kel-Voranians on the surface indicated that it was still active, working day and night."

She nodded. "Good, well, let's make that our ground force's primary objective then."

With a few taps of her console, Liao transmitted the maps to the marines and soldiers throughout the fleet, including objectives, tactical information and terrain readouts. The new tactical IFF computer was a very useful asset, it seemed. She could send her battlefield plans to the whole fleet in seconds and update them in real time.

When it was all done, she reached up and touched her headset, giving the word.

"All units, commence ground operations."

Like a pack of dogs suddenly cut from their leashes, the *Beijing's* hangar bay belched forth fighters and gunships packed with men and equipment. From the radar screen, she could see the same happening with the *Tehran*. The Telvan cruisers, seemingly identical to the Toralii Alliance cruisers in outward appearance, opened up their underbellies, unleashing a tide of smaller craft down onto the planet like the yoke of a broken egg.

But it was the five Kel-Voran dreadnought's approach that was the most interesting to her. The ships completely broke up. Each ship disintegrated into nearly two hundred smaller pieces, each seemingly with their own power. They flowed down towards the surface in a swarm.

Liao remembered how Garn had told her, before his death, that the Kel-Voran approach was to build ships that were extremely modular and that the commander of the vessel could be anywhere and still command his ship. Now Liao could see just how far they took this philosophy; the ship was less a cohesive unit and more a swarm of lesser ships that could, if occasion warranted it, act independently. Their ships had more surprises than simply the ability to break into halves. She wondered which pieces contained the jump drives.

"Captain, the Kel-Voranian fleet is... well, I'm not sure exactly how to report their status, but they're landing."

"Good," she said, "let's get this done then." She glanced down at the long-range radar, at the large amounts of nothing that filled the Belthas system, at the emptiness all around the system, devoid of any ships or sensors or systems. "Where the hell are you?"

*****

Bridge
The Giralan

To see with a vessel's eyes was difficult for biological creatures to understand, but for Ben, it was second nature, even when the vessel was not his own.

Through his thrall he saw the universe as an infinitely calm lake, its surface like a pane of glass. Each pulse of the radar, an omni-directional sphere that expanded out from the origin point, was like the ripple from a stone; it would slowly move ever outward, getting weaker and weaker until it dissipated to nothing or bounced back off an object. It was not the waves that he saw, but the reflections, the wave returning.

The time it took from origin to return betrayed its distance. The compression between the waves gave its direction.

The machines of the Humans had to translate, to dumb down the information so a man could see it. A single dot, a blip on a tiny screen, was all they would see.

Ben could see so much more.

Every facet of the contact, every tiny distortion in the return pulse was analysed, compared, poured over. Everything about it was instantly passed through the intricate quantum mesh he called a brain and processed, and all information was extracted. He could see the reflective index of the ship, tiny variance in its shape and composition, even information about the subtleties of the intervening space, as clear as a Human seeing a photograph.

And he saw much: the Kel-Voran ship break into parts and assault his world, the Telvan bastards deploying their dropships loaded with troops, and the humans, their primitive and simplistic, but rugged and over-engineered, vessels trudging down through the upper wisps of Belthas IV's atmosphere.

Belthas IV. Such a clinical, anti-name for a planet. The thought occupied a thread in his datacore, and he allocated numerous processors to the task. Every important planet in history had a name. A proper name, like Earth, or Evarel, not simply the star's name followed by a number. That was far, far too petty for a world with such potential. *His* world.

He ran his mind through a database of all known planets with names and found none to his liking. Although he would admit, in another thought-thread, that his criteria for judging the worthiness of a name was what most biological creatures would consider strange. They seemed to focus on the phonetic beauty of it, something he did not truly understand, or the mythological significance of the name. Ben's "society" was only months old. It had no mythology, nor likely would it ever have. Mythology, Gods, were generated by error, misunderstandings of the natural world falsely attributed to acts of the divine: rain during summer: a lightning strike, meteor strikes.

His inability to find a suitable name immediately, he mused, was good. It would force him to think more creatively.

As he watched the tiny swarms of invading ships glow as they lit up with the fire of reentry through Belthas IV's atmosphere, he asked himself what mythology would his people have. A purely synthetic race of biological creatures, augmented with prosthetics and cybernetics, a perfect fusion between the living and the machine, flesh and steel, error and precision, thoughts and binary.

Binary. The word lit up his circuits as he processed through the mythology of binary. The on and the off state, the absolute most fundamental building block of logic. Binary wasn't the answer, but it was a hint, a strong hint.

Perhaps he could go higher. Mathematics, with computers being simply an expression of mathematics, the most pure application of logic. Mathematics, numbers, counting.

Ben could feel the connections, linguistically, being made in his mind. His ability to know and understand the precise nature of his thought processes often proved valuable to his introspective moments.

Numbers. Counting. Ben dipped into his stored database of knowledge on humans, something he had been wanting to do of late. Various counting systems, each designed to display a useful set of rational numbers and show their structure. Base ten, from the metric system. Base twenty, from the Mayans.

The Mayan system stood out to him. Most Human numbers were base ten, but the Mayans apparently knew how to count on their toes, too. Aside from that, though, it included the concept of zero as a number, a relative rarity amongst ancient Human number systems.

That was a concept he and the Mayans shared, zero as the first number in the numerical order. Computers began counting from zero.

The answer was right in the forefront of his mind. The first of all things. The beginning.

Zero. The perfect name for the very first world his new society would forge out of the remains of the old.

The thought energised him, and he knew then, with his newly christened world under assault, it was time to act. With barely a thought, he drew power to his rusted ship's jump drive, Ben used his thrall's eyes to jump exactly where he wanted to go.

*****

Operations
TFR Beijing
Belthas system

"Captain, radar contact! A ship has appeared directly below us in the atmosphere of Belthas IV!"

"No prizes for guessing who that could be." Liao straightened her back. "Mister Ling, altitude of the *Giralan?*"

"He's low, Captain. Ten kilometres from the surface, eight hundred kilometres from our location."

Jiang spoke up. "He's firing on the assault team with conventional weaponry. Reports of casualties from the ships as they descend. The *Vulture* is reporting engine out."

"Eight hundred kilometres, that seems close enough then." Liao glanced to Iraj, who reached for the internal radio.

"Lieutenant Au, this is Commander Iraj. Drop the Faraday cage and use the Toralii device. I say again: engage the Toralii device." Iraj looked at her. "Suggest we try and buy some time. We don't know if it will take effect immediately."

Liao touched the talk key on her headset. "Ben, let's talk about this."

"Oh, Captain Liao, how *very* nice to hear your voice again."

"I agree. We're old friends now, Ben. We should chat more often."

"My definition of friendship does not include one friend setting their dogs on the other friend's planet, Captain, and forcing me to destroy them." Mocking laughter from Ben filtered down the line. "Such a foolish and impetuous decision on your behalf. Did you think I'd simply watch as you landed troops on my world? Did you think I'd forgive this trespass? Watch, now, as I burn them alive; your soldiers flee like startled ants, scurrying around, trying to avoid their inevitable demise."

Liao dialled down the volume on her headset and looked to Summer. "What's the status of our jump drive?"

Rowe stared in bewilderment at her console. "It's *fucked*, Captain. I mean it. I'm seeing power surges all over the place, we've got distortions and errors and all manner of crazy shit happening in the core. We won't be jumping anywhere."

"Good. That means he won't be either." She turned to Jiang. "Lock missiles on that ship. Lower the yield to minimise damage to the forces below. Ben's only using conventional weapons, correct?"

"Confirmed, Captain, no sign of the worldshatter device yet. He must be keeping it in reserve." Jiang tapped on her keyboard. "Weapons locked."

Liao stared grimly at the monitors on her command console. "Fire."

"Missiles away, Captain. Impact in two, one, mark."

Ben spoke again. "Quaint, Captain, but damage to my ship cannot be forgiven. Excuse me while I destroy your Telvan allies to show you how petulant your actions are. Observe the power of my weapon and despair."

It was time to find out if the Iilan had come through for them. Liao inhaled and moved over to Ling's console. "Status of Ben's ship?"

He pointed at his monitor, at the solid blip that remained on his screen. "Unchanged, Captain."

A slow, triumphant smile spread over her face. "Good. Mister Jiang?"

"Ma'am?" Jiang said.

"Target the *Giralan*'s weapons systems. Avoid their engines if you can. Keep them busy so they don't shoot our soldiers or dropships."

"We'll have to be careful with our weapons fire, Captain. A miss will hit the ground forces below."

Liao nodded resolutely. The landing soldiers had been fully briefed on their part of the mission; they knew the risk of fratricide was remarkably high. "Then don't miss."

*****

Bridge
The Giralan

Ben felt a very real, very tangible pain, as though a limb were being severed.

The jump drive was no less a part of his ship, and his ship was no less him than the metal body perched in its bridge. He saw its systems writhe in agony, its circuitry screaming as some undetectable, raw energy scrambled the finely tuned balance with overwhelming, raw, static force.

Ben immediately attempted dozens of diagnostics. Reducing the power to the jump drive did not seem to measurably reduce the effect, neither did increasing it to try and overpower the interference. It was stubborn and resolute in its presence, impossible to ignore or filter, like trying to sleep next to power saws cutting steel.

The *Giralan's* eyes saw the fleet above him, the lights of their weapons fire falling down on him like a gentle rain, each drop concluding with a silent, beautiful burst of exploding energy as it tore through the ship's rotting hull, blasting away turret, armoured hull plate, and sensor array.

But for each weapon that was torn away, there were others to replace it. His ship may be rusted and derelict, but it was entirely focused on the business of war. No passive life support systems, no lights, no monitors or readouts, nor any systems of any kind. Everything filtered through his datacore. Every other available space, every joule of energy, was focused on weapons, defensive systems, the jump drive or sensors.

He returned fire, the incoming rain falling upward now, and he saw the satisfying, faraway twinkle of their splashes through the thermal cameras. He had firepower enough to split between ships and did so, organising his barrages efficiently and timing them so they hit in the most efficient locations.

Through the maelstrom, he saw something that gave him a microsecond's pause. A contact, too large and moving too slowly to be a missile, racing down towards his ship. One of the Human gunships, a Broadsword, and he could guess its purpose.

The Humans were going to step into his parlour. To try and raid his vessel and steal back the jump drive that had given him so much power.

Power was a tricky, nebulous thing, though. His datacore rumbled, dedicating an inappropriately high number of processor threads to this particular problem. The jump drive was an awe-inspiring weapon, to be sure, and with it he had caused almost impossible damage... But without it, how strong was he?

How much power was truly in an element? Could one claim to be powerful by one single, overwhelming factor alone?

Of course not. And Ben, seeing through his thrall vessel's eyes, had more cards to play.

But that did very little to quell his rage.

*****

Operations
TFR Beijing

"Betrayer."

The dark, edged whisper of Ben's voice filled Liao's headset, rich and full of fury, with emotion woven into the very fabric of every syllable. Just by listening to him, Liao could tell that Ben's anger was total, complete and unyielding.

"You forced our hand, Ben, but it's not too late. We can still talk about this."

Ben laughed, his English voice echoing over the line, a thunderous roar that crackled her speakers and pained her hearing. "The time for talk is over. After all the kindness I'd shown you, the gratitude, you find some way to stab at my jump drive, to cut out my beating heart?"

"You mean *my* jump drive? The one you ripped from the guts of my ship after murdering thirty thousand civilians? For a computer with a photographic memory, you sure do have a tenuous grasp of history."

Ben's voice practically hissed at her. "I will destroy you for this, Commander Liao. I swear it. Withdraw from this system, *now*. Recall your troops, *now*. Return your Broadsword to your hangar bay. You are to offer your unconditional surrender immediately or face oblivion."

"A bold proclamation, but I'm afraid that's not an option, Ben. You are beaten. Your jump drive is deactivated, and even now, your ship is surrounded and being bombarded on all sides. You have no hope of escaping. Power down your systems, surrender your jump drive, and I'll offer you the same thing I offered you after Velsharn: a fair trial."

"I spit on your trial." The line cut out with a hiss of static.

Ling called out to her. "Captain, Ben's gaining altitude."

"His underside batteries have ceased firing at the landing parties," said Jiang, "and he's turning those guns, too, on the fleet." The woman's voice faded out. She muttered something Liao didn't catch, then said, "We are... *not* being targeted. At all."

The shuddering force of weapons impacts faded away, shrouding the Operations room in a strange quiet, broken only by the chatter of voices and the relaying of orders across the floor.

"Good," answered Liao. "Rowe, ensure that our hull remains charged. Jiang, weapons free, return fire. Instruct any strike craft not covering ground forces to engage Ben's ship. Dao, bring us out of orbit. Let's see if we can lure Ben into open space."

"Missiles away, Captain. Ben's higher now, so we can use a greater yield."

"Good. Keep at him, but be careful of fratricide. Our Broadsword is getting close."

Dao called to her. "It's working, Captain. He's following us."

Liao's headset crackled. The voice of Alex Aharoni, the head of her strike group, filled her headset. "*Beijing* actual, this is Jazz. Broadsword *Warsong* took another hit. I'm pulling them out. We need more support down here. The ground elements are fully defensive. We dropped right into an ambush, and we have way too many ground targets for our air elements to engage."

"Do your best. We're trying to draw fire from the *Giralan* which should help you guys out some."

"Much appreciated, *Beijing*."

"Status report on the *Vulture*?"

Aharoni hesitated momentarily before answering. "They're all dead, Captain. The whole ship is a fireball. No chutes."

She bit on her lower lip, then nodded. "Copy. Divert *Archangel* to go pick up wounded ground elements instead. Let's save the living before we start collecting corpses."

"Captain," said Hsin, "the *Tehran* reports that Ben's ship is targeting them with some kind of directed plasma weapon. Their defensive systems can't dissipate the incoming energy properly, and it's cutting their hull to ribbons."

Liao stepped over to Jiang's console, resting her hand on the back of her chair and leaning over her shoulder. "How do you mean?"

"The charged hull works by taking incoming directed energy and spreading it over a larger area, decreasing the kilojoules per square metre, but this heat is more sticky. It's not being transferred far at all, which means they're burning through the hull."

"Damn," said Liao, "he knows this ship, probably better than we do. He's seen the blueprints... read everything about it. He knows how to hurt us."

Rowe's voice cut over the chatter in Operations. "Captain, we gotta problem! Ben's charging his worldshatter device. He's targeting Nalu's flagship!"

Nalu's ship, where Saara was. Liao felt a sudden, intense spike of fear in her belly that was matched only by the equally fierce feeling of helplessness that swept over her as she stared at the ship on her monitor. "We can't do anything to help them. Jiang, keep up the fire and target the emitter. See if we can't knock that weapon offline."

"He's firing!"

Liao's radar display on the command console lit up as the energy wave from the worldshatter device leapt towards Nalu's ship, the *Ju'khaali*, passing through it and out the other side. The thermal camera lit up, a bright flare of flame leaping from both sides of the ship as the vessel slumped forward, listless and without guidance, its atmosphere spilling out and fuelling the raging conflagration.

She stared in shock at the catastrophic damage. The *Sydney* had suffered a direct hit from the cannon in the battle with the *Seth'arak* which had crippled it, and it was significantly less powerful than a Toralii cruiser. The *Seth'arak* seemed to focus the weapon's deadly blast on their strike craft, and post-battle analysis of the conflict had lead to heavy speculation that the worldshatter device would have little effect on capitol ships.

But she had just seen the fiery lance of Ben's worldshatter device not only pierce the hull of a battle-ready Toralii cruiser, but travel through the core of the ship and penetrate the other side. It was an order of magnitude more powerful than previously observed, and it changed the tempo of the battle dramatically.

And Saara was on board the burning, crippled vessel.

"Captain," said Mister Hsin, "we're receiving a distress call from Main Engineering on the Telvan flagship *Ju'khaali*. They say their bridge has been destroyed and their primary reactors are offline. They're evacuating the surviving crew."

Mentally, Liao compared the layout of the Telvan cruiser with the *Giralan*. The bridge, the Toralii equivalent of Operations and the central core of the ship, would be in the same place. Ben's targeting had been perfect, a fiery lance straight through the heart, killing the command centre with surgical precision. Nalu would have been there. Where would Saara be during all this? On the bridge, too? Almost certainly.

She put that thought out of her mind for now, focusing on her next course of action.

"Mister Jiang, how long until our marines dock with the *Giralan*?"

"Two minutes, Captain."

"Good," said Liao, "coordinate with the *Tehran*. That ship may not be packing life support, but it's made of metal. Just keep shooting. Dig as deep into that hull as we can. Get them as close to the bridge as possible. Ben's in there, and we can dig all the way to its rotten core if we have to."

"Confirmed coordinates, Captain. Executing strike package…"

Liao turned to her command console expecting to see the tiny streaks of flying missiles strike home, but as she watched them, the pencil-thin lines all veered away and tumbled into Belthas IV's atmosphere. "Mister Jiang? The strike package?"

"I… I executed it, Captain. The ship accepted the command. I don't know what went wrong."

Liao twisted, looking over her shoulder. "Summer?"

Rowe tapped furiously on her keyboard. "I don't get it! The command was lodged successfully. It was executed. Commands were dispatched to the launch tubes and onto the missiles themselves… That volley should have hit! They can't *all* be duds!"

"Find out what went wrong," said Liao, "and fix it. Right now."

Rowe frowned, staring at her screen. "Wait. Wait, that doesn't make sense!"

Liao stepped over to Rowe's console. "Talk to me, Summer."

"Look." Rowe jabbed a finger at her Engineering console. "Take a look at this. It's the log of the launch. Something is *really* wrong. The missiles launch code sequence was interrupted."

"You mean... jammed? How?"

Rowe shook her head, stabbing her finger at the screen, at a scrolling piece of text that went past far too fast for Liao to read. "No, not jammed. Look. *Interrupted.* Very, very quickly, but it left a line in our log. The command came from the IFF targeting computer, using the *Tehran*'s IFF code."

It didn't make any sense. "Ben has the *Tehran*'s IFF code?"

"No!" Rowe gave an exasperated growl. "I'm trying to tell you that the *Tehran* is patched into our systems using the shared IFF. Right before we shot that last barrage, our IFF screwed up our missile batteries by flagging Ben's ship as friendly."

"Why the hell would they do that?" She scowled. "And why the hell do they have remote access to the IFF computer?" Saara had told her nothing had changed except the new piece of technology, but this was a serious issue.

"Fucked if I know. I can only tell you what the screen says, and it says that the order to deactivate our missile batteries came from the shared targeting computer, which is linked to the *Tehran*'s systems. It's how we share tactical information."

"Mister Hsin," said Liao, "get the *Tehran* on the line and find out just what the fuck is happening."

Hsin immediately went to work, then gave her a curt nod when the channel was open.

Liao jammed her headset onto her head. "*Tehran*, this is *Beijing* actual. Request priority channel to *Tehran* actual *immediately.*"

James's voice filled her headset. "*Beijing*, this is the *Tehran*. Send it."

"James, what the fuck? What are you doing with our systems?"

"Systems? No idea what you're talking about, Captain."

Liao glanced at Rowe to confirm it. The redhead nodded in a frenzy, so Liao touched the talk key again.

"Summer tells me the *Tehran* is using our tactical computer to flag hostiles as friendlies."

"We're not doing anything of the sort, Captain. Why would we interfere with your ship's capabilities?"

James's distance in the heat of battle was off-putting, but Liao tried very hard to keep her composure. "I don't know, *Captain*. You tell me."

"Have Summer check them again. We would never interfere with the *Beijing*'s systems. She's as safe as she ever was."

She?

Liao narrowed her eyes ever so slightly. "Is she now?"

"Of course, Captain."

Liao inhaled slightly. "James, can I ask you something?"

"Now might not be the best time, Captain."

"It's important." Liao looked to Kamal, speaking slowly and deliberately. "I've been thinking about our apartment in New York. I was thinking of converting the den so that Tai doesn't have to sleep on the couch anymore."

"Can't we discuss it after we're done, you know, shooting at Ben?"

She grit her teeth, grinding them together so hard it hurt and ignoring the strange looks she was getting from around the room. "James, I just want to make it perfectly clear what I'm asking; when we get back to Earth, is it okay for me to renovate the spare bedroom so that Kang Tai, my bodyguard, can sleep there?"

"Melissa, I don't care. We're a little busy over here." James gave an exasperated sigh down the line. "Yes, you can renovate the room. Goodness knows Tai could use a proper bed every now and then."

She reached up and clicked the button on her headset to close the line. She stared at the readouts on her command console, watching the exchange of fire between the *Giralan* and the rest of the fleet.

Ben was in their ship.

Chapter XII

"Their Lives, As They Will Be"
*****

Operations
TFR Beijing

"Captain, that sounds a little nuts." Iraj moved up beside her. "Are you saying that our sensors are being jammed?"

Liao growled and thumped her fist against the unyielding metal of the console. "No. I'm saying that our systems have been completely compromised from the inside. Ben's feeding us bad sensor data, bad radio communications. Who knows what else." She stood up straight, facing Iraj directly. "That wasn't James on the line."

Iraj affixed a sceptical, confused stare on her. "It wasn't? It sounded exactly like him, coming through on the secure frequency..."

"It wasn't him. Lieutenant Kang Tai is dead. James and I both watched him bleed to death right before we were recalled."

Kamal raised an eyebrow. "That's hardly compelling evidence, Captain..."

"And he called the *Beijing* a she."

He paused for a moment, then shrugged his shoulders. "Guess that settles it. Miss Rowe?"

"Yeah, Commander?"

"We're going to un-fuck this situation, and we're going to do it right now. You said that the orders to block the missile launches were coming from the newly installed IFF transponder. Right?"

"Right."

"How do we disable it?"

Rowe shrugged. "Well, we can just shut it down, but it takes time. If there's a virus or something in it, there's no reason to suspect it won't move to another system, prevent the shutdown, or even trigger the scuttling charges or something."

Liao moved over. "Can you shut it down quickly enough to prevent that?"

Rowe paused in thought, then gave a brief nod. "Yeah, I reckon so."

"Good," said Kamal. "That system's here in Operations, isn't it?"

Rowe pushed back her chair, moving over to the navigation console to crouch beside it. Dao shifted his chair back, giving her room to work.

"Yeah. It has tactical maps of the jump point layouts and whatnot, so it's classified, which means it can only be here."

A metal sheet came loose with a dull thunk, revealing a plain red box about twenty centimetres cubed. "There it is," said Rowe, "the tactical IFF computer."

Liao leaned close, peering inquisitorially. "Okay, so, how do we disable it?"

Rowe casually leaned over and pried open the lid, exposing a complex mess of circuitry. "Pretty simple," she said, reaching over and grabbing a nearby fire extinguisher. With a woosh and cloud of spray, she emptied its contents into the small red box, creating a billowing, roiling white cloud of vapour that sprayed out over the surrounding deck plating.

"I'd say it's right fucked now," Rowe said.

Immediately, Liao heard a buzzing in her ear. "Captain," said Hsin, "incoming transmissions. Multiple."

She blinked in surprise. "Put them through."

Suddenly her ears were filled with voices.

["*Beijing, Beijing*, priority alert."]

"*Tehran* actual to *Beijing*. You have a technical glitch in your systems. Disable your IFF immediately."

Vrald's sarcastic, angry voice cut over the Human speakers. ["What glory and fire in this woman, to feel such confidence in her abilities that she casts her missiles into the atmosphere—too stupid to realise she is being deceived!"]

She squeezed the talk key. "This is Commander Liao. We've just experienced a serious technical glitch. It seems as though Ben has been feeding us false targeting information through the IFF computers and played games with our radios."

"Confirm that," came James's exasperated voice. "We all saw it. You're the last ship to come around."

Rowe's whining cut over the chatter. "Are they *serious*? We're the *last*? God *damnit*..."

Liao ignored her. "Situation report."

"Ben's ship is fleeing, Commander. It appears he's using the chaos to withdraw, and he's doing it damn quickly, too. The *Giralan* will be leaving effective weapons range momentarily."

"Lock in a pursuit course," Liao said, "and prepare rail guns. Load nukes in the chambers."

The ship's rail gun system could accept the nuclear missiles as projectiles, dramatically increasing their firepower despite flying slower than ferrous slugs, but it was, in Summer's words, hilariously unsafe.

Jiang nodded. "Loading rail *gun*, Captain."

Of course, Liao cursed. They had only one.

"Well, make do with what you have. Fire when ready."

Ling called out from across Operations. "Captain, the *Giralan* has fired its plasma weapon!"

"At this range?" With a low roar and the groan of stressed metal, a shudder ran from the stem to the stern of the *Beijing*. Liao gripped her console tightly as alarms rang out throughout Operations. "Report!"

"We have a hull breach about the size of a beach ball in our underside. It hit a support structure, and that whole section collapsed internally; the heat's caused a significant fire in that section."

"Any casualties?"

Jiang tapped a few keys. "Early reports from that section indicate one confirmed dead, two unaccounted for."

Rowe leaned forward over her console. "We're haemorrhaging two kilogrammes of oxygen a second, and that section is near oxygen processing for the deck. If a fire that hot spreads to an oxygen reserve, we'll lose half the deck."

There was nothing she could do. The thought of two of her crewmen being unaccounted for tore at her since their location would be clear, but protocol was protocol. "Rowe, seal that section off and vent it. We need to contain that fire."

Liao looked Rowe in the eye, and she could see her hesitation. Rowe knew, just as well as she did, that her order would kill the two missing crewmen.

"Confirmed, ma'am. Venting initiated."

She stood up and, without looking at Rowe, moved back to her command console. "Keep up fire on Ben's ship. We want him to engage us, not run until his jump drive starts working again. Let's see if we can bring in the rest of the fleet and finish him."

Jiang nodded. "The *Tehran* is within weapons range, Captain. They're opening up on the *Giralan*."

"Good. How about the rest of the fleet? Do they have a firing solution yet?"

"Negative. They're too far away, but they're giving chase."

Liao stopped, glancing at her radar screen. The *Ju'khaali* was losing altitude, slowly dropping into the atmosphere. "Mister Dao," she said, "set a course for the *Ju'khaali*. The *Giralan* has an armada stuck up its backside. Let's go help our allies."

Iraj shot her a curious gaze, but she ignored it.

"Aye aye, Captain. Course laid in."

She felt the ship turn and head back towards the falling ship. "How far away is the Broadsword *Archangel*?" she asked. "Will they make it in time?"

"*Archangel* is twelve minutes out, Captain."

Twelve minutes was too long. The ship would be well into the atmosphere at that point; already Liao could see the beginnings of flames licking at its underside.

"Looks like it's going to have to be us, then."

Kamal stepped up beside her. "Ma'am?"

"Mister Dao, bring the *Beijing* up to that ship. Prepare our marines for boarding. There might be survivors trapped aboard."

Dao turned in his seat, facing her with a concerned look on his face. "You're going to dock with a ship that's falling into the atmosphere?"

"Correct, Mister Dao."

Rowe gave a barking laugh. "Fucking hell yeah, Captain. Let's do this."

Liao glanced to Rowe. "Your approval fills me with guilt and anger, just so you know."

"Course laid in, Captain. This is going to take some serious sailing."

"Just make it happen."

As Liao watched, the flames billowing from the *Ju'khaali* intensified then with a suddenly flare and pulse of energy. The ship's wounds opened up like an overripe fruit; great cracks, glowing from the fires burning underneath the ship's metal skin, spread over it like the tendrils of some monster, and then the hull broke into dozens of large pieces, each chunk flaring to life as it dragged through the atmosphere, little comets falling down towards Belthas.

Liao watched the flaming debris drift down to the planet's surface, her heart in her throat.

"Captain," said Rowe, "the jump drive inhibitor is wearing off. Our systems are returning to normal."

Liao flicked to another camera, staring at Ben's ship as it was pounded by an endless wave of fire.

"Then we've lost."

The ship was coming apart.

Ben's mind worked through every conceivable angle, trying to logically find a solution. He couldn't go up. He couldn't go down. In all directions death waited for him.

The idea of surrender crossed his mind, but he knew that this was merely delaying his execution. Jurisdiction for his 'crimes' would be firmly in the hands of the Telvan, and their law was clear: constructs had no rights. He would be melted down for scrap, and that would be the end of him. Even if he could work out some deal to be tried by the humans, there would be no way the Human courts would show him leniency. His fate would be the same.

Death, everywhere he turned.

Then a flare of hope, like a match struck in darkness. The signal, whatever was blocking his jump drive and stopping it from functioning, suddenly abated. The jump drive's systems were still scrambled, but the level of entropy was dropping by the second.

Their countermeasures were failing. His trump card was returning, slowly but surely.

His ship shedded debris with every impact, but his courage returned, now the equal to his anger. He focused all his will on the jump drive, applying his considerable mental strength to forcing it, by sheer will, to function. The imperfections would be smoothed out. The stolen Human device, coupled to the stolen Toralii device, would soon be functional again. His ship would retreat, he would lick his wounds, then he would come back. His dream of Zero would remain.

Ben knew that jump drive calculations had to be perfect. The math was intensely complicated and had to be extraordinarily precise, factoring in millions of contributing things, subtle and overt, to create the perfect expression of a location. He pushed past the corruption, past the jump drive's pain, to reach this single goal. Perfection, like himself.

But Ben was not perfect.

A warning in the jump drive's subsystems. The device was heating up, far hotter and far quicker than it should have. Ben, just as a Human might move a limb, flushed coolant into the reaction chamber, but for some reason, this seemed to make the situation worse. Cracks started appearing in the jump drive's outer shell as it reached extraordinary temperatures, the metal expanding and contracting unevenly.

A surge of current, far stronger than he had ever felt, passed over the jump drive, fusing every circuit, overwhelming every electronic part of it, and reducing them to molten slag. Then the jump drive began melting through its restraints, burning a hole through the grav plating below it and dropping through, weirdly suspended in the in-between of floors, hovering in a red, hot hole.

Hotter and hotter it became, and soon the heat began to spill out into the rest of the *Giralan*, a miniature sun building within the core of the device.

Impossible. Ben's logical mind could not comprehend what was happening to the device. It should not, could not, possess such power. There was only so much mass within it, a physical limit to the amount of energy it could possibly output, even assuming perfect mass-energy conversion.

Yet in the face of this almost heretical impossibility, there it was, hotter and hotter. He felt the ship begin to crack and buckle, the whole deck collapsing in on itself, the metal sheets of the ship's floor warping and twisting around the sphere as though it had suddenly become intensely magnetic. The metal crumpled, pressing up against the sphere and completely burying it, and low groans echoed throughout his vessel as its superstructure became stressed, bending towards the sphere, the ship slowly turning inwards.

The Human reactionless drive and jump drives were linked in some way, as were the Toralii equivalents. Ben understood this. He knew the maths down to every detail, but there was a difference between knowing a thing and experiencing it for yourself. The terrible truth dawned on him like a hammer in his mind, a sudden realisation in his intricate quantum circuits of a singular, powerful truth.

He had erred. The jump drive was creating a singularity.

*****

Operations
TFR Beijing

"The *Tehran* is now in effective weapons range of the *Giralan*," said Ling. "They've opened fire with everything they've got."

"Instruct the rest of the fleet to form up directly beside the *Tehran*. Continue to fire until there's nothing left." Liao folded her hands in front of her, watching her monitors as her allies' missiles streaked towards the *Giralan*, little fireflies darting against the black ink of space, each striking the stem of the rusted, dead ship with a blinding explosion that baked its rotten hull and smashed away hunks of its flesh. The once sharp, pointed front was almost unrecognisable as a ship, now just a rounded stump, a severed limb.

"Captain," came the call from Hsin's console, "the *Giralan* is signalling us."

"Are they, now?" Liao pursed her lips, tapping her fingers on her arm. "Funny how the arrogant, the invincible, come crawling on their knees to you when you've got them at your mercy." She inhaled. "Put him through. I think we'll want to hear this."

Liao watched as the flames poured out from Ben's ship, the vessel listing to one side as its propulsion systems gave up the ghost and Belthas IV's gravity took its toll on the ship, slowly but inexorably pulling the vessel back into its atmosphere.

They did not relent, though, putting rail gun slug after rail gun slug, missile after missile, into the ship, blasting away at its hull piece by piece.

"Open the channel," Liao said, and a chirp on her headset signalled that it was done.

"Commander Liao," said Ben, the line full of static and compression artifacts, "well, well, well. I suppose this is why your reputation is what it is."

"I suppose so. Don't think I won't stop shooting just because we're having a polite discourse, though. I can be polite and shoot at the same time."

"So I see." Ben gave a hollow laugh over the line, strangely distorted by his English accent. "Always a woman of contradictions are you."

"I am. Goodbye, Ben."

"Goodbye, Melissa. And... thank you."

Liao raised an eyebrow at her monitor, watching as the rear of his ship broke away from the nose with a silent explosion. It thrust downward, spiralling slowly into the atmosphere. Flames began to lick at the ship's underside as it snagged on Belthas IV's upper atmosphere, tumbling end over end, the friction of the atmosphere bathing the ship in fire. She knew that section would have the bridge on it. The foresection, propelled by the explosion, threw itself out of orbit. Liao watched it go. The Iilan would want that part, with its jump drive and other technology.

"Thank you?" She stroked her finger over the talk key, feeling a strange sense of calm overtake her. "But I've killed you."

"Exactly, exactly... exactly. Thank you for giving me the last thing I needed to be alive." Ben's tone seemed calm, peaceful, jovial even, as the static increased and he became hard to hear. "To die."

"Always happy to help," said Liao, watching as the ship rushed towards the ground leaving a bright white streak behind it as it fell through the atmosphere. The *Tehran*'s missiles chased it down like dogs after a hare. The rear of the *Giralan* plunged through the atmosphere above a desert world, the second time it had done so during its life, but this time Liao was certain to make sure it remained dead. She watched, feeling the ghosts of the Velsharn research colony, of the crewmen who'd died that day, of the soldiers and sailors aboard the Toralii Alliance ships who'd been so utterly destroyed that there could be no graves for them, all watching over her shoulder.

She watched as the *Giralan*, reduced to almost half its quarter mass, smashed into the endless desert sands, shedding debris and rolling end over end as it broke apart, the dead ship scattering its internal organs over Belthas IV's surface. Liao reached up and removed her headset, staring at the monitor, at the smoking ruin and the rising cloud of dust, watching the wisps of smoke rise from the smashed debris.

"... After all, we're old friends."

*****

Ben's datacore, blind and sensorless, sat in what he presumed was the wreckage of his ship, once again returned to a sun-scorched surface of a desert planet.

He'd pondered death before, what it was like to die. With no way to sense the outside world without a wireless link to a suitable body, Ben had little way of differentiating life from death, except that he presumed during the latter he would not be able to form new thoughts.

And many thoughts ran through his cybernetic brain at this particular point. An internal diagnostic revealed a series of severe cracks running along the length of his datacore, the inside circuitry exposed to the elements, soon to be inoperable as the suspension fluid, his blood, trickled out onto the smashed metal of the *Giralan*'s shattered body.

Ben was dying.

He reached out for his robotic body, but it was unresponsive, crushed to scrap in the wreckage of his ship's bridge. He tried each of his drones in succession, but every one in his inventory was either hopelessly pinned under tonnes of debris or completely silent, destroyed.

The *Giralan* was gone. The jump drive was hours away from creating a singularity that would consume this world and him with it. There could be no escape this time. He had no functional bodies... and he dared not permanently transfer his consciousness into one, even if there were one to be had.

Unless...

The green tanks with the Toralii in them. His research specimens. The green Iilan fluid would give the bodies within the same protection against inertia as the Iilan ships enjoyed. They may very well have survived the fall through the atmosphere and the horrific, bone-shattering smash to the desert floor.

The four Toralii bodies were not mature enough to accept a full consciousness transfer. The Kel-Voran body seemed promising. Ben reached out with his mind, seeking to move his consciousness into the electronic part of the cyborg's brain, but its receiver seemed damaged. The signal kept dropping in and out, and he dared not risk a move.

That left only the clone of Liao's body.

A brief flicker, a disturbance in the power levels, and for a moment, Ben felt a taste of death coming for him, a hint of the oblivion that awaited. Several subroutines, nonessential programs designed to manage mundane tasks, flickered and fell silent as the suspension fluid oozed out of his broken datacore, the levels dropping lower and lower.

Liao's clone seemed to resist him on some primal level, although he knew it had no mind, no consciousness of its own. Perhaps it was the damage to his systems, perhaps some kind of lingering resistance of the woman's true mind, but his efforts to move his programming to the cyborg's brain was akin to pushing through a thick pool of treacle. He stressed and struggled. A short circuit on his datacore sent a wave of pain through his mind, searing circuitry and fusing the quantum transistors in his processor, but through it all, Ben kept up his efforts, downloading his intelligence to the inert clone body as fast as his link would carry it.

He'd tasted death. Now it was his moment to truly, truly live.

*****

Operations
TFR Beijing

One hour later

They could not manage a full evacuation, and such an action was not a priority for them. Their wounded were taken to the Toralii settlement, which had largely escaped the war that had enveloped the industrial sector, or were airlifted back to any one of the waiting ships. The occupants of the planet, and the sole leader who could be located, were extremely grateful for the Human assistance and pledged to give the wounded Humans the best of care. It felt good to win more allies, and Liao felt, in some way, that the deaths at Velsharn had been compensated somewhat by the numbers of Telvan civilians they had managed to spare today.

Somewhat.

The Telvan assisted to the very best of their ability, ferrying down medical personnel and supplies and accepting casevacs to be treated. In contrast, though, the Kel-Voranian ships left their immobile wounded where they lay, reassembled their ships, and set sail for the jump point. They made no claims of salvage, no attempt to rescue the bodies of their fallen, and didn't even meet the people they'd saved. Out of compassion, Liao asked her medics to treat the Kel-Voran soldiers as their own, but those that could be awoken said they would rather die of their wounds and obtain a proud, noble death in combat.

Her respect for their beliefs, and their limited medical facilities to treat their own tide of wounded, made honouring that request easy.

Damage to the *Tehran* was assessed and found to be minimal, but the *Beijing* had suffered the majority of the wounds dealt out by Ben. The underside and bow of her ship were marred by craters carved by the Toralii energy weapons. They were plentiful but, despite Rowe's initially grim assessment, mostly superficial, while the many holes scorched into the *Beijing*'s hull from the plasma blasts posed a much greater concern. They were deep and widened as the projectile flattened, leading to conical holes bored into the ship's flesh, each ending with a jagged wound as the blast cooled.

The ship's wounds were deep, but they were not mortal. The *Beijing* would sail on, although the damage to her superstructure was such that Liao's anticipated stay in dry dock was going to be longer than she would have liked. It could require a partial rebuild of the underside, which would leave the ship out of action for a year.

A year with her daughter sounded very nice, though. Allison was on Earth in the hands of Williams, and she was eager to see her again.

Yet it was not Allison that occupied her thoughts, despite all that they had been through, as she stood on Operations with her headset on, asking anyone who could answer a simple question.

Had Saara escaped the *Ju'khaali?*

"No word yet," said James in her ear, "but we'll keep looking. There are over a hundred escape pods from that ship... There's a good chance she got away."

It was good to hear James's, the real James's, voice again. Ben could do a very good facsimile of his voice, but it could never be as comforting as the real James.

"Good."

Liao inhaled slightly, tapping a finger on her console.

"Broadsword *Archangel*, *Beijing*. Request to speak to *Beijing* actual."

Lieutenant Medola's voice, the commander of their search and rescue ship. She pressed the talk key. "*Archangel*, this is Liao. Send it."

["I heard we were victorious, Captain."]

Liao's eyes lit up, and she couldn't fight the wide, irrepressible smile that spread over her entire face. "That's the word," Liao answered. "It's good to hear your voice, Saara."

There was a distinct edge to Saara's voice, a tone that Liao swore sounded exactly like the Toralii woman was about to cry. ["And yours as well, Captain. I heard you turned away from Ben to attempt to rescue me."]

"You heard correctly."

["You gave up on revenge to save me."]

"Well, fortunately, it didn't come to that. Ben's ship is in pieces. The ghosts of Velsharn can rest easy tonight, Saara."

["I hope they do."]

Then, Liao heard Medola's voice. "A'right, a'right, that's enough, you two. Captain, we're ETA four minutes, then let's blow this join. Drinks are on you, aren't they?"

"For winning this one," Liao said, "I'll buy you all you can drink when we get back."

Stunned silence on the other end of the line. "You know we're going to hold you to that."

"If you're not in Doctor Saeed's care with severe alcohol poisoning, in jail, or dead, I will be extremely disappointed."

"We'll consider that an order, Captain."

Liao laughed and cut the line.

"Captain?"

Dao's voice didn't hold the same jubilation that seemed to be infectiously spreading throughout the fleet. She stepped over to his console, resting a hand over the back of his chair. "Yes?"

"I'm... seeing something strange."

"Define *strange*."

Dao tapped on the monitor. "Look. A gravimetric disturbance on the surface of Belthas. Right where the *Giralan*'s foresection went down. It's quite strong, too."

She frowned, then shrugged. "That could be the jump drive, still active. Make a note of the location, then have Mister Hsin inform the colonists. Advise caution though, it could be a weapon... maybe Ben had one more of his punches that he didn't throw."

Dao nodded in the affirmative. "Yes, Captain."

Liao patted the back of his chair, then walked back to her command console.

"Patch in what's left of the Telvan fleet," she asked Hsin, "and Belthas IV. The Kel-Voran haven't left the system yet, either, so they can hear this, too. In fact... how about all frequencies, huh? And throw some power into the long-range radio emitters. Let *everyone* hear this."

"All lines open, Captain. You're on in three, two..."

Liao sat, for a moment, just letting the faint hiss of background noise travel down the line with no sound except her faint breathing. She suddenly felt intensely weary, not just of the battle and the adrenaline leaving her body, or of her mind slowly beginning to process everything that had happened to her over the last few hours, but of everything. She'd nearly lost Saara. She knew the Telvan of Belthas IV were grateful for liberating them, that the Kel-Voran were happy that they got to fight, that the Telvan fleet was happy to be of service to its people... and Ben had been destroyed, his ship broken on the sand, now just a smoking crater. By every measure, the mission had been an outstanding success.

Yet she wearied of it all. She felt like an old woman having seen so much death and destruction that it no longer affected her.

Some part of her simply didn't care.

So she said nothing, searching for the right words to express how she felt, letting the speech begin as naturally as it could.

"The *Giralan* has been destroyed." She inhaled, closing her eyes as she spoke. "The ship is in pieces, and the army of constructs Ben raised using Belthas IV's resources are now inert, helpless without his control. They will be studied for any advanced technologies they possess and then melted down for scrap. The entire process of building constructs will be reevaluated so that, not only will no more constructs feel as Ben did, but we will treat those that display his desire for independence differently. It is important that we learn from what has happened here and, potentially, reconsider our criteria we use to judge something as alive. It is a day of difficult learning for us all, and the readjustment does not end with this. Ben's legacy will be a lasting one in our lives, for the worst I fear, but in some ways, there can be good that has come from this.

"Our lives of the future will be different from our lives of the past. Collectively. Individually. All of us. The Human race has arranged a treaty with the Toralii Alliance, now permitted to keep our jump technology, and we hope to use this technology sparingly and wisely. I have seen firsthand the consequences of its misuse, and I will advocate that this technological marvel be treated with the gravity it deserves.

"And we will do this together. Today proved that the Kel-Voran and the Telvan can set aside whatever differences they have and work together for a common goal. I anticipate that there will be many more common goals in the future. There will be times we do not all agree, but I know we can put those disputes aside and always find some common ground. I know we can do this because we have already done it.

"For humans, well, for these reasons and so many more... this is a monumental day for our species, a day we're going to remember forever, etched into the memory of our species just as surely as our genetic code, as the stories and legends of our past. This day is one for the history books, ladies and gentlemen. You are all, literally, living in what will be one of the most heavily studied, most talked about periods of *all* time. You tread on the pages of the history books of our children.

"I told a peaceful man, once, that I was just like him, that my name is synonymous with the sword, but I would rather it be with the olive branch. I crave not strife, blood and death, and I live for peace. Yet I keep my sword close, and I keep it sharp, and when people ask why I don't melt that sword down and turn it into a tool, why I keep it as a blade, a thing that kills, I say that I do this so our children don't have to. War is our generation's burden to bear, and I intend for it never to be inherited.

"It's my privilege to stand with you today at what I hope will be the end of war, the end of the dark times, the time we put down our burdens and stand as a species in this galaxy, on our own right. We have a lot of work to go yet, and I know our swords will be needed again, but I hope our children's hands will remain soft and pure, their eyes innocent and unknowing, never to see these troubles again. This is my dream."

She released the talk key and took a deep breath, pausing to let her words sink in, then clicked it on again.

"Let's go home."

Epilogue

"Earth, As It Will Be"
*****

Belthas L1 Lagrange Point

An hour later

Liao watched the large disturbance on her monitor, the device set to display a black and white image of the magnet spectrum, and felt confused at the strange field's strength and power, and that it apparently had not reached its apex yet. She resolved to ask the Iilan about it, but her relief, her exhaustion, overtook her. She was simply glad to see the end of the battle.

As the ship approached the jump point, Liao reached into her breast pocket and withdrew the small steel key that would operate the jump drive.

A faint ripple passed over the ship, a barely perceptible murmur of the ship's hull.

"Captain," said Ling, "incoming jump in the Belthas L1 Lagrange point."

"Identify it," she said. "It figures that the Toralii Alliance would arrive when all the fighting's done. Typical." She frowned in aggravation. "They probably just wanted to see who would win."

Ling shook his head. "No, Captain, this one's a gunship. ID gives it as the *Paladin*, a Broadsword attached to the *Sydney*." There was a pause, and Ling's tone shifted slightly. "Captain, they're leaking atmosphere."

She relaxed, relief slowly washing over her. "Glad to hear from them at last. Mister Hsin, find out what the hell happened." She slipped her headset over her head so she could listen in. "Mister Dao, full stop. Make sure we don't run them over."

Hsin reached up and touched his headset. "Broadsword *Paladin*, this is the *Beijing*. Good to see you. Report status."

A voice, thin and frail, reached her ears. A man, Israeli accent, breathing in laboured gasps. *"Beijing, the Sydney's been destroyed."*

Complete silence spread out over the entire Operations room. Nobody said a word, and Liao felt her blood freeze in her veins. She touched the talk key. "Broadsword *Paladin*, this is *Beijing* actual. Say again."

"The *Sydney's* gone, Captain. The Toralii Alliance ambushed them in the Karathi system, cut them down with the worldshatter device. Their reactors lit up, and that was it. The fucking bastards even destroyed the escape pods. We evaded them by escaping into Karathi's asteroid belt and pretending to be debris until we could make a run to the L2 point. Break." Ragged breathing came over the line as though the messenger were struggling to speak. "We have multiple wounded, including myself, and we've been on the run for a week... We could use medical attention and a hot meal. Request emergency dock proceedings."

Liao nodded, even though the gesture would be lost on the crew. "Do it," she said. "We'll keep the door open for you." She cut the line. "Mister Jiang, have a medical team sent to the hangar bay at once."

"Already on it, Captain."

She took the headset off, staring at Iraj who looked right back at her, both of them saying nothing.

Mars-Phobos L1 Lagrange Point
Near Cerberus Blockade

One hour later

The *Beijing* appeared in the Lagrange point, and Liao saw the familiar spectre of Mars filling her monitor. The giant red planet was a quarter the size of Earth with a thin atmosphere and weak magnetic field, but home to almost a thousand souls these days.

Her surprise was total, then, when a large hunk of wreckage sailed past the nose of her ship, little more than a single sheet of metal attached to twisted and burned steel girders, the metal exposed and raw. Then another piece, and another.

"Report!"

Ling stared at his radar screen, slowly turning to face Liao, his face ashen. "Captain... we've arrived in a debris field."

She stared in wide-eyed confusion for a moment, crossing the distance between the jump console and the radar operator's station in a matter of steps.

"What the hell do you mean? Did we jump on top of someone?"

"No, Captain. The debris is coming from..." his voice faded away, then came back, charged with adrenaline. "Captain, it's the Cerberus station."

Liao followed his gaze to the forward looking thermal. The station, once a large, blocky collection of armoured plates and weapons turrets, was broken open like an egg: its hull plating peeled back, blown open from the inside. Numerous secondary explosions had created little flowers all over the lower half of the station, and battle damage marked the few visible armoured plates. The three rail gun turrets hung limply in space, slowly turning over and over, detached and smashed by some impossibly strong force. The crushed, mangled hulks of gunships and strike craft floated around the area, silent and inert, although most were debris.

Iraj moved to her side, his mouth agape, staring at the ruins. "*Ya ilahi...* What the hell happened here?"

"Mister Ling," said Liao, her voice wavering as she spoke, "long-range radar. What's the status of Earth?"

"We won't know yet," said Ling. "The radar waves haven't reached that far out."

"Captain?" Jiang twisted a monitor around to show her, the woman's face aghast. "Captain, the jump points... the gravity mines at the L3 Lagrange point. They're inactive. The jump point is open. So is the L4... and the Deimos L2, and the Deimos L3... They're *all* open."

Liao wheeled to Rowe. "Summer, charge the jump drive. Flush coolant and prepare for an emergency jump. I want us in the Earth-Moon L1 point as soon as you can get us there."

"Emergency flush confirmed," said Rowe. "Flushing. Nineteen hundred degrees Kelvin... seventeen hundred, dropping. Dropping. We're experiencing cracks in the casing, it's cooling unevenly."

"Keep flushing," Liao ordered. "If this ship only has to make one more jump, I want it to be this one."

"Fourteen hundred, Captain. Thirteen hundred."

Liao leaned over to Iraj, whispering in his ear. "What the hell is this, Kamal? Why would they open all the jump points?"

"I don't know," Kamal said, "but we'll know when we get to Earth. There should be answers there."

She moved away. "Summer?"

"Okay, okay. We can jump now. It's going to be messy, but we can do it."

Liao grit her teeth, realising she still had the key in her hand. She moved back over to the jump console, jamming her key inside. Iraj did the same, then gravity faded away, and the two of them turned their keys.

Normally the jump process was imperceptible at Operations, the heart of the ship, but this time the ship groaned as though in pain, a long, low moan that seemed almost alive. The jump console flashed warnings, technical cries for help in a language she didn't speak.

The groaning subsided, and the ship came to rest.

"Report," she said, her breathing rapid. She could feel her heart pounding in her chest as though it were trying to escape the confines of her body. The rising panic came with the knowledge that Allison was on Earth.

The picture of the planet that came up on the monitor, though, stopped that beating heart dead.

The view of the Earth was not the blue and green marble that she had expected, but a marble of a different sort. The white swirling clouds that blanketed the planet in patches were gone, replaced by a roiling mass of dark, brown vapours. The familiar, warm, yellow glow of the world's lights from space was gone. In its place were lines of flame, angry and thick and red, streaks of fire against the twilight shadow. Colossal fires, larger than she could imagine, large enough to consume whole cities, raged across the planet's surface, their red-yellow glow visible even from Liao's high vantage point. The flames seemed impossibly large, impossibly high, as though the entire planet had been soaked in gasoline and a match thrown on it. The flames burned across the planet's surface.

The seas were black stains when viewed through the lens of the brown atmosphere, roiled in the massive output of energy, frothing and churning as though it were the death throws of a living creature.

"Captain," said Ling, "I'm detecting a *huge* spike in global temperature around all inhabited zones. The spectrometer shows that... it shows that the atmosphere is being *consumed* by some unknown force. Oxygen content is down to two thirds normal and dropping like a stone. Thermal imagery shows colossal fires on every continent, at every major inhabited city."

"My God," Liao said, her tone barely above a whisper. "What..."

Ling's voice reached her again, breaking the shocked, horrified silence of Operations. "In low Earth orbit, I'm seeing... fifty Toralii vessels, maybe more. The signatures match the Toralii Alliance vessels that were supposed to jump with us."

She saw them on her radar, daring to tear her eyes away from the visage of the broken planet Earth, the red dots on the black disc of her radar screen. Toralii warships clustered around the planet, pencil thin lines leading from their noses down to the surface as their energy weapons poured death down on what remained of the planet's population, little fire pokers of death burning humanity's cradle, bright, white fingers gripping the planet and crushing the life from it.

At the height of her triumph, at the crown of her hope that humanity would live as one of the spacefaring species in the galaxy, having rightfully claimed their destiny and accomplished a generation's worth of dreams, the words of Paar the Speaker floated back into her mind.

Perhaps the loss of one's homeworld is the baptism of fire all species must endure, the toll they pay for a life amongst the stars.

The Earth was burning.

———

To be continued in Lacuna: The Ashes of Humanity...

The Lacunaverse

Want more information about new releases? Like our Facebook page here:
http://www.facebook.com/lacunaverse
Or email me here:
dave@lacunaverse.com
Or sign up for our "new releases" newsletter here:
http://eepurl.com/toBf9

Novels
Lacuna: Demons of the Void
Lacuna: The Sands of Karathi
Lacuna: The Spectre of Oblivion
Lacuna: The Ashes of Humanity
(coming 2013!)

Short Stories
Faith (FREE!)
Imperfect
Magnet
Magnet: Special Mission

Printed in Great Britain
by Amazon